THIS KING OF LO

THIS SPRING OF LOVE

Denise Robins

Chivers Press • Thorndike Press
Bath, England   Waterville, Maine USA

This Large Print edition is published by Chivers Press, England, and by Thorndike Press, USA.

Published in 2002 in the U.K. by arrangement with the author's estate.

Published in 2002 in the U.S. by arrangement with Claire Lorrimer.

U.K. Hardcover ISBN 0–7540–4993–0 (Chivers Large Print)
U.K. Softcover   ISBN 0–7540–4994–9 (Camden Large Print)
U.S. Softcover   ISBN 0–7862–4483–6 (General Series Edition)

The text of this Large Print edition is unabridged.
Other aspects of the book may vary from the original edition.

Set in 16 pt. New Times Roman.

Printed in Great Britain on acid-free paper.

British Library Cataloguing in Publication Data available

Library of Congress Control Number: 2002105458

PART 1

CHAPTER ONE

The sirens had sounded the 'All-clear.'

Christine Shaw, who had been standing by her ambulance during the two hours' alert, came out of the depot and made her way to the nearest bus stop, feeling a little thankful that tonight she would not be on duty. She was very tired and this was a Saturday afternoon, which meant a long rest, and she needed it. It had been a heavy week, what with the office where she worked as a typist being bombed and that awful business of trying to salvage what was left of files and letters and office equipment, and moving to temporary quarters in another part of London.

Besides that, there had been one big raid this week when she was on night duty, and although Christine had courage and determination, some of those long dark hours in a raging inferno had been trying, to say the least of it. All through that night she had been driving her ambulance, waiting for the A.F.S. and the demolition men to dig the dying and wounded out of the debris, and then driving back to the hospitals. All night she had witnessed grim sights, best forgotten—hard to forget. By night, the slender, delicately-built

1

girl must be as tough and resolute as a soldier on the battlefield. But by day she was just Miss Shaw again, quiet little typist in the service of Messrs. Tring and Locket, solicitors of Grays Inn Field.

It was glorious this September afternoon, she thought, and the sun warmed her face and her exhausted limbs, as she stood at the corner of the street waiting for a bus to take her to Warwick Avenue, where she shared a flat with a friend.

There were many others like herself to be seen in London in this year of our Lord, 1940. Just a tired girl in a uniform with a Service gas-mask, a steel helmet and the faintest look of strain in the eyes although the lips belied it with a laugh. But Christine at this precise moment was feeling neither valiant-hearted nor proud to be of service to her country. She was thoroughly tired and disgruntled. She knew that it was because she was so tired that this black mood was upon her. No doubt a hot bath, a good meal, and a long sleep would help her to return to her customary state of indifference to the 'slings and arrows of outrageous fortune,' many of which had pierced the armour of her joyous youth already, although she had only just come of age.

As she sat in the bus, homeward bound at last, and looked through the windows at the traffic, the crowds pouring out of shelters and

2

into the streets again, at the blue sky in which some high-flying fighters left a trail of exhaust, at the gaps here and there where a bomb from the Luftwaffe had sliced through a row of houses . . . at the sprinkling of uniforms, khaki, light blue and dark . . . she asked herself what it was all about. Why must there be terrible wars like this? Why should she, Christine Shaw, have been born into such an age?

Why hadn't she lived with the peaceful Victorians or the gay Georgians? Why had fate decreed that her beloved parents should have both died in India in an accident just before her eighteenth birthday (Colonel Shaw had retired from the Indian Army and was about to come home for good when that accident had happened and Christine, at finishing school in Switzerland, had been looking forward passionately to seeing him and the beloved mother who had been away from her so much all through her childhood).

Why should Uncle Alfred with whom she had gone to live on her return to England also have been taken from her, the victim of an influenza epidemic? Why should his only married daughter, Christine's cousin Alison, be such a horrid unattractive character, wanting everything for herself and her family and unwilling to let Christine remain in the home that Uncle Alfred had provided for her. Incidentally, *why* had poor Uncle Alfred died before altering his Will so that Alison had got everything and Christine nothing that he had meant her to have?

There seemed no answer to any of these questions which were running through Christine's weary young mind as the bus thundered down High Street, Kensington. At most times she did not let past problems or spectres trouble her. With all the ardour and resilience of youth, she had been able to fling off the cloak of trouble and face life anew. She had been badly disappointed and unutterably lonely for a long time after her parents' tragic death. There had seemed nothing to look forward to—that had been the worst of it, and that was the worst of it, today. She could do none of the things she had wanted to do if her father and mother had lived—or even if Uncle Alfred had survived, for he had been fond of her and was her last living relation except cousin Alison. She had had to stamp remorselessly on the dreams she had dreamed in her beautiful school in Chexbres. She had not been destined to settle down with mother and father in a country house (she had always adored the country) and have a marvellous time like many girls of her age and standing. Once Uncle Alfred departed this life, she had to become one of the world's workers. Out of sheer pride she had refused to take the meagre allowance grudgingly offered by cousin Alison.

She still had the small amount left to her by her father (it wasn't much because Colonel

Shaw had always lived up to, if not beyond his means) but Christine had managed to pay for her own secretarial training at St. James College, and soon afterwards she had found a job with Messrs. Tring and Locket. And she had had one stroke of luck . . . getting Barbara Jenkins, who had trained with her at St. James, and was also an orphan, to share the tiny flat in Warwick Avenue with her.

And then the war had come. Life had grown more difficult, more tense, less monotonous perhaps. Christine had wanted to leave the office and go into the A.T.S., but the senior partner of the firm had told her that he could not carry on if the whole of the staff left him. He had made her feel that it was her duty to stay, even once the raids began, so she had found a part-time job at the ambulance depot. And Barbara Jenkins—private secretary to a woman novelist—was an air-raid warden in their district.

So far, Christine had been through every one of the heavy raids on London. So far she had stood up to them without flinching, and she had met many courageous and delightful people in her depot; among them a man, once a stockbroker and now an ambulance driver like herself, who doggedly proposed to her almost every time they met.

Christine liked Kenneth Howell. He was ten years older than herself, a little bald and unprepossessing but essentially nice and with money behind him. It would have been a good marriage. It would have meant comfort and security and a husband who adored her and would never have to leave her alone. He was not fit for active service. But she did not love him, so she could not marry him. And now he was leaving the ambulance depot, because, as he had told her again today, he could not stand being near her and seeing her daily when he knew that there was no hope. The idea of losing Kenneth's friendship was one of the things which depressed her this afternoon. She liked him and she had stood shoulder to shoulder with him in many emergencies at the depot and they had shared some very pleasant evenings when they were not on duty. Christine wished she could have loved Kenneth. Then life would have seemed easy and her future settled. Alternatively, she wished that he had not loved her so that their friendship might have endured.

She seemed fated to lose the people and the things she loved, she thought dismally. Not only was Kenneth going, but Barbara had lately become engaged to a naval officer. They intended to get married on his next leave and that would mean an end for Christine to home life in Warwick Avenue, and to Barbara's companionship.

It didn't sound much. Just trifles in a world which was plunged into such frightfulness. She knew she ought to be glad she was alive and not one of those poor, shattered, maimed individuals whom she had helped to drive to the hospital. But it wasn't human to regard life with quite so much reason and logic. One's own little troubles mattered a terrific lot, and after all it *would* make a very great difference to her, saying good-bye to Barbara and to the home they had shared for the last two years.

Barbara was away this weekend. She had gone down to Reigate to stay with an aunt. When Christine got home it was to a deserted flat and to a muddle. She had slept late this morning and had to rush off without washing up the breakfast dishes. She grimaced as she saw the remains of her hastily-prepared and half-eaten breakfast waiting for her in the tiny kitchenette. The flat, which consisted of three rooms, was on the fifth floor of a big block, half-empty at the moment, since so many tenants had taken fright at the raids and left London.

It was stifling this afternoon and Christine hastened to open all the windows. The sun had been beating against the panes all morning. She adored the sun, but not in London when the summer was still aflame. But it would be lovely on the river . . . or in the country, in a rose-filled garden . . . or by the sea. She sighed at the very thought. She hadn't had a holiday in the country for eighteen months.

Yes, she was definitely at a very low ebb of depression today, she reflected. She felt like crying, here all by herself, and that was a weakness she scorned. She almost felt like ringing up Kenneth Howell and telling him she would marry him. But that idea horrified her. It wouldn't be fair to Kenneth, and hadn't she always sworn that she would never marry until she fell in love? Kenneth wasn't at all her type. She wanted somebody much more vital . . . She hadn't much use for the debonair man-about-town. Even Barbara's fiancé was more in her line . . . a sun-tanned, breezy naval officer. But she never really met the sort of man that she could love completely. He belonged, she told herself rather bitterly, to the many dreams which seemed out of her reach.

Somebody knocked at the door, and before Christine could say, 'Come in,' a girl had put her head round the door.

Christine jumped to her feet, almost upsetting her work-basket which she had just taken out.

'Why, Fiona—you!' she exclaimed.

Into the room came a slimly-built girl of her own build and age.

Fiona Challis was exquisitely dressed in a charming suit. Brown fox-fur, diamond clip in the organdie frills at her throat, chic turban swathing fair curls . . . a drift of perfume . . . a jangle of bracelets . . . an extravagant spray of orchids on her coat. All a marked contrast between Fiona Challis and Christine Shaw. The girls had been abroad at school in

Chexbres together.

Fiona said:

'Christine, darling. I've got to see you most urgently. Are you alone? Can we talk?'

'I'm quite alone. Barbara, my friend who lives here with me, is away.'

Then Fiona gave a little sigh, followed by something that sounded suspiciously like a sob.

'Oh, Christine, *Christine*!' she said.

Christine led her friend to the window seat, put a cushion at her back, and sat there beside her. With a sense of shock, she realised that something was very wrong with her old friend, Fiona. She had changed unbelievably since the last time they had met, which was some months ago, when they had tea in Fiona's house in Eaton Square.

Fiona had then been enjoying herself as well might the daughter and heiress of one of the richest men in England. So long as Christine could remember, Fiona had always been gay, pursuing a somewhat selfish existence perhaps, but so charming and kind that nobody begrudged her happiness.

Christine had loved Fiona ever since the days at school when the 'richest girl' had formed a friendship with the poorest . . . an attachment which had lasted through their education and long after they had left school, when Fiona became a popular débutante and Christine had gone to live with her uncle.

Christine had no idea what Fiona had been doing this summer. She had seen her photograph now and again in Society papers. Miss Challis helping to get up dances or fêtes in aid of the Red Cross. Miss Challis helping at an officers' club. Miss Challis dancing with this young guardsman or that.

What could have happened to bring her here in such a state? Christine could see that under the delicate make-up Fiona's face was pale, her eyes reddened as though she had been crying, and her whole body trembling nervously.

'Why, my darling!' exclaimed Christine. 'What on earth is wrong?'

'The most terrible and the most wonderful thing,' said Fiona Challis, 'I'm in love, Christine . . . desperately, hopelessly in love. So much so that I can't eat or sleep properly . . . I can't think of anyone but *him*. It's killing me!'

Christine stared.

'But why? Why shouldn't love make you happy?'

'Because father has put his foot down and absolutely refuses to let me marry my Peter,' said Fiona. She flung herself into the other girl's arms and burst into tears. 'Oh, Christine, I've been half-mad for days. You're the only person in the world who can help me, so I've come to you.'

It took some time for Christine to get a

10

coherent story out of Fiona, who was obviously distracted. But gradually it was unfolded to her. Three months ago at an officers' club dance, Fiona met Peter Hollis, a subaltern in the 'Gunners.' She had realised at once that Peter was the one and only person in the world for her. He felt the same way about her. He was twenty-five, charming, amusing, but dependable . . . even her father had to admit that Peter Hollis was 'a good lad.' But, although Mr. Challis had nothing concrete against Peter, he disapproved on principle of war marriages. Nothing would induce him to agree to the immediate wedding which Fiona demanded.

'He thinks I'll change my mind,' finished Fiona, looking at Christine with wet, tragic eyes. 'He won't see that it means so much more to me than an ordinary love affair. Why, *it's life itself!*'

For a moment Christine hesitated to give her opinion. She had known Fiona to pass so quickly from one light-hearted 'affair' to another, and crowds of men were after the girl who was remarkably beautiful, with her primrose hair, her grey-blue, dark-lashed eyes, coupled with a sunny disposition, and a fortune behind her. But a few minutes' more conversation with Fiona made Christine decide that this affair was different from the rest.

'I would die for Peter,' Fiona declared

passionately. 'I'd give up everything and be poor with him, if necessary. Oh, Christine, I know I've been a butterfly up till now but Peter has found the *real* me. Daddy won't see it, but Peter can make me the woman he's always wanted me to be.'

She rambled on about Peter. He was stationed near London at the moment, but there was a rumour that his battery might shortly be going abroad. Then she might never see him again. She said:

'Christine, I must marry him at once. I must belong to him. If Peter was killed before our marriage, I should never get over it. You do believe me, don't you?'

Christine looked at Fiona's tear-stained woeful face, and she *did* believe. Yes, Fiona was desperately sincere. Christine could not doubt that, and as she sat there, listening, it gave her a queer psychic sensation, as though this thing were happening not only to Fiona, but herself. For she knew that if and when she loved, she would feel as Fiona did. The same blinding need to go to her lover against the world itself.

It seemed shortsighted and stupid of Mr. Challis, who had always indulged his daughter's every whim, to refuse now the thing that mattered most to her. Naturally he was afraid that she might rush into a mistake, in wartime. But if he sent this man away from Fiona, mused Christine, it might destroy all that was best in her. It might hurt her irreparably.

Fiona went on with her story. Her father was going to America at once on Government business of some urgency. She knew that he was terrified she might do something mad while he was away so he had got in touch with an old friend, Robert Standing, who owned a big property on the borders of Westmorland and Lancashire. His home, Wyckam Manor, was in a wild, lonely, lovely spot. He ran three big farms up there. Despite all Fiona's protests, her father had arranged for her to go to Wyckam Manor as a paying guest until his return from America.

'He thinks I'll be out of mischief up there,' Fiona told Christine, 'and you can imagine what it would mean to me never to see Peter, and for him to leave England and perhaps never see me again!'

Christine stood up and moved restlessly round her small sitting-room. Fiona's story was beginning to depress her. She had meant to be comforting and practical, but what could she say or do to help this girl whose whole soul was bound up in urgent need of her lover?

Fiona, dashing the tears from her eyes, caught at Christine's hand

'Help me, Christine, help me!' she implored.

'I'd do anything on earth for you if I knew a way,' said Christine huskily.

'Well, I know a way,' said Fiona, her eyes wild and bright and her young face pale. '*You* can go to Wyckam Manor in my place.'

Christine stared.

'Darling, are you mad?'

Fiona broke into a fresh argument, unfolded fresh plans which had obviously been formulated before she came.

Robert Standing had not seen her since she was a baby . . . would never know the difference if Christine went up North to stay with him. She, Christine, loved the country. She would be happy wandering around the farms. Meanwhile, Mr. Challis would be in America, and Fiona could marry her Peter the day after Mr. Challis left. By the time Mr. Challis returned, it would be too late for him to make a fuss.

'I shall be Peter's wife and nothing can separate us,' Fiona finished breathlessly.

Christine's eyes, hazel-gold, looked into the grey-blue ones of her friend. She laughed nervously.

'Darling, it's a crazy scheme . . . I couldn't . . .'

'You can, you *must*,' interrupted Fiona. 'It will only be for a few weeks. Please, *please* go in my place. It's all so easy. You've no ties. You've only got to give notice in the office and tell the girl you live with that you're going off for a hiking tour. You leave no address. Nobody will know you up in the North. I'll

14

write letters and send them to you to post to Daddy from the village. Peter and I will have our honeymoon, and then, when he goes abroad, I'll go up North and tell Uncle Bob Standing the truth. But it won't be any use then his cabling Daddy.'

'But, darling . . .'

'No, no, you mustn't refuse me. I'll help you find a better job when you come back. And you're tired, Christine. You look thin and worn. It will do you a world of good to have a few weeks on the farm. Oh, Christine, *Christine*, do it—for it means the whole of my life to me.'

Christine shook her head blankly. Her head was in a whirl. She was stirred and impressed by all that Fiona said, but hesitant to impersonate another girl. On and on pleaded Fiona, pointing out that if she, Fiona, defied her father openly now, he might refuse to go away and leave her. It would be fatal for him to refuse the Government's offer to send him to America to pull off a big deal at a time of crisis. It was for *his* sake that Christine must do this thing as well as Fiona's.

'And it will only be for a few weeks,' Fiona kept assuring her.

Somebody knocked on the door.

At once Fiona dashed to the mirror to powder her face and arrange her hair. Her eyes grew starry-bright.

'That's my Peter. I asked him to call for me.

I knew you wouldn't mind.'

Christine stood speechlessly thinking over all that Fiona had said. The idea was beginning to appeal to her vastly. Not only the idea of helping her friend to gain her heart's desire but of spending a lovely autumn month in the country. It *was* tempting.

Fiona opened the door, Christine caught a glimpse of a tall young man in officer's uniform, of a hand going up in a salute, then of two arms enfolding Fiona's slender figure. Her fur dropped to the ground. The fair head was tilted back. The lips of the lovers met in a long, passionate kiss.

Christine Shaw felt her heart rocketing and her cheeks grew warm. She was curiously stirred by the sight of that close embrace. It decided her. She knew that she could no longer refuse to do what Fiona asked. She *must* help these two to find their heaven.

Fiona came back into the room. Peter Hollis came with her, his fingers twined with hers.

'I suppose you think we're both crazy,' he said to Christine with an apologetic smile.

'Quite,' she said, and smiled back at him.

'Oh, but darling,' exclaimed Fiona, 'I've explained how terribly urgent it all is and what it means to us, and you do agree with me, don't you, Christine, that we're justified in getting married like this without Daddy's permission?'

'I wouldn't exactly use the word "justified,"'

16

said Christine, 'because I don't really know whether one is ever justified in telling lies or going behind someone's back. But in this case I sort of feel that your father is making a mistake and that you *ought* to be allowed to get married.'

'There!' said Fiona triumphantly, 'I told you she'd see our point of view, didn't I, Peter? When we were at the *Institut Préalpin* Christine was always terribly romantic. She believes in romance. She believes in *ours*, don't you, Christine?'

'Yes, I think I do, but I don't know why. I never had much in my life,' said Christine with a short laugh.

Peter Hollis, one arm still enfolding his Fiona, glanced speculatively at the other girl. He thought she looked rather sweet, although she had none of Fiona's spectacular beauty. She was too pale and thin and—perhaps only for the moment—lifeless. But he could well believe that with Fiona's chances and in Fiona's clothes, Christine might well become a beauty. Those hazel eyes of hers were very lovely and the short hair, brushed up into waves around her head, was as bronze as a copper-beech. She looked sensitive and delicate and yet there was a certain strength in the curve of her lips, the tilt of her chin.

On an impulse Peter Hollis said:

'One of these days you're going to find romance, I promise you, and just as much as I

17

want to give my life for Fiona . . . so some man will want to give his for you.'

Christine flushed and laughed in some embarrassment, although despite herself those words held a definite thrill for her.

'Thanks,' she said; 'that's one of the nicest things I've ever had said to me.'

'Oh, you've no idea how nice my Peter is,' put in Fiona.

Christine turned to her.

'Isn't it possible, my dear, for you two to fix things up without all this impersonation business? It does worry me a bit.'

'Darling, I've already explained that Daddy *won't* give his permission and I don't want to defy him openly just as he's going to America. And you needn't worry about the impersonation. You are only going to take my place for a short time and no one will be any the wiser, but it will keep everyone happy while Daddy is away.'

Christine lit a cigarette and stuck her hands into the pockets of her slacks.

'And what explanation do you think I'm going to give to Barbara Jenkins?'

'Just that you're staying in the country with me, and you've said yourself that they've told you at the ambulance depot to get away for a bit. You've done your bit for the war for long enough without a rest, and they can quite well do without you for a few weeks.'

'I suppose so, but I feel I'm walking out on

18

them.'

'But you owe yourself something. Honestly, Christine, you're an old goose. Always so conscientious. You can carry that too far. I used to tell you so at Chexbres.'

Christine smiled and turned to Peter again.

'She's a madcap. I suppose you know what you're taking on, Mr. Hollis?'

'I think so,' said the young man, and bent and dropped a kiss on Fiona's blonde head. 'But I don't know that she's doing very well for herself. I ought really to face her father and get his full permission, or else refuse to marry her. I'm not being very conscientious myself, am I?'

'Oh, darling,' exclaimed Fiona in a desperate young voice, *'don't* let's start all these qualms of conscience again. It's all fixed now. Christine is going to help us. She believes in our love.'

'Yes, I do believe in that,' said Christine.

'And you will go up to Wyckam Manor *as me*?'

Christine Shaw hesitated only for a moment longer. It seemed to her suddenly as though her world was topsy-turvy and that somebody might have to pay dearly for this crazy scheme, but it had a strange fascination for her. She was in the mood to do something crazy . . . just to get away from the old life, and to get into the country . . . up to those wild, beautiful fens and fells of Lancashire and Westmorland,

19

which she had read about and thought about, and which drew her by the very magic of their names.

'It may be wrong of all of us,' she said, 'but I'll go.'

CHAPTER TWO

It was not until the following Monday when Barbara Jenkins returned to London and Christine had a chance of talking to her that she realised a little more fully the seriousness of the thing she had promised Fiona she would do.

On the Saturday afternoon, Fiona and Peter had stayed with Christine for several hours discussing their plans, and when they had left Christine had felt in a kind of daze, a state in which she had remained over the week-end. On the Sunday she had spent an extraordinarily exciting morning with her old school-friend getting together a *trousseau* for this trip up to the North. It was fortunate that the two girls were of the same build and that all Fiona's lovely clothes fitted Christine— even down to the shoes. They had had a dress rehearsal and Christine had experienced for the first time in her young life the intense feminine satisfaction of seeing her reflection in the mirror and knowing that she was a hundred per cent perfectly dressed.

It was pretty good to feel the soft silkiness of Fiona's exquisite lingerie—creamy satin, gossamer silk georgette—each garment embroidered with her initials F.M.C.—*Fiona Mary Challis*. The real silk stockings (a guinea a pair) were pure delight, like the smart American shoes. Those daring little hats which Fiona wore perched on her blonde curls looked just as attractive on Christine's chestnut head, and Fiona, watching her, had taken a childish delight in decking out her friend.

'You look enchanting, darling,' she had said. 'And you'll soon impress all the old stodges up at Wyckam Manor that you're *me*. All you want now is an hour with my beauty specialists and another hour at Antoine's, who'll cut and set your hair divinely. Then you'll be Miss Challis complete.'

Yes, it had all been very exciting, and Christine had driven back to the flat in Warwick Avenue in a taxi, taking with her two rawhide expensive-looking suitcases, already packed with the borrowed plumes.

But on Monday some of the thrill evaporated. Two difficult moments awaited Christine. The first was when she had to face her employer and hand in her resignation, using the excuse that she was not well, and the doctor had ordered her to stop work and go away at once. Of course, she told Mr. Locket,

21

whom she had interviewed, she would forfeit her salary (Fiona, the millionaire's daughter, could recompense her for that, and Fiona's case was more urgent than Mr. Locket's if it came to a case of deserting one or the other).

And the second was when she had to talk to Barbara . . . B.J. as she was affectionately called, that distinguishing name having been given her at College because there were so many Barbaras.

At first Christine had made up her mind not to tell Barbara anything, but on second thoughts she had decided to confide in the friend who had shared her life for the last two years. So, over their supper that warm summer's night, she unfolded the story of Fiona's visit and its astonishing sequence.

'I know you'll think me mad, B.J.,' she finished. 'And I don't much like all the deception entailed, but I have a queer sort of feeling I *must* help Fiona. All her life she has been a spoiled, selfish sort of girl, rushing from one boy-friend to another. Now the real thing has come her way—I can see it has—and I want her to marry Peter. I don't want Mr. Challis to step in and put a stop to it all. He is making a mistake in not agreeing to the marriage right away. Later on I think he'll see how settled and happy Fiona is and he will admit he was wrong.'

'But meantime,' said Barbara Jenkins, 'what you are going to do could hardly be called right.'

That somehow roused the spirit of defiance in Christine.

'But why not? What harm can it do?' she argued. 'Not a soul knows Fiona up North. She loathes country life and I adore it. I shall enjoy it far more than she would have done, and she will be with Peter, so we will both benefit.'

B.J. opened her grey-blue eyes widely and cast a slightly reproachful look at her friend.

'But, Christine, my lamb, can't you see that it might lead to all kinds of complications?'

'Such as?'

B.J. shrugged her shoulders.

'Oh, I don't know,' she said weakly. 'But it just might. Somebody who really knows Fiona might turn up at Wyckam Manor.'

'Fiona says that's not possible. Wyckam Manor is absolutely in the wilds. This man, Mr. Standing, runs three farms there, Stonehead, Stack End and Burnt Hollow, and he doesn't know anybody in Fiona's circle.'

'Stonehead, Stack End and Burnt Hollow,' repeated B.J. 'I must say they sound attractive.'

A dreamy look came into Christine's hazel eyes.

'I'll say they do! Oh, I've always had a mad longing for country life. I'm crazy to go, B.J. Now that I've given in my notice at the office and burned my boats, I'm longing to lose myself in the fens and fells and all that wild, glorious country. It should be perfect now that autumn is on the way.'

'I'm only too glad you're going to have a rest and a real one at that,' admitted B.J. 'Especially as I've got Alan coming home— and my aunt at Reigate to go to at week-ends. I've always felt life has cheated you, poor little Christine. I want you to get some happiness. But it doesn't seem to me that this is the right way of getting it.'

Christine reached out a hand and took the other girl's.

'Angel, don't lecture me and don't start pointing out the evil of my ways. I know you're dead right and if you say much more to me I'll get wind up and chuck it.'

'Oh, don't do that,' said B.J. inconsistently. 'But I wonder Miss Challis can't see that she is asking a great deal of you.'

'She does, but she's so much in love with her Peter she has no other thought.'

'And what sort of a young man is he, allowing you to do all this so that he can get married without the permission he ought to get from the old man?'

'Darling, don't be so devilishly logical and clear-headed and sane about it all,' laughed Christine. 'Every word you say is right and yet I like Peter. He is young and rather shy, and terribly in love with Fiona, and he's due for service abroad at any moment. I haven't the heart to criticise him. I *want* those two to get married at once in case he gets killed. And that's why I am helping them. Oh, I'll admit it is against some of my better instincts, but I'm going to shove them into the background. Don't think too badly of me, B.J.'

'I could never think badly of you, Christine. You are one of the most courageous people I've ever known. You've had rotten luck ever since you left Switzerland, and you've stood up to it all marvellously. I just don't want to see you get into a fix.'

'Oh, what's the good of anything if one doesn't take a chance occasionally?'

'You must be a bit of a gambler, Christine. I'm afraid I never have been.'

'The whole of life's a gamble,' said Christine grandly. 'Every night when there's a raid we may all be killed or hopelessly injured. I've reached a state of mind, B.J., when I want to enjoy life before I die . . . or go into a home for cripples.'

B.J. looked at her with some curiosity. It was queer, she thought, that one could live for two whole years with a person and not really know them. She didn't really know Christine Shaw. She hadn't thought her capable of indulging in such an escapade as this. Certainly Christine was not by nature as equable as herself. She was more moody and felt much more intensely about things. And she could recall now a conversation which she had once had with Christine's admirer, Kenneth Howell.

Kenneth, whilst admitting his own inability to win Christine's love, had said to B.J.:

'One day some lucky fellow is going to attract her and then Christine will surprise herself and everybody else. Look at that mouth of hers, and those eyes . . . she is capable of a *grande passion*, is our Christine.'

Well, this evening, B.J. had to admit to herself that Christine was capable of anything. There was a wild streak in her and here she was about to impersonate her friend, cut adrift from her old life, and embark on an entirely new one. She was taking a risk—but she might have a marvellous time up North and it would do her a lot of good. Yet B.J. in her practical mind was still worried by the suspicion that it might have repercussions, and they would be upon Christine. She didn't care what happened to Fiona and Peter, but she did mind what happened to Christine.

The two girls talked over the matter for a bit longer. B.J. had finally to agree with Christine that the repercussions could not be very severe, whatever they were. Christine could only be severely censured by Fiona's father and by Mr. Standing, of Wyckam Manor, once the truth was out. Christine did not seem to mind about that. She did not mind about anything, she said, so long as Fiona and Peter were safely tied up.

'It's really going to be fun,' was Christine's summing up of the whole affair, 'a glorious adventure. Just imagine me, B.J., as the rich Miss Challis. Come and look at my heavenly clothes.'

B.J. was about to respond when the door bell rang. Christine answered the call. It was a telegram for Miss Jenkins. Christine's heart constricted as she took the orange envelope from the boy. Telegrams always frightened her in war-time. Her greatest anxiety whenever she took one in at this door was in case it should be bad news for B.J. about her man at sea.

B.J. opened the telegram with her usual calm, although Christine fancied the girl's cheeks paled a little. There was a moment of tense expectancy and then Christine saw the blood fly to her friend's cheeks and B.J. raised a pair of shining eyes.

'Oh, Christine,' she exclaimed, '*look!*'

Christine read the wire. It was a cable from B.J.'s fiancé. It announced that Lieutenant Alan Torcross expected to be home the first week in October and asked Barbara to make all the necessary preparations for their wedding. Christine's romantic heart beat fast with joy for her friend. The two girls danced together round the tiny sitting-room, waving the cable aloft.

'What wonderful news. Just two or three weeks more and you'll be B.J. no longer!' cried Christine. 'We'll all have to alter the J. to a T.'

For once B.J. actually seemed to have lost her customary *sangfroid*. She was flushed and trembling.

'I can't believe it, Christine. It's much earlier than we expected.'

'His ship is probably coming in to refit or something.'

'I'll be able to put up the banns at once,' said B.J.

Christine nodded.

'All the more reason why poor lonely little Christine should take that illegal holiday on a Lancashire farm.'

'But what about attending my wedding?'

'I'll come if I can, darling. Miss Challis can always slip away to town for a night.'

B.J. dropped into a chair and read her cable again. Christine lit a cigarette and looked with a sigh at her friend. Dear old B.J. She was so glad for her. *And* so envious. Just as she was envious of Fiona. It must be grand and glorious to find the right man and be married to him. Would it ever come *her* way. Would she ever meet a man who would make her pulses beat faster and her heart leap at the thought of him?

She had better stop worrying about whether it was right or wrong to take Fiona's place. She could see, now that this cable had come, that B.J. would be leaving the flat—leaving her alone—before another month was out. She had nothing to look forward to except this visit to the North. She was going, now, whatever happened.

She went into the hall to telephone to Fiona and make definite arrangements for her journey.

CHAPTER THREE

Twilight was falling when Christine stepped out of the train at Grange-over-Sands and stood looking around her.

She had had the thrill of travelling first-class, and of being deferentially treated by porters anxious to carry her rawhide cases. Wearing a beautifully-cut tweed suit, short Persian lamb jacket, and *chic* little hat—all Fiona's—Christine felt that she was acting a part in some play.

During the long journey, Christine had had a few more qualms of conscience about it all, but they had speedily vanished when she remembered the radiant faces of Fiona and Peter who had seen her off. They were going to be married as soon as possible. Mr. Challis had already left by Clipper for the United States. The road was clear for Fiona and her romance.

Christine felt well-primed in all that she had to do. So far as she could see, there would be nothing to give away her real identity. Mr. Standing had wired that he was sending a Mr. Farlong, the factor of his estate, to meet the train, on which there would also be two landgirls who had been engaged for work on the farm.

As Christine stood hesitant, she noticed a tall dark girl, wearing a sensible Burberry and felt hat, walking toward the barrier, carrying two heavy suitcases.

The girl hailed the porter at the barrier in a voice loud enough for Christine to hear.

'Is there a Mr. Farlong of Stonehead Farm here to meet me?'

This, thought Christine, must be one of the land girls. Stonehead Farm was part of the Wyckam estate.

Christine approached the big dark girl.

'Excuse me, but I'm expecting to be met by Mr. Farlong, too.'

The other girl stared at the fashionable young woman with some surprise.

'Oh, are you? I'm Molly Deacon. I've been working down Exeter way, but they've made a change there so I took the job up here. There should be another of us on the train . . . I suppose you aren't—'

'No, I'm not a land-girl,' cut in Christine smiling, 'but I'm going to Mr. Standing's place. Would you recognise Mr. Farlong if you saw him?'

'I wouldn't, and I'm not keen on working for him either,' said Molly Deacon gloomily. 'One of our girls in Exeter has an aunt living at Stonehead. She heard from the aunt who says

Mr. Farlong's a grand factor, and Mr. Standing's right-hand man, but that he doesn't half make everyone under him work. He hates women, too, I hear say. Not much fun having a woman-hater for a boss, eh?' she ended with a half laugh.

Before Christine could answer, both girls came suddenly aware of a man's clear, rather dominating voice. It came from one who was obviously used to giving orders. It said:

'Where the devil are these women? I can't go up to every girl who arrives at Grange and ask if she's for Stonehead.'

Christine and the land-girl turned their heads in the direction of that voice. It came from a very tall man who was talking to the station-master by the bookstall.

'Whole thing's a waste of time and petrol,' he added. 'This is the second train I've met. Typical of the sex . . . no punctuality . . . no discipline. It's taken the war and a shortage of men for me to hire a pack of females for *my* farm.'

Molly Deacon pushed her hat over her eyebrows.

'That,' she said, 'must be my woman-hating boss. Crikey! What a welcome!'

Christine looked curiously at Mr. Standing's factor. She was not impressed by what she had heard. On the contrary, it made her rather scornful. She disliked 'cave-man' stuff. At the same time, she was forced to admit that

31

Martin Farlong was an interesting-looking creature. The epitome of physical fitness, tall, lean, wide-shouldered, with a rough head of thick dark hair, and a face tanned to a rich brown.

Suddenly he turned his head and caught Christine's gaze. Now she had almost a sense of shock. What a fierce direct look the man had. He came striding towards the two girls and when he was near enough Christine could see that his eyes were a brilliant blue. He would have been unusually handsome but for the thinness of his lips and that sombre, almost ill-tempered expression.

'He's stepped right out of *Wuthering Heights*,' she thought. 'What a bitter face!'

Martin Farlong touched his cap and said curtly:

'You for Stonehead Farm?'

'That's us,' said Molly, no more pleasantly than her future boss.

His deep-set eyes swept past her and rested upon Christine. He looked her up and down almost derisively. She felt her cheeks growing scarlet.

'Car's outside,' he said, and turned on his heel.

'What a bear,' said Molly. 'Aren't you glad you're not going to work for him?'

'It's obvious that he thinks I am,' said Chris with a smile.

Molly Deacon looked at the charming and

expensively-dressed girl and then laughed aloud.

'What a sell for him.'

A ramshackle old Ford stood outside the station. Into the back climbed Molly the land-girl, slinging her luggage beside her. The porter placed Christine's suitcases with the land-girl's shabby luggage. Martin Farlong, scarcely giving the girls a glance, swung himself into the driver's seat and lit a pipe.

Perforce Christine seated herself in the front at his side.

As they drove up the hill and through the main street of the town, she said:

'How far are we from Mr. Standing's place?'

'Twenty miles, and let's hope we make it before black-out. The lights on this car don't work.'

'What fun,' said Christine coldly. 'We're liable to land in the ditch.'

'You girls have got to get used to ditches,' he said.

Christine raised an eyebrow. So Molly Deacon was right. This man thought she was the second land-girl. He hadn't much discrimination, she reflected.

The air struck cold once they left the town and got out into the country. Christine let it blow upon her face. It was pure and crisp after the close, sticky atmosphere in London. Around her lay the beauty of the open country. But she shivered.

'It's much colder here than down South,' she ventured to say to the factor.

He gave her a quick sidelong look in which she read contempt.

'No good you girls getting soft ideas. You've got to get used to the cold, and I'll not apologise for forgetting to bring you a hot-water bottle.'

Christine was half amused and half angry. Whether he thought her a land-girl or not, he had no right to be so rude. His attitude began to rouse the fighting spirit in her.

'Don't worry about hot-water bottles. Worry about your lack of manners,' she flung at him.

He gave her another swift look and this time it held surprise and no small annoyance. He was unaccustomed to having girls work on his farm and he certainly was not used to criticism from any of the men he employed. If there was one thing he detested, it was a woman about the place, except old Emmy, the housekeeper, who looked after him at the farm. And what in the name of fortune, he asked himself, was he going to do with a cheeky slip of a girl like this one, with her smart clothes, her red lips, those delicate-looking hands? The beauty of her long-lashed hazel eyes which she flashed upon him was not to be denied. Deep down in himself, Martin Farlong could never remain unmoved by beauty, but this girl's glamour, the subtle perfume which drifted from the charming figure so close to him, roused resentment in him rather than admiration. He was afraid of glamorous, pretty women . . . he avoided those who rarely came his way as an animal would avoid a snare.

There were dark bitter memories of his past . . . things stored away in the recess of his inner consciousness, which made Martin Farlong feel that way.

Christine was trying to converse with him again.

'As I'm going to live up here, I'd like to know something about the place.' She had to raise her voice as Martin was driving fast and the wind was rushing noisily through the battered side-curtains. 'Where are we now?'

'On Cartmel Fell,' he said.

'It must be beautiful in the sunlight.'

'It's beautiful any time,' he shouted back in a surly voice, and would not let her know that he was impressed by the fact that she appreciated the scenery. For he loved it—it was his country. He knew every stick and stone of it. He had been born and bred in the village of Cartmel.

Christine turned her attention from the factor to the panorama, which was thrilling her to the roots of her being. In a way it was no more welcoming than this queer man. In the grey twilight the wild beauty of the Fell was harsh, even forbidding, and there were heavy clouds banking in the sky, threatening a fall of rain.

Below them the valleys were shrouded in a mist that curled like a human thing about tree, bush, and thicket. Close by, she could see stone dykes, little circles of trees under which cattle were huddling, and the thick purple mat of the heather.

They passed sturdy grey stone houses and lonely farms. Everything upon this Lancashire soil seemed to her full of stern simplicity.

Soon they came to the borders of Westmorland, where the hills rose higher, and far below she could catch a glimpse of silver water . . . one of the Lakes . . . then mile upon mile of grassy, uncultivated land . . . sombre woodlands, boulder, and fern. And this was where she was going to live for the next few weeks, thought Christine! The spell of it touched her to the core, never to leave her again.

It was almost dark by the time they reached Stonehead Farm, another of those sturdy granite houses built bravely to face the wind and the rain, surrounded by straggling farm buildings, sheds, and labourers' cottages. Martin Farlong pulled up the car and almost reluctantly opened the door for Christine because the handle stuck and he knew she couldn't manage it.

As Christine stepped out, one of her high heels turned over in the gravel path. She almost missed her balance. Against his will, Martin Farlong put out his hand to steady her.

She was never to forget the sensation of tremendous power from those long brown fingers closing about her forearm. They were like steel, she thought, remorselessly strong.

But whatever effect she had upon him, he merely laughed derisively.

'You'll want to wear more sensible shoes when *you* start work, my girl.'

Christine looked up at him furiously.

'How dare you speak to me like that!'

'Come, come,' he drawled, 'you've got to get used to taking orders. Where did you have your training?'

She was on the defensive now, thoroughly nettled.

'You seem to think you're delivering me here as though I were a sack of potatoes,' she flared. 'I should think you'd give more care to a bottle of milk.'

He began to laugh. Molly Deacon stood by listening and staring. Then through the small, well-kept garden in front of the farmhouse, came a thin grey-haired man in plus-fours. He was carrying a gun and had a retriever at his heels.

Immediately Martin Farlong stiffened and his hand went up to his cap.

'Good evening, sir,' he said—then muttered to the two girls: 'This is Mr. Standing, so mind your manners.'

The anger in Christine's heart boiled down. She saw that her revenge was at hand and she was feminine enough to take it. She ran forward to greet Robert Standing, remembering all that Fiona had told her.

'Why, Mr. Standing,' she exclaimed, 'it's good to see you. Daddy said I wouldn't recognise you as I haven't seen you since I was a little girl. But do you know me? I used to call you Uncle Bob.'

Robert Standing held out both hands.

'My dear Fiona! How very nice to see you. No, I can't say I'd recognise you, my dear child. But how did you get down here? You ought to have come up to the Manor House. Hi, Farlong . . .' he turned to his factor, smiling . . . 'What made you bring Miss Challis down to Stonehead?'

Martin Farlong stared. Blinking he looked from his employer to the lovely girl who was hanging on to Mr. Standing's arm in such a familiar fashion. Then as he realised his mistake a slow flush crept under his tan. *This was Miss Fiona Challis.* He had heard that she was expected as a guest at the Manor. And he had thought her a land-girl and treated her as one.

He stood speechless with confusion and chagrin. He saw 'Miss Challis's' hazel eyes mocking him. It was certainly her turn to deride. But she smiled sweetly enough and said:

'I think poor Mr. Farlong thought I was going to work on the land. I hope he isn't disappointed.'

Martin forced an apology to his lips, touched his cap, then turned on his heel and followed Molly Deacon into the farmhouse.

Robert Standing took the girl whom he believed to be Fiona Challis along to his shooting brake which stood outside the gates.

'Just as well I was down this way delivering a brace of birds to old Emmy. I'm sorry, my dear, I'm afraid you haven't had a very attractive welcome. But it was a day's shooting I couldn't get out of, so that's why I wasn't there to meet you in person.'

Christine, seated in the car, sat thinking about Martin Farlong. Her moment of triumph had passed, and she did not feel particularly pleased about it. The man wanted bringing down a peg or two, and yet . . . it had been no fun doing it.

Mr. Standing asked a lot of questions about his old friend, Challis and she answered them mechanically.

A few minutes later she was being introduced to one of the loveliest old houses she had ever seen. One of those small perfect Queen Anne gems, Wyckam Manor stood high on a hill. It was too dark now to see the country but Christine was certain that in daylight the view would be incomparable. Inside the Manor, she saw exquisite panelling, polished walnut period furniture, fine rugs on yew floors and a museum collection of beautiful glass and china, all of which went to make up a perfect country residence.

Robert Standing had spent a lot of money on his home, and his wife, now dead, had been a woman of rare taste. The Manor, blacked out from the night, welcomed Christine and enchanted her. Here were soft lamplight, big log-fires in all the main rooms, flowers, books, a radiogramophone—every luxury. After her little flat in London, it would certainly be heaven, she reflected.

Her bedroom, too, was perfect with its rose and white chintzes, and the luxurious modern bathroom leading out of it. A rosy-cheeked Lancashire maid in frilly cap and apron came up to help her unpack. Later, dining with old Standing, it seemed obvious to Christine that life for the next few weeks as Fiona Challis would be exceedingly lazy and pleasant.

Robert Standing, although nearing seventy, was a good companion, cultured and interesting, of course, he knew everyone in the neighbourhood. He had asked several people over to the Manor to meet 'Fiona' tonight, so that she would not be bored or lonely. He had been warned by his old friend to keep the girl well amused and out of mischief. So Christine, playing her part creditably as Miss Challis, and looking lovely, spent a pleasant evening. But when the guests had gone, she found herself thinking again about that sullen, handsome young factor who had treated her so rudely.

She asked Mr. Standing a few questions about him. Standing had nothing but praise for his factor. He was invaluable here, he said, and because of the fact, he had refused to release the factor for Army service. Farlong had been told that it was his duty to stay and manage the three farms now that times were more than ever difficult.

'I think he feels not being in khaki,' Mr. Standing told Christine, 'but I tell him that he's doing just as much good for his country here, making a success of farming.'

Christine considered this. But she disagreed with Mr. Standing. She could see that it would be a thorn in the flesh to a man like Farlong, not to be in uniform during the war.

'Perhaps that's what made him so bitter,' she said.

Robert Standing smiled and told Christine that she mustn't take any notice of Martin's surly ways. His 'bitterness' was due not only to present war conditions but his whole upbringing. He had been disciplined and hardened to life from early youth. The son of a Cartmel doctor, life had once been full of promise for Martin. But he had had a pretty frivolous mother who had left her husband for another man. The subsequent divorce and loss of his mother had left a deep mark on the boy's soul. It had been the beginning of his antipathy toward all women.

'But I always say he'll get over it one day

and marry,' Robert Standing told Christine. 'I'm very fond of Martin. He's a good fellow and well educated. It's surprising what a lot he's read, and how much he knows outside farming. By the way I must ask him to take you over the farms tomorrow. That is if you are interested?'

Christine said that she would be very interested. She went to bed that night, thinking not so much about this new amazing life which she was leading as Fiona Challis, as the 'woman-hater' living down there alone at Stonehead Farm. She could not get away from the fact that his history intrigued her.

When Martin Farlong was asked that next morning by his employer to show 'Miss Challis' round, he had no choice but to say 'Yes.' But he was secretly irritated. He was a busy man with three farms under his control. It was a waste of his time, in his opinion, showing a pretty, useless society girl places and things which he was convinced could not interest her.

Mr. Standing left Christine with his factor and went off on business to Ulverston.

Christine greeted the factor as though nothing untoward had happened between them yesterday. But Martin was still smarting from the fact that he had made a fool of himself and that she had helped to make a fool of him by not telling him at once who she was.

He had tried last night in his lonely farmhouse to forget her existence, but had found himself remembering her voice, the softness of her arm beneath his fingers, her subtle perfume, and the challenge in her lovely eyes.

This morning he had to admit she looked attractive enough in her tweed suit, and with a bright blue scarf tying up her beech-brown hair. She greeted him cheerfully and could not resist teasing him by pointing to the thick brogues with the crepe rubber soles which she had put on.

'Are these the sort of shoes you approve of, Mr. Farlong?'

He flushed.

'When I criticised your high heels, Miss Challis, I was still under the impression that you were going to work on my farm.'

She shook her head at him.

'Oh dear! I don't believe you've got a sense of humour.'

His handsome, sulky face burned a deeper red.

'If you'll come with me, I'll show you Stonehead,' he said curtly.

Still smiling, she went with him. Then for a little while hostilities between the two were forgotten. There was so much for Martin Farlong to show, and for her to see, and he could not disguise his pride in the five acres of pastureland; the beautifully-kept modern dairies; the well-equipped milking sheds with the newest type of machinery; the handsome

Jersey cows.

Harvesting was still in progress, later up here than down South. At the end of the tour Christine stood beside Martin Farlong watching Molly Deacon drive a binder which cut the corn, and thought that she had never seen anything so perfect as this great field of grain under a clear blue sky and with a fresh wind blowing from the Northern hills.

The sound of the binder chuffing over the field, the song of the skylarks, the distant bleating of sheep on the fell, formed a symphony which seemed to Christine the grandest she had ever heard.

She took an active interest in everything that Martin showed her. As they walked across the fields to the farmhouse she was thrilled when, passing a clump of bushes, they put up a pair of pheasants which whirred into the spinney beyond.

She plied Martin with questions about the farm which he answered shortly, yet impressed by her intelligent interest in his beloved work.

He told her that the sheep would stay out on the hills until the winter when the snow drifted, and then they would have to be brought down for feeding.

'It must be pretty severe here in winter,' said Christine.

'At times, but you get used to it.'

'I've never known anything about farming before,' she said, 'but I think it must be enthralling work.'

'It's been my life,' said Martin Farlong, 'but I'd sooner be away in the Army now.'

She remembered about his disappointment over this matter, and her voice was gentle as she said:

'That must be rather tough for you.'

Sympathy was the last thing Martin wanted from this girl or any woman. Deep down in him he would like to have thanked 'Fiona Challis,' but a lifetime of inhibitions prevented him from making any such response, just as he would have died rather than admit that he had enjoyed showing her around Stonehead.

He looked at his watch:

'Quarter to twelve. If you'll excuse me, Miss Challis, I've got to drive into Cartmel.'

'Where is that?'

'About ten miles from here.'

'I think Mr. Standing mentioned it to me last night. Isn't it a particularly lovely little place?'

A faint smile curved Martin's lips.

'I was born there and to me it's the grandest village in the world. It has an historic interest, too. Cartmel Priory and the Gatehouse are gems of architecture which no one ought to miss.'

Christine was genuinely interested. She had always had a passion for old buildings, inherited probably from her paternal grandfather, who had been one of the leading

45

archaeologists of his time. Even as a very young girl, wherever Christine had been taken on holiday, she had wanted to look at old churches and houses and find out all she could about them.

On an impulse she said:

'Lunch isn't until half-past one at the Manor. Do let me come with you and see Cartmel.'

Martin hesitated. In a manner he was pleased by her enthusiasm, because the little village of his boyhood—happy only in the days of his mother's lifetime—was always dear to him. He loathed the tourists who rushed through in cars without appreciating Cartmel to the full. On the other hand, he felt diffident about being seen in a place where he was known so well in the company of Mr. Standing's 'heiress' guest.

'Please take me,' Christine said; 'I can look around while you're doing whatever business has to be done.'

Martin felt it would be more than churlish to refuse, so a few minutes later, much to his own surprise, he found himself driving with the girl through the soft September sunshine, across the rugged fell toward Cartmel. Somewhat grudgingly he had to own to himself that she was not a dull companion, neither did she talk a lot of rubbish such as he might have expected from a young woman who led an artificial London life. She seemed candidly interested in all that she saw around her and all the questions she asked him about the country through which they were driving, he was only too pleased to answer.

They came to Cartmel and as they turned round a bend in the road, and Christine had her first view of the charming little village with its wide main street and the market cross, she bowed from side to side in the car in royal fashion.

'Salute to Martin Farlong's birthplace,' she said.

Martin eyed her dubiously. He had a sense of humour and was ready to appreciate hers, but his own had not been much developed in the hard, lonely life he led, and he was half afraid that this girl was laughing at him. She did laugh at him, but with such gay, honest eyes that he could not be offended.

'I really do salute it,' she told him. 'It's enchanting, and I wish I'd been born in such a gem of a place.'

'Where where you born?'

It was on the tip of her tongue to say 'India.' For she had, indeed, drawn her first breath in an English hospital at Delhi, where her father had been stationed at the time. Then she had to remind herself that she was Fiona Challis. She had no real idea where Fiona had been born, so she said 'London' and left it at that.

Martin parked his car outside the King's Arms Hotel and then opened the door for

47

Christine.

'I've got to meet a farmer in the pub about some sheep, so if you don't mind being left alone, Miss Challis . . . .'

'Go right ahead,' she broke in; 'I shall be quite happy wandering about.'

And she spent a very pleasant half hour looking at the village. She was enraptured by the Priory—one of the loveliest churches she had ever seen; by the tiny cottages with their flower-filled gardens; the little old-fashioned shops; and most of all by the Priory Gatehouse with its Norman archway.

She was going to be late for lunch, but she did not mind. She walked into the little post office and bought some postcards—views of the Priory Gatehouse, which she intended to send to B.J.

When Martin finally left her outside the Manor, she thanked him warmly for the expedition.

'I've enjoyed every moment of it,' she said.

He believed her, and he could not but feel more friendly towards her than he had done yesterday. Touching his cap, he drove away, leaving the slim, beautifully-dressed girl outside the portico of the Manor House.

Mr. Standing had waited lunch for his guest. Christine apologised for being so late, sat down at the table and broke into rhapsodies about Cartmel village.

'I'm enchanted by it,' she said. 'It's the sort

of place I've always wanted to explore.'

Mr. Standing smiled.

'Oh, most people who live this way get Cartmel fever,' he said. 'Your father has been up here in his time and he was a great admirer of the Gatehouse.'

Christine's enthusiasm faded and she dissolved into sudden silence. She knew that Mr. Standing alluded to William Challis. It was at moments like these that she chafed under the thought of her impersonation of Fiona— and disliked it. She would so much rather have talked candidly to Mr. Standing about her own father who had died, and about her own life.

Mr. Standing, looking at the girl under beetling brows, thought how pretty she was. A real 'charmer,' Bill Challis's girl, and he could not quite understand why her father had described her as being pleasure-mad and difficult. 'Fiona' seemed far more interested in country life than her life in town, and there was a simple friendliness about her which pleased him. He was also amused about what she had to say about his factor.

'You've achieved a triumph, my dear, to get Martin to take you sight-seeing. Well, it's good for him to have a little female company. He is far too inclined to keep away from them. But don't turn his head. That would never do.'

'That's not likely to happen,' said Christine with a laugh. 'But he is rather an exceptional character, isn't he? I mean, he's not at all like

49

a farmer. He knew the history of every building we passed.'

'You people from towns have a wrong idea of farmers,' said Mr. Standing. 'They're not all uneducated churls. I've met a lot of very cultured men on farms who know as much about Beethoven or Michelangelo as they do about grain and sheep.'

'Oh, I like farmers and everything to do with farms,' said Christine. 'And I like Martin Farlong. He interests me.'

'Well, I expect he'll annoy you one of these days. He has moods,' smiled Mr. Standing. 'Wants a lot of knowing, does our Martin.'

'Oh, I am so enjoying being up here,' exclaimed Christine.

'I'm glad, my dear. I shall be able to write very happily about you to your father.'

Christine lapsed into silence again.

CHAPTER FOUR

Following upon that day when Martin took Christine to Cartmel, she did not see him for the best part of a week. She did not know whether it was deliberately or not that he kept away from Wyckam Manor. She was rather disappointed, but could only suppose that he had no wish to cultivate any kind of friendship with her. And she had to keep reminding herself that she was Miss Challis and he in a subordinate position, as Mr. Standing's factor.

But she was given no time in which to feel dull, or to regret coming up here. Each day was filled with a new delight, for Mr. Standing saw to it that she visited all the places of interest so far as the petrol would allow him.

The week of sight-seeing ended with visits to several of Mr. Standing's friends, who occupied houses in the district. Christine liked some of them. All of them extended cordial hospitality to her, which made her feel embarrassed because she felt she had no right to it.

She wrote long letters describing her reactions to everything and everybody, both to B.J, and Fiona.

She had had two letters from Fiona since she came here, telling her that she was extremely happy, and then three days ago a telegram announcing that she had become Mrs. Peter Hollis and was the happiest girl in the world.

'You are responsible. We both bless your name.'

That was how the telegram had ended and it had cheered Christine immensely and helped her to brush aside her misgivings about the deception she was practising for Fiona's sake.

Then this morning had come an ecstatic note which Fiona wrote from the South during her week's honeymoon and enclosing a letter for Christine to post to America.

Mr. Standing knew nothing of this, but he saw the cable which reached Christine here from William Challis, giving his 'daughter' news of his activities in New York. And Christine gave Robert Standing a cable to send to America in return. There was no earthly reason for Mr. Standing to suspect that this girl was any other than Fiona Challis.

It was toward the end of the week that Christine came face to face with Martin Farlong again. She had taken a walk towards Stonehead and met him coming up from the turnip fields. He had had a busy morning helping the men make fresh folds for the sheep. When he saw 'Miss Challis's' attractive figure, he touched his cap and would have passed on but Christine stopped him.

'Mr. Standing tells me that you'll soon be sowing the winter wheat. Do you think I could come and watch?'

'Please do exactly as you wish,' he said with an icy courtesy which immediately put her on her mettle. She challenged him:

'Don't you think you might offer to show me a bit more of the three farms?'

He struck a hazel switch against his leather gaiters.

'I must ask to be excused,' he said. 'The days are getting shorter and I've all I can do to get through my work. I really haven't time for this sight-seeing.'

Christine flashed:

'You really are disagreeable!'

'I'm sorry,' he said, in a voice which showed little real contrition, touched his cap and moved on.

She stood looking after the tall figure of the man, with a feeling of frustration. Never in her life before had Christine come up against a thing like this . . . a man like Martin Farlong. In some undefinable way he appealed to her. She could not get him out of her mind, and yet she detested his arrogant rudeness. He roused in her an almost passionate desire to *make* him like her and be nicer to her. It was impossible for her not to admire his management, and, too, she had to admire the pride of the man. Whether she was 'Miss Challis' or not did not seem to matter to him. He was not kow-towing to hear just because she was a personal friend of his employer's.

The following morning Robert Standing went away for the day. He had wanted to arrange for friends to keep Christine company but she preferred to be alone. She intended to go down to Stack End and later to Burnt Hollow, which was the smallest of Martin's three farms. If he would not show her what was going on, she would see for herself.

She took one of Robert Standing's golden retrievers with her. She felt well and she knew that she looked a different girl from the one

53

who had left London ten days ago. She was well fed, rested and had plenty of fresh air and exercise. There seemed no shortage of rations at Wyckam Manor. There were great jugs of cream and dishes of butter on the table every day.

For the last forty-eight hours the weather had been glorious. The air was full of the odour of ripe blackberries and sunburnt gorse. The fells were lovely, enchanting under the autumn sky. Tomorrow was the first of October.

Christine thought uneasily of London and life as Christine Shaw. In her bag lay a letter from Fiona telling her that Peter's leave was up, but that he was still in England and that she was staying near his Depot for the moment.

'I'm so utterly happy . . . go on being me for a bit longer,' she had written. 'Don't get fed up with life up there.'

Christine knew definitely, today, that far from being fed up, she was in love with life up here. She could hardly bear the thought of it coming to an end, and of going back to the old grey existence as a typist and an ambulance-driver. The war seemed so far from this place. Occasionally they heard sirens in the distance, heard planes overhead, that was all. The place was a paradise and she was only too willing to impersonate Fiona for weeks and months if need be.

As she passed the gates that led into Stonehead Farm, she met Molly Deacon driving a dray-load of turnips on her way to one of the cattle-sheds. She stopped the horses as she met Christine and climbed down from the seat. Christine noticed that Molly's face looked grey and damp with sweat and that her features were contracted,

'Why, you oughtn't to be driving that load,' she exclaimed, 'you're ill, Molly.'

Molly admitted that she wasn't too well. She had a bit of a pain in her side, she said, and was worried about her appendix.

'Then you must stop work and go to bed at once,' said Christine.

Molly climbed down from her seat and wiped her forehead.

'I must get this load down to the shed. Mr. Farlong said it was important.'

'Well, never mind him, you get to bed. I'll take you to Emmy myself,' said Christine.

Molly, nothing loath, allowed Christine to take her along to the farm and to the old housekeeper. She was groaning with pain as she said:

'I've left that load standing there. I shan't rest until someone's taken it along.'

'All right,' said Christine, 'I'll take it myself; I haven't a thing to do.'

Old Emmy glanced at 'Miss Challis.'

'I reckon if you're doing that job, you'd better get into Molly's things and not spoil that pretty dress of yours, Miss,' she said.

Christine smiled. That seemed to her a good idea. It would amuse her to be the land-girl for whom she had once been mistaken.

She was feeling in high spirits when at length, clad in breeches and shirt, and with Molly's old felt hat on her head, she climbed on to the dray and took up the reins of the horses. She had told Molly that she could drive. She had thought it would be easy enough to lead a couple of old farm horses down to the shed, but she did not know what she was in for. The horses, knowing they were off home, started trotting. They were soon aware that the hands holding them were new, and in another moment they were cantering along the road. A very shaken Christine with crimson cheeks and pounding heart tried in vain to check them.

Along the rough road the dray clattered and swayed. Desperately Christine tried to pull the runaways in. Half-way down the road, Martin Farlong met the horses, saw what was happening, and sprang into the road to check them. The dray stopped with a jerk and Christine, losing her balance, tumbled out on to the road at the feet of her rescuer.

For a moment she lay in a little heap, winded, barely conscious of what had happened.

Martin, not recognising Christine in that attire, bent over her, more angry than sympathetic.

'These damn fool land-girls,' he thought, 'can't even handle a pair of horses.'

Then as he turned the girl over, wondering if she was hurt, he saw that this was no land-girl but 'Miss Challis' herself. For a moment he was startled, wondering what she was doing in those clothes and on that dray. Then he saw a tiny trickle of blood on her forehead, knelt quickly down and began to fan her with the hat that had fallen from her curls. His heart-beats quickened as he looked down at the lovely young figure, the sun-browned throat, the half-open, flower-red mouth, and he knew that in spite of all his antipathy this girl had a strange and disturbing effect upon him. He was seized with a mad longing to pull her into his arms and kiss that red mouth which had so often challenged him, mocked him.

Then Christine became aware of his hand chafing hers, and of his voice saying:

'Come, Miss Challis, come on . . . wake up . . . come along!'

His voice sounded as though he was anxious, she thought. His touch was extraordinarily gentle. He had forgotten to be bitter and sarcastic. Perhaps he was really concerned about her. She wasn't really hurt except for a scratch and the shock of the fall. But for a moment she stayed quiet, alive . . . all too intensely alive . . . to the fact that she wanted that hand to go on holding and stroking her arm . . . that she wanted that vital brown face of his to draw nearer, and it was near enough now for her to see how amazingly blue were his eyes in that thin, hard face.

'Fiona!' The name tumbled out from him unaware. 'Fiona! Are you all right?'

That use of her name from him—the name to which she really had no right—sent a wild confusion through Christine. She opened her eyes widely now and smiled up at him. At once he drew back from her as though he had been stung.

'You little fool,' he said furiously. 'Trying to break the necks of two good horses as well as your own. What the devil are you doing playing about in my land-girl's shoes anyhow?'

CHAPTER FIVE

Slowly Christine sat up. The smile had left her face. The thrill which she had experienced just for that moment vanished. It was no use, she thought, even trying to persuade herself that Martin Farlong liked her a little and had been anxious about her. He was just a surly brute. She passed a hand over one cheek and drawing her fingers away saw a smear of dust and blood. She could imagine what a sight she looked and she resented the way Martin's blue eyes scowled down at her. She decided to scowl back.

'So that's all the gratitude I get for trying to do a job for you,' she said.

'Who asked you to do it?'

'No one. I took it on myself, Mr. Factor. Molly is ill and it looks as though an ambulance will be required to take her into hospital for an operation. Appendix!'

Martin slapped a hand against the steaming neck of the big grey mare nearest him. His scowl deepened.

'What a devilish nuisance,' he muttered.

Christine scrambled to her feet, brushed the dust from her breeches and grimaced at the sight of her sleeve which was torn to shreds.

'You aren't human!' she flung at Martin. 'You don't think of anything but work, work, work! You are not sorry because poor Molly is ill—only because you think you will be shorthanded now.'

His face burned crimson. This girl was always getting at him . . . striking him in a raw place. He knew perfectly well that she was right. The whole of his life was bound up in the farm and its prosperity. Not human! But that wasn't at all the case. What right had she to make such an accusation? What right indeed had she to come to Stonehead and disturb his peace of mind? He felt ashamed of the all-too-human way in which his pulses had leapt when he had bent over her just now . . . so close to the tempting curve of her lips.

'I am extremely sorry that Molly is ill,' he at length blurted out.

Christine laughed shortly.

'And I suppose I ought to say I am sorry I couldn't manage the dray. I daresay I am better at driving a car than tackling horses.'

He gave her a swift look, more concerned than he would let her know by the sight of the scratches on that soft young cheek, and her grazed elbow. He whipped a handkerchief out of his pocket.

'This happens to be clean,' he mumbled, 'perhaps you'd like to bind up that arm.'

'Oh, it's nothing,' she said, but took the handkerchief and made an effort to turn it into a bandage. Martin then volunteered to bind the elbow for her. She allowed him to do so, smiling a little at his clumsy efforts. But once again she noted the gentleness of his fingers. What finely shaped fingers they were! Not the huge coarse hand that one might have expected from a farmer. But then the whole man, in spite of his height, was built on fine slim lines.

The ice between them thawed a little. Martin said:

'Jump up on the dray and I'll drive it into the yard and then take you back to Wyckam in my car.'

'I'll come in the dray,' she said, 'but I'm not going back to the Manor House. I'm taking Molly's place and I'm not going to back out of it just because I've had a tumble. No doubt there is a job you can give me that I can do with more success.'

Martin hesitated. Taking off his cap he rubbed the back of his rough black head, and through the short black lashes, those gentian eyes of his regarded her with a certain amount of bewilderment. She could see that he really did not know what to make of her.

'Poor old Martin,' she thought, 'he is so inexperienced with women. So tied up in knots with his repressions!'

She added:

'Honestly, I can do a job of work. I have never worked on a farm before but I am used to typing . . .'

She broke off, checking herself just in time. The guilty blood rushed to her face and throat. Heavens! she thought, she had been just about to give herself away; to tell Martin that she had worked for her living in a city office. And he thought of her as Miss Challis. Of course, there was some excuse for his doubts, his slight contempt for her. Society débutantes going from one dance or cocktail party to another would not be at all in his line.

He stared at her. He did not know why she had not finished her sentence, but he could see that she was embarrassed.

He said:

'Typing an occasional letter won't have made you fit for farm work, Miss Challis.

However, it's . . . it's . . . good of you to offer.'

Her embarrassment vanished and she was once again challenged by his inference that she was not capable of work. She tilted her head.

'Well, I insist on taking Molly's place for the time being,' she said.

Martin shrugged his shoulders.

'As you wish. I doubt if Mr. Standing would think it suitable . . .'

'I shall do as I like,' said Christine, with a petulance worthy of the real Fiona.

'Hop on to the dray then,' said Martin curtly.

She found it difficult to 'hop on.' Her body was sore and stiff after that fall but she would have died rather than let Martin know it. A few moments later they were clattering at a slow even pace down the lane. Ruefully Christine watched the way in which Martin managed the horses. They were docile and obedient to his touch on the reins; to his coaxing 'Come on then, Susy . . . come on, Betsy-girl.'

With Molly's felt hat on her knees, she sat there beside Martin and closed her eyes a moment, letting the soft air blow against her face. It was good up here, like this, with the sunshine on her uncovered head and the farm smells which she was beginning to know and like. The warm rich odour of the steaming horses, the hay lying in the fields, the hot apricot odour of burnt gorse, and perfume of hawthorn hedges.

She did not want to go back to her old life in London as Christine Shaw. Her whole soul recoiled from the prospect. And curiously enough, she had no more wish to be Fiona Challis, spoiled and pampered up at the Manor House. It was fun and a novelty living in luxury, but to be Molly Deacon . . . a land-girl working here at Stonehead Farm . . . that would be something real . . . something with backbone and purpose to it. She began to realise why a man like Martin Farlong was so wedded to the land. It was a wonderful thing to be a farmer. To sow and to reap, to be close to the mother earth from which you had sprung, and out of that earth, watch the new life springing.

A rabbit darted across the roadway.

'Oh!' said Christine jumping. 'Don't run over it.'

Then Martin laughed. It was positively the first real laugh she had heard from him and it had a pleasant ringing sound. She liked the way his blue eyes crinkled at the corners . . . she liked to see that stern hard mouth of his relax.

'Why do you laugh?' she asked.

'At the idea of a land-girl worrying about running over a rabbit.'

She coloured.

'I don't like killing things.'

'Nor I, particularly, but farmers have to get

63

accustomed to it. Rabbits eat the young corn and the greenstuff. They have to be exterminated.'

'All the same I wouldn't like to run over one. I used to have tame rabbits when I was a child.'

'So did I,' said Martin grimly; 'but you alter your point of view as you get older.'

'I shall never like seeing a warm living young thing done to death,' she said.

He flicked one of the horses with the rein and then glanced at the girl beside him. He did not despise her for being tender-hearted. On the contrary, he remembered very vividly a boy named Martin Farlong, who, at the age of ten, had kicked another boy for torturing a kitten, and then, when the boy's mother had got him into a row for the kicking, had taken his own beating gladly, and resolved never to be cruel to animals. He hoped that he was not cruel, but certainly a farmer had no time to worry about a dead rabbit. When he had thought about Miss Challis he had put her down as being a hard, spoilt, society girl. He could not altogether associate that young lady of his imagination with this one today. She had 'guts,' he had to admit it. She might have gone up to the Manor weeping after her accident and taken to her bed for the rest of the day with a magazine and a box of chocolates, but this girl was sticking to the job she had set herself.

Her last words echoed in his ears. The way her voice had softened when she said those words 'a warm living young thing.' She might have been describing herself, he thought. She was warm and very much alive with her sun-kissed skin (it was satin-smooth to touch, and he knew it), that waving hair tumbling about her head, as brown as the beech trees were brown, her eyes hazel-bright. A man wouldn't want to take that soft brown throat under his hands and squeeze the life out of it. He would want to bury his face in it and kiss that proud young mouth until it lost all pride and beseeched for more kisses.

Then he was angry with himself for such thoughts. Angry with her for arousing them. She would insist upon thrusting herself into his life—into his peace. He would show her that she couldn't fool around. If she was going to take Molly's place, then she could darn well take it.

He drove the dray into the yard and pulled up in front of the sheds. He stepped down and Christine, without waiting for him to offer a hand, jumped down after him.

'Think you can get the turnips out of the dray and into stacks in the shed?' he asked curtly.

'Certainly.'

'After that it will be lunch-time,' he said. 'This afternoon there is mash to be prepared for the pigs. I shall be down at Burnt Hollow,

65

but you can get one of the cowmen . . . George will be about . . . to show you where the stuff is.'

'Thanks,' said Christine, and realised that the moment of friendliness between them was at an end. She was vaguely disappointed because she would have liked to have gone on talking to Martin Farlong . . . to have heard his views about things in general. She could see what Mr. Standing had meant when he told her that Martin was cultured . . . much more so than the average factor. But if he wished to be the 'boss' to her as he was to Molly Deacon, let him get on with it; she wasn't going to complain.

'If you don't mind I'll just go along to the farmhouse and change my shirt, and wash the dirt off my face,' she said.

'O.K., but don't worry about your make-up down here,' he said.

'You just can't help being offensive!' she flashed.

'You told me I hadn't a sense of humour. Now where's yours?' he retorted, laughed, and walked away, whistling.

She stared after him, her hands clenched. She had never in her life before met a man with such power to annoy her, to stir up all her most primitive feelings. But she was going to get that work done and show him she could do it if she died.

She went back to the farm and found old

Emmy had already been on to the doctor about Molly.

'It is appendix, that it is,' she said with her strong North-country accent. 'Reckon doctor will get her to hospital soon enough.'

'Will she be all right until he comes?' asked Christine. 'Poor Molly. I can't offer to stay with her. I am going to do her work for Mr. Farlong.'

The old woman looked at Christine's dishevelled figure.

'Eh, but you've got yourself in mess, Miss Challis. Had tumble, have you?'

Christine explained. A moment later she had washed and tidied herself and found a fresh shirt of Molly's to slip over her head. She left Martin's handkerchief round her elbow. She would return that for him tomorrow. She said a few kind words to the land-girl who was in some pain, but relieved to find that her work was being done.

'You are a sport, Miss Challis, and you look grand in that outfit. You're one of those that looks good no matter what they put on.'

Christine laughed.

'Thanks for the compliment. But as you see I have washed my face and left off the make-up. Boss's orders!'

'Oh, him!' said Molly scornfully. 'Don't take any notice of him. He may be a good looker, but he has gone sour on women.'

'I expect he has reasons,' said Christine

lightly. 'Anyhow, I'm not going to be intimidated by him. But I just thought I'd leave my face as Nature made it.'

A few more words and suggestions for Molly's comfort till the doctor came, then Christine told Emmy to look after Mr. Standing's retriever and went back to her job of unloading the turnips.

CHAPTER SIX

Dusk had fallen before Christine finished the jobs which would have fallen to the lot of Molly that day. She stood outside the shed wherein she had been mixing pail after pail of mash for the hundreds of pigs which she had helped George to feed an hour ago. She had never in her life been so physically tired. Her very brain felt numbed after the unaccustomed manual labour. She had not had a break since lunch, which she had speedily eaten at the Manor, and it had been hard work unloading those heavy turnips, but she had persevered.

She stood wiping her hands with a handkerchief, horrified at the sight of her nails. No more varnish! They were cracked and broken. And for the first time in her life she had known what it was to have the sweat pouring down her cheeks. Now what she needed more than anything was a hot bath. It was growing cold. Once the sun went in, it was by no means warm up on these Fells.

She heard the sound of nailed boots clumping over the stone courtyard. Turning she saw Martin Farlong. As he came up to her she said:

'If there is nothing more to do I would like to go off.'

He looked at her as though surprised to find her still here. He had hardly recognised her in the gloaming. Now that he was near to her he could see how exhausted she looked. And he was not blind to the fact that her nose was shining and her lips their own natural pink. But he liked her like that.

'You ought to be home,' he said gruffly. 'You look done in.'

Back went the bronzed young head.

'Not at all. If there's anything more to do I'll do it.'

'You've done enough for today, thanks. Remarkably well in fact from what George told me just now.'

'Thank George for the compliment,' she said coldly.

'And you oughtn't to be standing here in the night air,' he said. 'It is dangerous when you are hot and perspiring.'

Her eyes widened.

'Don't tell me that you nurse your land-girls so tenderly!'

He twisted his lips, pulled a pipe from his

pocket, and began to fill it.

'You seem to think that I'm a first-class bully,' he said; 'but I assure you that isn't my reputation. I expect people to do their job, but I don't want them to overdo it, nor do I wish them to be stupid enough to catch chills that can be avoided.'

'That being so, I'll get along to the Manor,' said Christine. 'Good night.'

An impulse made him say:

'I'll get the Ford and drive you up.'

'That really is kind, but it is only ten minutes' walk. Save your petrol.'

'I'll drive you,' he said stubbornly, and walked towards the garage.

She stood alone shivering a little as the night wind struck her. It was growing darker every moment. From the distance came the sound of the cows lowing, and of Emmy's big Airedale barking, then the sound of a car being started up.

She did not really know why Martin should bother to get his car for her unless he thought he had better do something for Miss Challis. Mr. Standing would be home by now, and it might look better for the factor to be courteous to a privileged guest. Then Christine dismissed that idea as spiteful. Martin was not the sort to curry favours. No, for some strange reason, aware that she was tired, he was taking pity on her.

She was really thankful beyond measure

when she found herself in the Ford. Her feet ached. There was a blister on one heel and she had dreaded even that ten minutes' climb up to Wyckam. The Ford stopped outside the Manor House almost simultaneously with Robert Standing's big limousine. Mr. Standing greeted them, then stared at the girl with amazement. He burst out laughing.

'Good gracious, Fiona, my dear child . . . what have you been doing?'

'Molly Deacon has gone sick . . . in fact, Dr. Fielding took her himself into Ulverston to the hospital this afternoon,' said Christine, 'so I've taken her place as Mr. Farlong is so shorthanded.'

Robert Standing eyed her in the dusk.

'Well I'm blowed,' he laughed again. 'And what does Farlong think of that? Has she been sprinkling perfume on the pigs, Martin?'

The factor said:

'As a matter of fact, Mr. Standing, she has done a good day's work.'

Christine was surprised at the praise and absurdly pleased.

Mr. Standing said:

'Come along in and have a spot of food with us tonight, Martin. I've got some business I would like to talk over with you and we've no one coming in.'

Martin did not want to accept. Spending the evening with his employer was one thing . . . but with this girl as a third, it was another. She was far too disturbing to him and he found himself alternating between the desire to be nice to her and be thoroughly 'offensive' as she accused him. But it would have been discourteous of him to refuse Mr. Standing, so he had to accept.

'I'll change and come back,' he said.

Inside the warm lighted Manor House, Robert Standing chaffed the girl whom he thought to be William Challis's daughter, about her new role.

'Very sporting of you to do it, my dear; but I don't think your father would like you to work on the land like this. You'll ruin your hands.'

'I don't care about that,' she interrupted. 'I know labour is hard to get, and I would rather like to do Molly's job for a bit.'

'Well, I don't know,' said Mr. Standing doubtfully. 'The winter is coming on, you know, and you may be up here a long time. Your father said he might have to stay over in the States till Christmas.'

Christine bit her lips. If Robert Standing but knew, she would only be here a couple of weeks. It all depended on Peter . . . if Peter went suddenly abroad, Fiona would come up here and give the whole show away.

Christine went upstairs to her room and it struck her more forcibly than usual that this deception she was practising for Fiona's sake was going to reflect upon her integrity to no small degree. She liked and respected old Mr.

Standing. He would be disgusted with her impersonation. As for Marlin Farlong, she could imagine his withering criticism. And somehow, stupid though it was, she would not like to give Martin real cause for scorn.

She felt rather miserable about the situation as she lay in the bath relaxing her aching limbs in the hot water. She wished indeed that she were really Fiona . . . or that she had come here as Christine . . . anything rather than as an impersonator. She tried to recapture her former feelings of pleasure—in the fact that she had done something big for Fiona; tried to concentrate on the thought of Fiona and Peter together in all their passionate happiness; but she was distinctly uneasy when at length she dressed and went downstairs.

Martin had come back, and was drinking sherry in the library with his employer. The two men rose as Christine entered. Martin Farlong had to admit, with a slight sense of shock, that it was a very beautiful young woman who walked into the room, in her exquisitely-tailored dinner dress of some brown silky material which toned with her hair. It had long sleeves and fitted tightly to her lovely young figure. Her hair was brushed and shining, her face delicately made up, and there was a sophisticated touch about the gold earrings, the gold twisted necklace about her throat.

Yes, he admitted she was a lovely, *soignée*

73

creature, but his mind still held a vision of the untidy, dusty land-girl with her scratched cheek and torn elbow. That was a Fiona he could deal with . . . This was the glamorous Miss Challis to whom he hardly dare speak.

Christine, on her part, looked with approval at a Martin she had never seen before, in a dark-grey lounge suit. She liked his taste in ties and socks and the well-fitting white silk collar showed up the extreme brownness of his throat.

His unruly hair was combed and flattened, but he did not look out of place in those clothes . . . the 'farmer dolled up' . . . he was at his ease in them.

But they were neither of them at ease with each other as they sat down and Christine took the sherry Mr. Standing poured out for her.

During dinner, Christine became more and more conscious of being in an unreal world as she sat at the beautiful oval table, with its lace mats, shining crystal and Georgian silver, the big silver trophy cup in the centre (won by Robert Standing, steeplechasing in his youth) full of roses.

The parlourmaid served an excellent meal . . . home-cured ham and hot peaches . . . apple pie and jugs of cream. No sign of rationing here! On one side of Christine sat Robert Stauding, whom she was supposed to have known in her youth but who was an entire stranger to her; on the other his factor, the misogynist . . . a man who treated her with small courtesy on the farm but who was stiffly deferential to her here.

When she spoke to him, he answered with the same stiff politeness.

He passed her the salt, the butter, the toast . . . he did not refer to her work or any former discussions they had had. And for the most part during that meal, Christine kept silent and let the two men talk about shooting or the estate; matters which were of mutual interest to them.

Every now and again Christine's hazel eyes met the full gaze of Martin's blue ones, and all the time she was conscious of his fine, attractive hands, so brown against his white cuffs; of the gulf between them which, somehow, she would like to bridge . . . and perhaps he felt likewise . . . but it seemed unbridgeable.

Dinner over, they had coffee in front of the library fire. They discussed an air-raid which had taken place yesterday in a town twenty miles off.

'There has been one bomb on Cartmel Fells since the war began,' said Mr. Standing, 'but that was obviously a pilot jettisoning his bombs when he was being followed. We are pretty lucky here.'

'It is marvellously peaceful,' said Christine. 'You don't know what it is like in London.'

Both men looked at her. Martin Farlong

became conscious of something approaching horror at the thought of a girl like this one being in an air-raid . . . a really bad one. She had bothered about the killing of a rabbit, but heaven help them, women and children were being blown to pieces in this accursed war. Bitterly, Martin wished he could fling over the farm, get into uniform and do his bit against the Nazis.

'I suppose you had a good shelter in your place, my dear,' said Robert Standing.

'No, there is no basement in my place, and . . .'

She broke off stammering. That was the second slip she had made today. She *must* remember that she lived in Eaton Square.

Mr. Standing was quick to remind her.

'Surely you have a good basement in that London house of yours?'

'Yes, I was thinking of another place I was in,' said Christine, nervously lighting a cigarette.

Mr. Standing said suddenly:

'By the way, my dear, there is a letter for you in the hall. You saw it, didn't you?'

'No,' began Christine.

At that moment, the butler came in to clear away the coffee cups. Mr. Standing told him to bring the letter to 'Miss Challis.' The man handed it to her on a silver tray. Both Mr. Standing and Martin Farlong noted the American stamp.

'Ah!' exclaimed Mr. Standing. 'It is the first letter from your father. Came by Clipper, eh?'

'Yes,' said Christine.

'Open it, my dear, and tell me how he is and what he has got to say about New York.'

Christine became first hot and then cold. Her cheeks scorched. She hardly dared look at either man. For she knew that this letter belonged to Fiona. It had been arranged that she should send Fiona's letters on to her. She did not want to open a personal missive like this, written by a father to his daughter. She was conscious of Martin Farlong watching her with his penetrating eyes. She sat there, feeling in a trap.

'Farlong won't mind, and I want to hear how your father is,' added Mr. Standing.

She lifted her head and caught Martin's gaze.

'I don't mind. By all means open your letter, Miss Challis,' he said.

CHAPTER SEVEN

Christine only hesitated for a moment longer. Whatever these two men thought, she was not going to open Fiona's letter, so she forced a laugh, and slipped the envelope inside her evening bag.

'Oh, I'll read it later! I . . . I want to linger

77

over every word from dear old Daddy . . .'
How she hated that false representation of
facts, but it had to be done . . . 'I'll tell you all
the news tomorrow.'

Robert Standing looked disappointed.

'Well, well, you're a queer girl! I always
thought young people found it hard not to tear
open a letter as soon as it arrives.'

Martin Farlong, still watching 'Miss Challis,'
thought:

'She's concealing something. I wonder what.
She's certainly being secretive and she's
blushing . . .'

But Christine stuck to her ground. And
anxious that there should be no more
conversation about the letter, she tried to start
a conversation about the war news. But that
was not a success. Martin immediately looked
grim and sank into silence. She was reminded
then of his bitterness at being in a reserved
occupation. She could not help thinking how
well that tall, beautifully balanced body of his
would look in a uniform. He would make a
good officer . . . he was a born leader of men,
was Martin Farlong.

Mr. Standing, lighting a cigar, harped back
to the subject of his old friend.

'Your father will be visiting Washington,
won't he, my dear? I wonder if he mentions
anything about that?'

'I'll tell you at breakfast,' she smiled, with
an attempt at nonchalance. And added: 'I

78

must write and give him all the news from home.'

'Well, I'm writing to him myself tomorrow,' said Robert Standing, 'so if you'll give me your letter, I'll take it in with mine to the post office at Grange. I can send them off by air-mail. It'll be quicker.'

Christine's heart knocked a little. This was getting more and more difficult. She could not write to Mr. Challis. She had to wait for Fiona to send her a letter to forward. Between now and tomorrow she must rack her brains for an excuse for not having written to her 'father.' Oh, how she hated this enforced deception. And somehow she hated it all the more because Martin Farlong's deep penetrating eyes were scrutinising her.

Restlessly she got up and moved about the room. It struck her very forcibly in this hour that she was not at all the type to undertake an impersonation. There was a strong streak of honesty in Christine which rebelled against the whole thing.

Suddenly she said:

'Uncle Bob, do you mind if I go into your little study and use the telephone. I want to get a trunk call to a friend of mine down South.'

'With pleasure, my dear.'

Martin watched the slim, graceful figure of the girl vanish through the doorway. In her brown dress, with her bronze head, her golden, peach-bloom face, she was like a wood-nymph of the autumn, he thought, and then jeered at himself for his poetic fancy. In reality he breathed a sigh of relief now that she left him alone with his employer. Whenever that girl crossed his path, he was conscious of tension, and of her feminine allure.

He began to talk to Mr. Standing about matters of the farm.

In Mr. Standing's sanctum, Christine paced up and down waiting for her trunk call to come through. She knew she was doing a dangerous thing, but she *had* to speak to Fiona. She had put through a personal call to Mrs. Peter Hollis at the hotel where she was now living with her husband. Once the connection was made, Christine sat at the desk, and with burning cheeks spoke to Fiona.

'Don't say anything indiscreet,' she began tersely. 'People may be listening this end; but I want you to know that I can't stand this any longer.'

Back came Fiona's voice full of dismay:

'Oh, darling, but you *must*! You must wait till Peter goes.'

'When is he going?'

'Any day now.'

'Any day may mean weeks and months more,' said Christine, 'you know what the Army is.'

'But, darling, we're so divinely happy together, it would be a disaster if I had to come up there and tell the truth now. It would spoil things and Uncle Bob would cable to you-know-who, for heaven's sake, hang on a bit longer.'

'I don't like it.'

'What's happened to upset you?'

'Nothing and everything.'

'Is there some man . . . ?'

Christine gave a little laugh. *Some man!* No, that wasn't the reason . . . and yet . . . she would hate to face Martin Farlong and tell him what she had done.

Fiona went on pleading.

'Every night of our lives we bless you, darling. You don't know what it's like to be married to a man you love. I'm a different person. I just live only for Peter and he grows more precious to me every minute. Can't you understand? Couldn't you feel like that?'

Christine bit her lip.

'Oh, I suppose So! But it's awfully difficult, About letters . . . everything.'

'Hang on for a bit longer,' broke in Fiona. 'Peter is sure to go soon, I must stay with him and make him happy until he does.'

'Your three minutes is up and I'm going to cut you off,' broke in a cold, detached voice.

'Wait,' said Christine frenziedly. 'I want to say some more . . .'

'I'm sorry, but there are priority calls waiting,' said the operator.

'Good-bye darling, and hang on for my sake!' from Fiona. Then silence. A dead line.

As Christine went back to the library, her nervous trembling ceased. She became philosophical about the situation again. After all, she had gone so far—what use to worry now? Let matters take their course, and she really was enjoying every moment at Wyckam Manor. Still more was she enjoying her work on the farm. She had had a gruelling day yesterday but it appealed to her.

Martin Farlong came out of the library.

'Martin's going,' said Mr. Standing from behind him. 'He keeps early hours, you know.'

'I shall have to keep them, too,' said Christine, with a faint smile to Martin. 'What time do I have to report for duty, Mr. Factor?'

He looked down at her in an embarrassed fashion.

'Are you sure you want to go on with this work?'

'Quite sure.'

'I think I ought to look for another hired girl,' said Martin.

Christine turned and appealed to Mr. Standing.

'Don't let him, Uncle Bob. I love the work and it's good for me, and you don't have to pay me. It'll all add to the profits.'

'Oh, very well, if you want to, my dear,' he said laughing, and added to his factor: 'Will you retain the services of this charming young lady, Martin?'

Christine saw the blood mount up beneath

82

Martin's tan. He avoided her eye.

'Just as you wish, sir,' he said stiffly.

Christine felt almost annoyed with him. He didn't want her down on the farm, he made that so obvious. Well, she was going—in spite of him.

'What time am I wanted?' she persisted.

'If it's Molly's place you're taking, then Molly would be down at the milking sheds at 6.30,' he said in the same stiff voice. 'But that may be too early for you, Miss Challis?'

'Not at all, I'll be there at six if you want,' she said, with a tilt of her head.

And she left a message with the maids to call her at 5.45 because she knew she would never waken herself. She was dog-tired.

To her annoyance, Agnes, the maid who received the order, herself overslept, and had to confess, guiltily when she handed Christine her morning tea, that it was seven o'clock.

Christine, usually sweet-tempered, was furious with the girl. Of course, Martin would think that it was just laziness on her part. It was strange how anxious she was not to give that young man cause to sneer. She left the tea, sprang up and hastily put on her working clothes. Heavens how stiff she felt! Her elbow was very sore. Her eyes were still drugged with sleep as she swallowed the breakfast which the repentant Agnes rushed up to her. A glance from the window did not help to cheer her. The fine weather had broken during the night.

Agnes had said there had been a thunderstorm, but Christine had slept so soundly she had not heard it. Blue skies and sunshine were replaced today by heavy banks of grey cloud and that steady driving rain which comes down with such drenching force across the Fells.

In Fiona Challis's wardrobe there was a smart white silk mackintosh but Christine borrowed an old and more serviceable one from Agnes, jammed Molly's felt hat on her curls and ran rather than walked down the road toward Stonehead.

By the time she reached the byres, the milking had been done and the cows were turned out. She found Martin wearing a heavy mackintosh and tweed cap, talking to one of the cowmen. As he turned and saw her, he lifted the cap but was curt and unsmiling as he bade her good morning.

Before he could speak, she said:

'Oh, I know you think I couldn't get up at such an early hour, but you're wrong! Agnes forgot to call me, and I'm just as angry about it as you are.'

The cowman walked off, leaving them alone. Martin, hands in his coat pockets, looked down at the girl with a faint derisive smile which maddened her.

'I'm not angry, Miss Challis. It doesn't concern me what you do. It's your right to stay in bed the whole morning if you so wish.'

Already cross and put out, Christine lost her temper.

'Don't be so hateful,' she flashed at him, 'you know perfectly well that I want to take Molly's place, and take it properly.'

He shrugged his shoulders, and looked up at the skies. The rain was driving like a grey curtain between them.

'Not much of a morning for you, but if you want a job you'd better get on with mash for the pigs like you did yesterday. That'll be an inside job.'

'I don't want to go inside. I can stand the rain,' she said, crimson, tight-lipped.

'If you're taking Molly's place, then you must take her orders,' he said.

Christine could have hit him, he was so granite-hard. So untouchable, and always so right. There were moments when she had wondered whether she had dreamt he had pillowed her head on his arm and called her Fiona, anxiously, humanly, yesterday.

'All the same,' she said to herself. 'I'm not going to fall off a dray every time I want a decent word from you, Martin Farlong!'

Without another word to him she turned and walked into one of the sheds.

He looked after the small rain-drenched figure and now quite a broad smile relaxed the harshness of his face. What a queer girl she was! She didn't give in any more easily than he did. He respected that stubborn spirit in her.

85

All the same, in his opinion she was too pretty and soft and the sooner she stopped hanging around Stonehead the better.

CHAPTER EIGHT

Martin only saw Christine at odd moments during that day. She worked doggedly and knocked off only when the rest of them did, at midday, for her lunch. When the rain lifted late that afternoon, she went out with some of the other hands and helped drive the cows from the pastures back to the milking sheds.

Martin stopped to speak to her after tea.

'You say you can drive a car?' he asked her.

Only a whit less tired than she had been yesterday, Christine wiped a wet forehead with the back of one grubby little hand and nodded: 'I can.'

'Then you might take Bastable's job on the lorry tomorrow morning. I want him for something else. Take the milk churns along to the main road. There's a platform there and you can leave the churns to be collected at 9 a.m.'

'Very well . . .' Then impishly she added the word 'sir.'

'Please don't call me that, Miss Challis.'

'Then please don't call me "Miss Challis" while I'm working for you.'

'I don't know that it would be right for me to call you "Fiona",' he said uneasily.

Looking up at his face which was almost friendly in that moment, she wished ardently that she could have asked him to call her 'Christine.' She said:

'Oh, "Fiona" will do.'

He hesitated. He knew that he liked that name. It had a haunting attraction for him, like the girl herself. She spoke again.

'And who collects the churns from the platform?'

'Allgood's men. Allgood's are the big chocolate manufacturers' in Barrow. They buy a lot of our milk.'

'How amazing,' said Christine. 'I've eaten heaps of Allgood's milk chocolate, but I little thought I should ever handle the milk it's made of.'

'Well, we're going to have some bother soon,' said Farlong. 'There's talk of chocolate being rationed, and milk, too.'

She was pleased because he volunteered to discuss such things with her. But her pleasure was short-lived. For after a sudden look at her, he turned, and with a curt 'Good night' walked away.

While she made her way slowly and wearily back to the Manor House through the gathering dusk, Martin Farlong returned to Stonehead Farm. He was drenched through and wanted a change of clothes. And he was more tired today than he ever remembered feeling. It was not merely a physical fatigue. He was mentally weary—of the three farms under his control, of the war-time restrictions on farming and of his whole life as it must be led at the moment.

Some of his mental depression was due, he knew, to that girl who had come to live at Wyckam and thrust herself, unwanted, into his life.

He had never allowed women to interfere with him. He didn't trust them. The sweeter, the prettier they were, the more suspicious he became. He could not forget the tragedy of his own boyhood. His mother had left him just at an age when he had been most impressionable. The divorce had smashed an ideal: his ideal of his mother. It had made him wonder if any woman could be trusted, or if any marriage was worth a trial.

Yet for all his instincts against the opposite sex, he knew that his present life was lonely and incomplete. Some of his men friends with wives who were decent women, and good mothers, seemed fulfilled and content. He had to admit it. Yet he shrank from the very thought of marriage for himself. Shrank from it, even while the desire crept insidiously and continually into his mind.

He couldn't stop himself thinking about that girl, 'Fiona Challis'. The fearless way she stood up to him, the brave manner in which she tackled a job for which she wasn't really fit. There had been nothing of the spoiled society pet about her these last two days, trudging around the farm.

'Damn you, Fiona,' he said softly to himself as he walked into the little grey farmhouse where he knew old Emmy would be waiting with a hot bath and his supper. But there was nothing much to look forward to after that but a lonely evening with his dog in front of the fire; a daily paper, a book perhaps, the radio . . . (he liked music). Or a walk down to the village for a glass of beer at the Royal Oak with a few of the farmers from outlying districts.

'Damn you, Fiona,' Martin repeated, when at length in old, dry clothes, he sat in the little living-room, smoking a pipe, waiting for Emmy to bring in his meal.

He thought of that girl up at the Manor as he had seen her last night in her silky evening dress, remembered her subtle perfume, her feminine graces . . . the softness and elegance of her surroundings.

It seemed austere and cold here in Stonehead Farm after Wyckam Manor. It had never struck him before how grim it was despite its antiquity, which made it a gem from an architectural point of view.

In the living room there was an old faded paper on the walls which had not been changed, so far as he knew, for fifty years or more, like the gloomy black and white pictures in heavy maple frames . . . scenes of fishing or shooting. The massive furniture, and ugly red serge curtains, the well-worn red and yellow Turkey carpet were unlovely. There was no electricity. Up at the Manor House they had their own plant, but down here they were still in the age of oil-lamps. And Emmy was economical. She only allowed one to be lit. The big standard, with its old-fashioned frilled shade of faded yellow silk, gave out a dim, depressing light.

The room seemed full of shadows this autumn night and it had begun to rain again. Martin could hear the heavy drops pattering against the casement windows.

Into the room came old Emmy, bearing a tray and, to Martin's astonishment, followed by a girl. An attractive girl in a short blue skirt and yellow knitted jumper which showed a neat young figure. For a moment Martin stared blankly at her olive face, the bright narrow dark eyes under heavy brows, and the long black hair which curled down to her shoulders. Then he exclaimed:

'Good gracious! *Susan!*'

Emmy set the tray on the table.

'Ay, and a couple of days before she was expected, Mr. Farlong. You don't mind her being around the place, do you?'

'No, of course not,' said Martin.

'Good evening, Mr. Farlong,' said the girl

demurely.

He eyed her a trifle dubiously.

Of course he knew her now. Susan Blythe was old Emmy's granddaughter. Her parents lived in Manchester and from time to time, as a child, she used to come up and stay on the farm. But as she had gown older, her visits had become less frequent because she was being trained as a seamstress in a dressmaking establishment where her mother formerly worked, and only got very occasional holidays.

Martin had grown used to the sight of little Susan running around the farm with bare legs and pinafores. But tonight he noticed that the child had become a woman. Vaguely he said:

'You have gown up, haven't you, Susan?'

She looked at him with bright, bold eyes.

'Ay! I'm eighteen come Christmas.'

'Ay, and with all the Manchester lads after her,' put in Emmy with a chuckle.

Martin stuck his pipe in his pocket. All the Manchester lads, eh? That made him feel suddenly elderly, although he wasn't thirty himself yet. Susan Blythe had certainly grown into a 'gradely lass.' Charming curves and ripe red lips and those sloe-black eyes. But he wasn't so comfortable about having a pretty eighteen-year-old girl living at the farm, although he had liked the curly-haired child in the pinafore to whom he used to give pennies and sweets.

Susan lingered to talk to him after her

grandmother had gone out of the room.

'I've been looking forward to this holiday, Mr. Farlong. After city, it's grand up here and there's plenty doing, I hear. Soldiers billeted everywhere and what with them and aeroplanes, and a bomb on the Fell, it's not what it used to be.'

'It certainly isn't,' said Martin curtly.

She went on staring at him. As a child she had adored the gentleman at Stonehead Farm whom grandmother looked after, but, of course, he had appeared quite old to her in those days. This evening, he seemed young and very handsome with his magnificent figure and brown strong face, after the weedy youths in Manchester who ran after her.

She fingered the coral beads round her neck.

'And I hear there's a young lady up at the Manor who wears wonderful clothes and that,' she added.

'Well, she's not wearing them at the moment,' said Martin, with a faint smile. 'She's working on the farm.'

'Gran says she's a fair beauty. Do you think so, Mr. Farlong?'

He did not wish to think of 'Fiona's' beauty at all. He hedged:

'What about you, Susan? Your grandmother says all the lads are after you. Not thinking of marrying too young, are you?'

'Wouldn't you approve of that, Mr.

Farlong?'

He looked away from her, slightly uneasy. The little minx made no bones about her 'sex-appeal.'

Women, he thought, had suddenly become an active menace in his life and he had not time to bother about them. He said:

'Anyhow, don't you marry too young, Susan.'

'Not till I get the one I really care for,' she said, and pouted her lips at him, with a little deep laugh in her throat.

Martin was made well aware that Emmy's granddaughter was certainly no longer a child to tease or give pennies to. It was plain that she was coquetting with him. Plain that if he wished, he need not have a lonely evening. But something much deeper than the fleeting desire of the male for a young and pretty companion made him brush aside that temptation. The persistent maddening thought of that Other girl up the Manor House.

'Just let me know, Mr. Farlong, if you want any mending done,' said Susan softly. 'I sew properly these days and would dearly like to do a job for you.'

'Many thanks,' he said, 'and now, my dear, run along, as I've some accounts to do.'

Susan vanished. Once more Martin was alone. He ate his dinner without enjoying it. Even his healthy appetite seemed to have deserted him. And immediately afterwards he put on his raincoat, called to Jess, his spaniel, and went out into the stormy night to walk over the Fells.

It was still raining that next morning.

Up at the Manor it seemed to Christine, when she got up (she was on time this morning—an alarm-clock had ensured that!) that the fine weather had gone for good, and that soon autumn would be merging into the rigours of the winter. The countryside looked bleak and forbidding with that everlasting curtain of rain across the Fells and there was a wind with it this morning, sweeping the rain against one's face, tossing the branches of the trees and scattering the rich red and golden of the autumn leaves on to the muddied soil.

Prepared for another hard day's work, Christine trudged down the dirty road through slosh and puddles, and before presenting herself at the milking sheds went to Stonehead Farm. She intended to give Emmy the handkerchief which Martin had lent her. Agnes had washed and ironed it.

She knocked on the door. There was no answer. Christine knew that Martin must be already up if not at work. She pushed open the door. There seemed nobody about, so she walked further into the square, red-tiled hall. It seemed to her full of Martin Farlong's personality. Austere, harsh, a couple of gun cases here, some fishing rods there, a pair of rubber waders, an old cap and a coat. Not a flower, not a feminine touch.

Taking sudden interest in the old farmhouse, Christina stepped a little further into the factor's domain. Then suddenly a swing door was pushed open from the kitchen quarters and Christine saw a young girl with long, dark, curly hair, and wearing a blue cardigan over a flowered cotton frock. For a moment Christine stared at the girl blankly. The girl stared back, then looked down at the tiled floor and uttered an exclamation.

'Eh! . . . just look at you tramping in on Gran's clean floor with your dirty boots. Go on out! You land-girls are a dirty lot, ay and you are.'

So taken aback was Christine by this rude and unexpected greeting that she looked dumbfounded at the younger girl. Then she flushed scarlet and found her voice.

'I'm sorry if I've marked the floor. It was thoughtless of me, but may I ask who you are?'

Susan tossed her head.

'I'm living here. I often stay with Gran and Mr. Farlong.'

'Oh, do you?' said Christine, coldly, and wondered if she had been wrong in thinking that Martin Farlong always debarred women from his life. Forgetting all about her reason for coming here, she turned, and was on the point of leaving when Susan said:

'It'll be me that'll have to clear up the marks. Pity you don't come back and wash the tiles yourself.'

Christine forgot that she was no more than one of the land-girls and a farm labourer in the sight of this cheeky child. She swung round with blazing eyes:

'What right have you to speak to me like that?'

The next moment there came the sound of heavy boots clamping on the floor, the living-room door opened, and Martin Farlong, with a piece of bread and butter suspended in his hand, came out and confronted the two girls.

'Here, here, what's all this!'

Christine turned to Martin, indignantly.

'I don't know who this young person is, but she's been extremely rude to me and . . .'

'Mr. Farlong, it was only that she's bringing in mud all over Gran's tiles,' broke in Susan, equally indignant. 'I told her of it.'

A faint glimmer of amusement came into Martin's sombre eyes. He raised an eyebrow at Susan.

'My dear, you don't know who you're speaking to. This is Miss Challis from the Manor House.'

Susan stared, went crimson to the eyes, muttered something under her breath, and fled back to her kitchen.

Martin laughed outright.

'Now you've upset our little Susan.'

Christine bit her lip, conscious of chagrin and the usual baffled feeling that Martin was always mocking her. She was also vaguely conscious that she did not like 'our little Susan.'

'Who is that girl?' she demanded.

'Emmy's granddaughter. Have you any objection?'

Their eyes met. Christine felt herself trembling. There were a dozen unspoken questions in her eyes and mockery in his. Then she said:

'I haven't the least objection, except that it's time you and Em taught her some manners.'

Turning, she marched out of the farmhouse. Martin, bread and butter still in his hand, stared after her.

CHAPTER NINE

At a quarter to nine, George, one of the cowmen, lifted the heavy milk churns of fresh creamy milk on to the lorry which Christine had been detailed off to drive to the platform.

George was a curly-headed, bright-eyed Lancashire man with a dialect that Christine could scarcely understand, but he had a kind heart. He maintained that those churns would be too heavy for 'yoong lady' to lift down by herself. He volunteered to go with her and give his aid.

Christine accepted the offer. The factor was nowhere in sight. She had not seen him since

97

her visit to the farm and her unpleasant encounter with Emmy's granddaughter, and she was still furious at the treatment she had received at the hands of both the girl and Martin.

At home with a car of any sort, she drove the lorry quickly and neatly down the country lane, directed by George, found the platform and waited while he unloaded the churns. He then went off on foot to another job and left Christine to turn the lorry round and drive it back alone.

Just before reaching the farmyard at Stonehead, she encountered the tall figure of Martin, with a gun under his arm, and Jess, the spaniel, close at his heels.

With tight lips and tilted chin, Christine prepared to drive on as though she had not seen him, but he hailed her:

'Hi! wait a minute, there.'

With a grinding of brakes, she drew the lorry into the side of the lane and gave him a stony look.

'Yes, sir.'

'Don't call me that,' he said, irritably.

Christine made no answer. Martin looked up at the small unbending figure with faint humour in his eyes. Such open antagonism from any one was new to him. And for the last two or three hours, ever since Christine had marched away from the farmhouse, he had been conscious of some compunction. After all, 'Miss Challis' had not received a great deal of courtesy whilst under his roof . . . he was a bit remorseful.

He felt a new desire to tease her.

'What sort of orders would you like me to give you for the day?' he asked. 'Like to borrow my car and take Susan for a joy-ride?'

Christine crimsoned.

'If that's meant to be a joke, it isn't very funny.'

He laughed and, pulling a pipe from his pocket, and a packet of tobacco, began to fill it.

'You needn't be so cross. Susan didn't really mean to be rude to you and I didn't intend being so inhospitable. If you'd waited a second, I'd have asked you in for a cup of coffee.'

'I wouldn't have had it,' she said childishly.

'Then we're fine as we are.'

She felt exasperated. Yet she could not help thinking what an attractive face this man had when he chose to smile, and what curious power he had to upset her equilibrium, whether he was being rude or affable.

Martin said:

'Got those milk churns in place?'

'Yes. George helped me to lift them. I suppose asking for his help wasn't too marked an indication of my useless femininity?'

Martin stuck the pipe in his mouth and proceeded to light it.

'Sarcasm so early in the morning! I say!'

'If you've no orders for me, I'll drive on,' she said.

He made no answer but lifted his head to watch a flight of starlings which whirred over them suddenly and across the arable field, where they came down like a soft black cloud, and settled.

'Sign of dry weather,' said Martin, puffing at his pipe.

That interested Christine, despite herself.

'What? Starlings flying like that?'

'So they say in these parts.'

She looked up at the sky. It was a pale, almost luminous blue, and although cold, the morning was glorious, touched by the frosty finger of autumn. After the recent rains, the whole countryside looked fresh and washed. On the other side of the fields the woods seemed to Christine to be a shade redder today than they had been yesterday . . . the inevitable change from the green summer to the russet gold of the fall.

She had to admit that it was good to be alive, sitting here on the farm in this gracious country so far removed from the noise, the odours, the hemmed-in feeling of the city. The war! Where was it? Somewhere, of course, there were hordes of khaki-clad men, training . . . prepared for invasion . . . somewhere there were hidden guns and army lorries and all the equipment of war. But here in this farm lay

100

only the essence of peace and quietude, and the manifold glories of Mother Nature.

Christine felt, deeply, a love of the country and the spell of these wild fells and moors in particular.

Involuntarily she broke out:

'I think this is the grandest part of the world!'

He saw that she meant it and was vaguely pleased.

'It is grand,' he nodded. 'And in farming you'll soon learn that what you do for the soil never goes unrewarded. That's what I've learned. What you reap, you sow, and even if it's a bad crop, you gain something. Nature is rich with her rewards for labour.'

She turned her gaze upon him. A strange man, this. Somehow one wouldn't expect such words, such thoughts, from a factor, and yet she remembered Mr. Standing telling her that Martin Farlong was an unusual person and that behind that iron mask of his lay much real humanity.

'*What you reap, you sow* . . .' he had just said.

'That applies to one's actions, too, I suppose,' she said thoughtfully.

'Certainly.'

'H'm!' said Christine, and drew in her lips. She had the uneasy feeling that those amazingly blue eyes of his were reading into her soul at the moment. Would she reap an unpleasant harvest of this thing she had done in coming here in place of Fiona Challis? She wished that whenever she talked to Martin Farlong, or encountered him in any way, he would not always make her feel ashamed of her complicity. She was a living lie, sitting here at this moment, letting this man think of her as William Challis's daughter.

'What's troubling you?' asked Martin.

She flushed and shrugged her shoulders.

'Nothing at all.'

He kept his grave gaze levelled upon her, unaware of the fact that he was making her feel so self-conscious.

'Well, I'd better drive on,' said Christine awkwardly.

'I'm giving myself a morning's shooting,' he told her, 'going after the jays and the magpies, and I daresay I'll get a few rabbits.'

Then, as he saw her expression, he laughed, and said:

'Oh, I remember now, you don't like killing rabbits.'

'I don't like killing anything.'

'You women are funny creatures. Tender-hearted about a rabbit, but there are plenty of you that wouldn't mind killing all that was best in a man.'

She was startled by this unexpected bitterness, but remembering the story of his mother, was immediately sympathetic.

'Oh, you mustn't say that. All women aren't the same, you know.'

102

Her brown charming face was no longer haughty and hostile. He found himself looking into a pair of hazel eyes which were so soft that they reminded him absurdly of Jess's eyes, and he could never resist the soft liquid gaze of his little spaniel.

Who was it, he thought, had said something about '*A woman, a spaniel, a walnut tree—the more you beat 'em, the better they be . . .*' There was probably truth in it, but he had never beaten Jess in his life and he couldn't picture himself hitting 'Fiona Challis.' If a man laid a hand on *her*, it would be to stroke that copper-beech head and those tanned cheeks, he thought dreamily. How proudly she sat up there on the old lorry; much too attractive in the blue woollen jersey with the high polo collar she was wearing this morning, tucked into the corduroy breeches.

An emotion so unusual seized Martin Farlong that he was afraid of himself. Afraid of this girl. He'd wasted enough time with her, he told himself. In a rough voice he said:

'Well, you'd better get on! You might ask Walters to show you how they work the binders. That is, unless you're sick of this job.'

She stiffened again. Moments of friendliness with Martin Farlong seemed to be rare and as speedily over as the light of those starlings overhead. She answered him with equal curtness.

'I'm not sick of it, thanks.'

103

Then she switched on the engine, which throbbed noisily, thrust in the gear, and moved off. In the agitation of the moment, she let the clutch in sharply and the lorry sprang forward. She was furious because she did not wish to display herself to Martin as an amateur driver. She prided herself upon being a good one. But what Martin thought about it, she did not see. She did not look back, but rattled on in the lorry back to the farm.

Martin walked on a few yards, puffing at his pipe. Why the devil did this girl want to come here and get him all worked up he didn't know. He spoke sharply to the spaniel who was careering into the thicket.

'Heel, you little devil!' he thundered, giving vent to some of his feelings.

The spaniel capered back, and looked up at him, wagging her tail, her golden eyes pleading for pardon because it was such a lovely morning, and she was dying to get after a rabbit.

Mechanically he bent and patted her silky head. And once again he found himself comparing those dewy hazel eyes with the eyes of the girl who had just driven away.

'Confound it!' he said to himself. And was glad that at that moment a magpie flew across his pathway. He levelled his gun at it and shot it dead.

Christine heard the report of that gun as she jumped off the lorry outside the farm

104

buildings.

'Now I suppose Mr. Factor's killed something, he's feeling better,' she reflected wrathfully, and that wrath increased during the morning, because she found that whatever she did she could not escape from the thought of him.

CHAPTER TEN

That same evening when Christine was back at the Manor House and the 'land-girl' had once more become a fashionable young woman, sitting before the library fire drinking sherry with Mr. Standing, she was conscious of a growing uneasiness and dislike of her position.

To begin with, Fiona had not sent the letter for Mr. Challis which she had been expecting daily, and which she could post up here.

Almost as soon as she had come in from work Mr. Standing had started to reproach her for her apparent neglect.

'If you were my daughter, young woman,' he had said, 'I'd be exceedingly annoyed with you. Do you realise that you haven't answered that long letter from your father yet?'

Christine had made some vague excuse about being busy. She supposed she could have lied outright and assured Mr. Standing that she had, herself, posted an air-mail letter to New York. But she had been loath to do that. First of all because she so hated this lying and secondly because she knew that it was just possible that Mr. Standing might find out that she had sent no air-mail letter from this district. He knew, for himself, that she had not given him one to post when he drove into Grange.

'Now you sit down and write tonight,' had been his last words on the subject. 'I'm not going to have my old friend cabling to know why you haven't written. I'm going to bully you, young woman, until you do it.'

While she sat there talking to Mr. Standing, Christine wondered why on earth Fiona had not sent the necessary letter. It was putting her in a most awkward position. Of course, like so many people blissfully in love, she thought, Fiona was selfish, living in a world of her own with her Peter, regardless of any difficulties which her impersonator might be experiencing up North. Christine decided to write a really cross letter on the subject to Fiona this very night.

'So you're enjoying your farm work, are you?' she heard Mr. Standing's pleasant bass voice.

'Immensely,' she said with enthusiasm.

'Getting on well with Farlong?'

She laughed.

'He annoys me at times, but I do what I'm told.'

106

'Oh, he's a good fellow and sometimes I'm sorry for him. He seems a lonely chap.'

Into Christine's mind leapt the remembrance of a certain almond-eyed, olive-skinned girl from Manchester living down at Stonehead Farm. Half resentfully she said:

'Oh, I think he has his amusements. There's a very pretty granddaughter of Emmy's living just now at the farm.'

Robert Standing smiled.

'I don't think Farlong would look long at *her* type.'

Before Christine could either agree with this or deny it, Mr. Standing added:

'By the way, Fiona, I'm giving a little party next week. Happens to be my birthday, and I've always been an old fool about birthdays. I can't have sixty-five candles on my cake, but I can have some friends, and feed 'em as far as rations will allow. We're lucky enough to have a Cumberland ham hanging in the kitchen and I think Cook can make us forget there's a war on just for one night.'

Christine smiled back at him. She had grown sincerely attached to 'Uncle Bob.' She hated deceiving him. She was glad to take any chance of pleasing him.'

'We must make it a really fine party,' she said. 'Who are you asking?'

He gave her a tentative list: General Whitely, the Millers from Three Acres Farm, Miss Youngton, Sir John and Lady Greene

107

from Windermere, Sir John's sister, Mrs. Anson, and her two daughters, who were in the local A.T.S. but could get away no doubt for a night.

'Pretty girls,' added Mr. Standing, 'and yourself, another very pretty girl.'

'Thanks,' said Christine gaily.

'And we must rake in the bachelors. I hear Dickie Newbury is on leave . . . he's a captain in the Gunners. And, of course, we'll ask Martin.'

Christine suddenly coloured and sipped her sherry. Martin at a party! Surely he'd be rather awkward and out of place and yet . . . there wouldn't be a more arresting-looking man in the room, she had to admit. She also admitted to herself that it would be rather fun to get Martin away from the farmyard, in a dinner jacket, and at his employer's birthday party. She would tease him. Yes, she would make a point of teasing him.

Then Mr. Standing said:

'Oh, and by the way, I knew there was something I wanted to tell you, my dear. You remember last Sunday when I took you over to Lingford House for tea . . . the Renwicks' place. Remember a photograph of a young man in Air Force uniform on the piano? I think I saw you eyeing it. Rather a good-looking fellow.'

'Yes, I remember,' said Christine vaguely.

'That was Gilfred, her son you know. He

108

came up on leave last night. Mrs. Renwick rang me up just before you came in this evening. She tells me that Gilfred has met you many times at parties in London and is quite delighted to hear you're in the district.'

Then Chris put down her glass and sat bolt upright, aware of the scorching blood that rushed to her cheeks and throat.

'He . . . knows . . . me?'

'Yes, didn't you recognise his photograph? I suppose you didn't, as you made no mention of it to me or to Mrs. Renwick. I believe he met you for the first time at a Red Cross fête when you and several débutantes last year took part in some kind of tableau.'

Christine did not speak for a moment. She was racking her brains wildly for an explanation of this. But she knew nothing. It was easy enough to surmise that Fiona and 'other débutantes' had posed in tableaux at a Red Cross fête, and easy enough to believe that Pilot-Officer Renwick had met Fiona at several London parties.

Mr. Standing continued, unaware of the dynamo that he had set racing in Christine's heart.

'Young Renwick, according to his mother, won't be in such a hurry to tear back to London if there's a chance of seeing the fair Fiona again. I've accepted their invitation for us to dine at Lingford House tomorrow.'

'Oh, have you?' said Christine stupidly.

109

'That suit you?'

She stammered.

'I . . . I'm pretty tired after a day's work . . . and . . .'

'Oh, take the whole afternoon off, or knock off before tea. I'll drop the hint to Martin not to put you on a long job.'

She looked at Mr. Standing wildly, but he was quite unconscious of her distress. Picking up the bellows he started to blow the logs into brighter flame in the big open fireplace and went on making suggestions for the party. They would put fires in the big drawing-room, which was not generally used at the Manor, he said, and polish the floor. The young people could dance to the radiogramophone. They must teach poor old Martin to dance, etc., etc.

And Christine listened with a sense of panic, for here was a denouement which she certainly had not anticipated. When she and Fiona had discussed the possibilities of their scheme, they had both been fairly sure that Christine would never encounter up here, in this out-of-the-way spot, anyone that Fiona knew.

'I suppose,' thought Christine, 'Fiona forgot this man in the R.A.F., or maybe she didn't know that he lived up here.'

What in heaven's name was she to do? She could pretend to be ill tomorrow night and not go to the Renwicks' house, but that would only postpone the disaster. She could hardly feign a longer illness and spoil old Uncle Bob's birthday party for him by her absence. And anyhow, if Gilfred Renwick was keen about Fiona, he might turn up here at any time to see her.

The maid announced dinner. Christine led the way into the dining-room, wondering how she would be able to eat a bite of food without choking. For the moment she simply could not see a solution to this new problem confronting her. For, of course, as soon as young Renwick saw her, he would know that she was not Fiona, and there would be instant complications. He might even denounce her as an impostor before she had a chance to explain and then the fat would be in the fire. There would be no possibility of a quiet explanation to Robert Standing. There would be a public scandal to electrify the whole neighbourhood. And that was a thing Fiona had certainly not wanted to do for the sake of her father's old friend. They had meant to tell him the truth quietly one day after which 'Fiona Challis' would vanish and never be seen again in the vicinity of Wyckam Manor. Then there would be no scandal.

Mr. Standing was not an observant man so he did not notice how distrait and nervy 'Fiona' was during dinner. Neither was the subject of dinner tomorrow night at Lingford House brought up again. Christine realised that he took it for granted that she would go.

For the rest of the evening she struggled with herself, feeling rather like a helpless fly caught in a spider's web. A web largely of her own spinning. One thing was certain; she *must* get in touch with Fiona at once.

She pretended to be busy writing letters and did not go up to bed that night until after Mr. Standing had retired. Once alone, she sent a telegram over the telephone to Mrs. Peter Hollis, wording it carefully: *Ring me at once.*

She signed it 'Fiona' which would avoid suspicion this end. She must inevitably disappoint Mr. Standing about tomorrow night. He must dine alone with the Renwicks. She would take to her bed with severe headache in the afternoon and stay there. She *must* put off meeting this man, Gilfred, until she had spoken to Fiona.

All through that next day she was worried and nervous. She kept wondering whether she would return to the Manor to find a man in R.A.F. uniform waiting to see her—and give her away! But Gilfred did not come because he expected to see her at his own home that night. And it was not until tea-time that she carried out her plan, told Martin Farlong that she had developed acute neuralgia and gave up work for the day.

Martin was always sympathetic with those in pain. He looked at Christine and noticed her pallor, her gravity. She had none of her usual brightness or capacity to make a pert reply.

Obviously she must be ill.

'Why, you must go home and get to bed at once,' he said kindly.

She avoided his eye, muttered a 'So long' and went home.

He found himself thinking about her frequently after she had gone. He missed the sight of the trim young figure about Stonehead Farm. He enjoyed even a battle of words with 'Fiona.'

That night after dinner—it was a misty autumn night with white vapourish mists curling softly over the Fells—Martin left his comfortable fireside and walked up to the Manor House. He had a twofold purpose. He wanted to see Mr. Standing on a business matter, and he wanted to enquire after 'Fiona's' health.

At the door of the Manor, a maid informed him that Mr. Standing had gone over to dine at Lingford House.

'But Miss Challis is in if you'd like to see her,' the girl added.

Martin fingered his cap awkwardly.

'Isn't she laid up?'

'She was this afternoon, Sir, but she's down in the library now, expecting a trunk call, I believe.'

Martin hesitated, then decided that he would see 'Fiona' for a few moments. He was astonished by his own secret longing to make sure for himself that she had recovered from her neuralgia, and would be back at work tomorrow morning.

Nobody was more astonished . . . or put out . . . than Christine when the library door opened and the maid announced:

'Mr. Farlong, to see you, Miss.'

The one thing she wanted tonight was to be alone . . . to be able to speak rather more openly than usual to Fiona. If that call came through while Martin was with her, she would be able to say nothing and she would be put into a worse quandary than ever. For as it was, Gilfred Renwick had rung up to say how disappointed he was. about tonight, and had announced his intention of calling first thing in the morning to see her.

CHAPTER ELEVEN

Christine had no option, however, but to greet Martin with the courtesy which he expected in this house.

'Oh, hallo!' she said, rather lamely. 'Don't tell me you've got a nocturnal job for me, Mr. Factor.'

It was the old bantering tone which used to irritate Martin. But this evening he almost found it a welcome. Christine had been so off-colour all day and looked ill into the bargain. He hoped and believed that she was better, and expressed these sentiments with some awkwardness. Clearing his throat, buttoning and unbuttoning the heavy mackintosh he was wearing, he said:

'Glad to see you're about again. I thought perhaps you'd be laid up . . . I . . . really came to see Mr. Standing.'

'Oh,' said Christine, with a nervous little laugh, 'not me.'

'To see you, too, of course,' came from Martin hurriedly. But that admission brought a considerable colour to his cheeks, and he passed a hand uneasily over the thick dark hair which the wind had blown about his temples.

He could never feel really at ease, he thought, with this girl who had disturbed him strangely from the first hour he had met her. When she was on the farm doing her land-girl's work, and under his orders, he could be masterful. He was capable of dealing with any situation that might arise. But in the Standing library . . . luxurious, softly lighted, warmed by a leaping log fire, alone with 'Fiona' . . . he really had not the slightest idea what to say to her. He was all for turning and running out of the house. Yet, fascinated, he stood still staring at her. She wore a house-gown of soft dark blue wool with a wide cyclamen-coloured sash about her small waist. Her coppery curls were tied up in a chiffon scarf; her face was flushed and her eyes held a queer excited troubled look which Martin could not fathom. She seemed nervous of his scrutiny. She dug both small hands into the deep pockets of the tailored gown which flowed down to the slender feet in their thin satin sandals.

'How you do stare!' she said, with another short laugh.

He grew scarlet. 'I beg your pardon.'

'Oh, not at all; have a cigarette . . . have a drink,' said Christine vaguely, and pushed a box of cigarettes toward him.

He unbuttoned the mackintosh and put a hand in his coat pocket.

'If you don't mind my pipe . . . I'd rather . . .'

'By all means,' she said, in that nervous excited way which he had noticed before. He had a quick perception, and intuition told him that something was worrying 'Fiona Challis.' With the pipe suspended in his fingers, he said:

'Am I intruding? Shall I go away?'

It was what she imagined she wanted him to do. She was on tenterhooks waiting for that call to come through from the real Fiona. She had been haunted by the problem of meeting this man, Gilfred Renwick, ever since Mr. Standing had spoken about him. She foresaw nothing but disaster if Renwick gave her away, and she saw no reason why he shouldn't. Really, it was high time Fiona put an end to this affair and owned up to both her father and Mr. Standing, and let her, Christine, go away from here.

Martin filled and lit his pipe. She looked at

him through her lashes. In this state of nervous irritation she really did not know whether she hated him or the reverse. There was something . . . something she could not deny . . . which made him curiously attractive to her. She had always been fascinated by his hands and she watched them now as he fingered pipe and matches . . . such fine well-bred fingers, brown and strong as steel. At the back of her mind somewhere was a secret yearning for his friendship and counsel. Martin was so rock-like, so wise, so full of vision; of that she was sure, despite all his mistrust of women and life as he imagined she led it. She wanted to be able to tell him the truth and ask his advice. Yes, she would like to draw him to that sofa by the fire and tell him the whole thing. But it was the last thing she could do. It would disgust him. He would be first incredulous, and then full of contempt for her for consenting to impersonate Fiona Challis. And she could not face becoming the object of Martin Farlong's contempt.

Worried and harassed, Christine was not at all herself. She felt caught up in a little whirlpool of difficulties and troubles. She had one predominant sensation . . . a fear that if Martin stayed she would not be able to talk openly to Fiona when her call came through.

'Shall I go away?' repeated Martin.

She felt that it was impossible to be discourteous to him in this house, and said:

117

'No, of course not. Won't you . . . take off your coat . . . sit down . . . let me offer you a drink.'

He took off his coat, put it over a chair, and followed her to the sofa in front of the fire. Once they were seated he tried not to feel ill at ease with her, but his heart was hammering because of her nearness and the beauty of her. How brilliant her eyes were . . . and her colour so high that she might be feverish.

'Are you sure you oughtn't to be in bed,' he stammered; 'you haven't been fit and . . .'

'I'm all right,' she interrupted, and then added, 'Uncle Bob is dining at Lingford. There's . . . there's an old friend of mine there on leave . . .'

'Yes, that would be Mrs. Renwick's son, Gilfred.'

She bit nervously at her lip. She had brought the conversation around to the Renwicks because she could think of little else except this young officer in the R.A.F. who was threatening her peace and the destruction of Fiona's plans. She began to question Martin.

'Do you know Gilfred?'

'I've known everybody up here since I was a boy. Renwick and I played village cricket together.'

'What's he like? I mean, how do you like him?' (She had to correct herself.) She wanted to find out as much as she could about Gilfred, yet disliked these lies which she was telling to

118

Martin right now, pretending that Gilfred was her friend.

'He's all right,' said Martin.

'That's poor praise.'

He gave a half smile.

'In this part of the world we never flatter people unduly.'

'I'll say you don't!' Christine exclaimed, 'and *you* are more critical than anybody.'

He looked at her keenly. He would have liked to have offered her criticism of a new kind, by no means adverse, as usual. He would have liked to have told her how attractive she was looking tonight and what a mad desire he had to snatch her in his arms and bury his face against that soft young throat, draw in her fragrance as a man draws the breath of life.

He found himself only half listening to her talking about the Renwicks. He was much too conscious of her physical nearness and her intoxicating scent. At length he said:

'Tell me more about yourself, what you used to do in London; the sort of life you used to lead.'

She dragged her worried thoughts away from Gilfred Renwick, and for a moment she gave herself up to what solace could be derived from a *tête-à-tête* with Martin. This was a Martin whom she liked more than a little, and not the curt dictatorial 'boss' of the farm. Those very blue eyes of his scrutinised her with unexpected kindliness. She could *feel* that

119

he was trying to understand her and she would have given much for his understanding; but her eyes kept wandering to the telephone. Her ears were strained, waiting for that call. Why, why, she asked herself impatiently, was there not another instrument in this house? Robert Standing had rigid ideas of economy for a rich man and he was not one who used the phone overmuch.

She answered Martin's questions vaguely. It was so horrible, she thought, that she could not tell him a word of truth; could not describe the hard work that the real Christine used to do in London. He must continue to think of her as Fiona Challis . . . just a 'butterfly.'

Martin gradually became conscious of her distraction . . . her ill-concealed anxiety. At length he said:

'Is anything wrong?'

She coloured and looked away from him.

'Why should there be?'

'It seems to me you have something on your mind,' he said gravely.

She tried to laugh.

'What nonsense . . .'

And she wished that he would go away. Alternatively she wished that she could seize one of those strong brown hands, hold on to it, and pour out a full confession.

In desperation she turned the conversation round to himself.

'Don't you ever get sick of Stonehead, and

the narrowness of the world *you* live in?' she challenged him.

He knit his brows.

'I love the farm. And I don't think I would ever get tired of this country. But, as you ask me, I'll tell you straight away that I hate being in a reserved occupation. Do you think I don't envy a fellow like Renwick his uniform? Do you think I didn't feel it when all those chaps went through Dunkirk? I wanted to be with them. I'd like to join up now, only Mr. Standing . . .'

He broke off, fingering his pipe, brows fiercely knit. He was amazed at himself for letting this girl see so far into his innermost heart. And Christine was suddenly remorseful, remembering the difficulty of his present position.

'Don't let it upset you, Martin,' she said. 'You can always remember that your work on the farm is just as valuable as anything a soldier can do, and just as much work for the war.'

He looked down at her with a sudden warmth in his eyes,

'Thanks,' he said, 'I'm glad you said that.'

Her lashes flickered before that look. It was suddenly disturbing to her. She felt that she must offer him some hospitality and was on the point of ringing a bell for drinks, when another bell suddenly shrilled through the house and made her heart jump furiously.

The telephone at last. And inevitably it would be . . . Fiona.

'Excuse me,' she murmured to Martin, and walking to the instrument, lifted the receiver to her ear.

CHAPTER TWELVE

Martin watched Christine. She was a lovely thing, he thought, so straight, so slender in that dark blue house-gown. Fascinated he found himself staring at the cyclamen sash, thinking how incredibly small was her waist.

Christine, meanwhile, waited for that long-distance call to come through, and while the connections were being made, floundered desperately in her mind as to what she could say in front of Martin. It was hopeless having him here at this precise moment.

She heard Fiona's voice:

'Hello, hello. Yes, it's me! What is it? Your wire scared me . . . what's wrong?'

Christine darted a look at Martin. He was looking straight at her and her whole body trembled with nervous agitation as she answered:

'It's all rather awkward . . . but listen . . . you know Gilfred Renwick, don't you?'

Fiona wasted a few seconds the other end, thinking about this. She had met so many young men during this war. Then she recalled Pilot-Officer Renwick.

'Yes. We had rather a gay evening or two, why?'

'He lives up here. He's coming to see me . . .'

'Gawd!' came from Fiona.

'What shall I do?'

'You mustn't see him. You must avoid it.'

'How can I? It will look so curious. When are you coming up?'

'Not yet. Not till Peter goes abroad. He's expecting embarkation orders almost daily. Hold on, you must.'

Chris set her teeth. If only she could speak more plainly. What must Martin be thinking? and how *could* she avoid meeting Gilfred Renwick?

Martin, in fact, was not an inquisitive man and he did not wish to intrude upon 'Fiona's' private business. At the same time he could not avoid hearing what she said, and it filled him with perplexity. It seemed mainly about Gilfred Renwick, and obvious that 'Fiona' had no wish to meet him. Why not? All kinds of conjectures sprang to Martin's mind. And the chief of these was a suspicion that 'Fiona' might have had an affair with this man and was anxious not to reopen it.

A few more broken sentences, then the telephone operator broke in upon the conversation. Frantically Christine endeavoured to hold Fiona for a moment longer, but she was told that three minutes was the limit, and there were priority calls waiting.

Fiona's last words were:

'Don't see Gilfred . . . wangle something . . . I'll write . . .'

Christine put down the telephone. She was white now and her eyes looked enormous. The conversation had been utterly unsatisfactory. She began to feel that it was unfair of Fiona to force her to face such a situation.

Martin stood up and approached her.

'You don't look too well. Won't you come and sit down? I'm sure something is wrong.'

'Oh, be quiet, leave me alone,' she exclaimed excitedly. An hysterical feeling suddenly engulfed her. She sank down on the sofa and buried her face in her hands, struggling to regain her self-control.

Aghast Martin looked at her and saw that the slender shoulders were shaking. 'Fiona' was in tears. If there was one thing that floored Martin, it was the sight of a woman in tears, and particularly when the woman was this one, who was as a rule so cool, so spirited.

He sat down and impulsively put an arm about her.

'My dear, what is it? Can't I be of help?'

'Oh, Martin, I wish you could,' came from Christine in a muffled voice.

'Tell me what's wrong?'

'No, no . . .' Then she added, desperately,

'Please go home . . . please.'

'By all means if you don't want me here.'

She looked up at him, her face wet with tears and her eyes tormented.

'It isn't that. I just can't tell you. You wouldn't understand . . . you wouldn't.'

His heart began to race again, and a longing such as he had never known before in his life filled his whole being. This girl in tears, in some kind of trouble, appealed to him irresistibly.

He said:

'I don't want to seem interfering . . . but I rather guess it's something about young Renwick that's upset you. Is it that you don't want to see him?'

She was terrified because his intuition had led him that far.

'Perhaps . . . no . . . Oh! What can it matter to you, anyhow?'

Martin's breath came unevenly.

'Is there something between you and him?' he asked abruptly

'Oh, don't be silly.'

'How can I help you if you won't answer me?'

She felt cornered.

'What's it matter to you, *anyhow*?'

'It would matter,' he said tersely, 'if I thought you'd had an affair with Renwick down in London and he was objectionable to you, and was going to force his attentions on

125

you again up here.'

Christine put her hand to her lips. So that's what he thought. A hysterical little laugh escaped her. The sound of that laugh filled Martin with a kind of primitive fury and jealousy combined. The beauty, the defence-lessness of her and the thought that perhaps she had known what it was to love . . . to be loved . . . went to his head.

'Don't laugh!' he said between his teeth. 'Don't you realise that you're driving me crazy?'

And before he could restrain himself he had caught her in his arms, kissed the tears from her lashes, her moist flushed cheeks and then brought his lips down to her mouth. It was a long searing kiss Martin Farlong gave to this girl, not only the first passionate embrace he had ever given to any woman, but all the pent-up emotion of a lifetime . . . the depths of his very soul.

Christine was without resistance, helpless, annihilated by that kiss. Other kisses she had received in light fashion from men she had known. But never a kiss like this, and never from such a man. She was burnt up by it. Trembling violently, she surrendered to Martin's mad embrace. Without thought of the past or the future, she gave herself up to the incredible delight of this moment in his arms. His kiss was an almost agonised entreaty for her love, and she responded to it. She felt that hostilities between them hitherto had been only an expression of love.

At last she gave a little moan and moved her head aside.

'Oh, don't! Don't!' she said. 'Martin . . . let me think . . . let me breathe . . .'

He mistook that cry for one of appeal to him to let her go. At once his arms released her. He was like a man shaken by a tempest. White . . . trembling as she had trembled. But he had no clear analysis of his emotion in this moment. He only thought that he had offended her unpardonably. He said:

'Forgive me, please.'

And snatching up his coat, he walked out of that room like one in the grip of a wild dream from which he must wake himself or perish.

Christine looked at the door through which he had vanished and put both her hands to her burning cheeks. She could not think. She only knew that she wanted him to come back, and before she could restrain herself, she called him.

'Martin . . . Martin!'

He did not hear her. He had reached the front door and opened it. With mind and body in chaos, he walked rapidly away from the Manor. There was only one clear thought in his head. He loved 'Fiona Challis.' For the first time he was madly and desperately in love with a woman. He was both exhilarated and crushed by the knowledge. Exhilarated because he had never known such sweetness, such perfection as the loveliness of her in his arms. But she was Fiona Challis, far, far out of his reach and probably after tonight she would loathe the sight of him.

He walked blindly down the road he knew so well. There was a thick mist curling over the Fells tonight. The air was cold and raw. But Martin was hot and shaking like a man in a fever. He felt that he was walking in the wrong direction. He wanted with all his soul to turn back, and run to her and gather her again into a close embrace.

The yellowish lights of a car broke through the fog. Martin heard the warning hoot-hoot of a horn. He stepped aside to let the car pass him. It was not a closed car, but an open sports tourer, and through the mist Martin saw the driver quite plainly as he passed slowly by. A man in Air Force blue uniform.

Martin's pulses jumped.

Gilfred Renwick! And he could only be going in that direction for one purpose. To call on 'Fiona.' He must have broken away from the party at Lingford and come here, seized with a sudden desire to see the girl.

Martin stood staring after the car. And now his whole being was filled with an ungovernable jealousy. Why should that fellow be calling upon 'Fiona' at this time of night? Did she want to see him? Had he been wrong in his surmisal that she did not? Was there *something between those two*? If so, it must be serious because the girl had acted so strangely tonight.

Martin had to force himself to walk on to Stonehead. He did so, tormenting himself with pictures of the young airman up there, alone in that warm fire-lit library with *her*.

Meanwhile, Pilot-Officer Renwick accelerated up the hill toward the Manor House. The mists and the cold did not deter him. He was young and strong and used to flying in all kinds of weathers, and he was urged by a very keen desire to see Fiona. The young heiress to the Challis fortune had attracted him more than ordinarily when he had known her in town. They had had some amusing evenings together. There was nothing he wanted more than to see her again, and he had been bitterly disappointed when old Standing had turned up at Lingford without her tonight. So much so, that he had made an excuse to slip away from the dinner party . . . said that he was meeting some friend in the Air Force in Windermere . . . and had come along here.

Fiona was supposed to be in bed, but he bet she'd come down and see him. She had always been such fun, and her presence was going to add considerable spice to what might have been a rather dull leave.

Renwick drew up before the Manor House and knocked on the front door. While he stood waiting, he lit a cigarette and whistled the bars of a tune which he always associated with the charming Fiona. They had danced to it together at the Dorchester.

A maid opened the door, and in answer to his inquiry said that she very much regretted that 'Miss Challis' was laid up.

The young pilot gave her an ingratiating smile.

'You tell her that a great friend wants to see her just for a moment. I'm sure she'll want to see me, and come down.'

The maid melted. He was good-looking, the young airman, with his forage cap on the side of his fair curly head, and his tanned young face.

She went upstairs, fully under the impression that 'Miss Fiona' was in her room,

But Christine was still in the library. She had sat there on the sofa; smoking, trying to pull herself together ever since Martin had left her. And she had been facing the extraordinary revelation that she loved the man who had kissed her so violently . . . loved him as she had always believed that one day she might love a man. *The* man in her life! And she could see that she was in a far worse tangle now than she had been before.

She did not hear the knock on the front door. She did not know what was in store for her, and she chose that moment to turn out the lamp in the library and go up to her room. Once in the hall, she saw that the front door was wide open, and standing just outside was a young man in uniform. She stood stock-still, her heart sinking, for she at once recognised the young man from the photograph she had seen at Lingford.

It was Gilfred Renwick.

CHAPTER THIRTEEN

Young Renwick looked with surprise and some appreciation at the russet-haired girl in the blue house-gown. She looked scared and wide-eyed for some reason which he did not understand. His hand went up in salute.

'Good evening. I've come to see Miss Challis . . .' he began cheerfully.

Christine gulped. Her face was now a burning sheet of colour. She looked around swiftly, hoping that Agnes, the maid, was out of earshot. She knew that it was useless to fly in the teeth of this danger. Gilfred Renwick would only go back to Lingford and say that he had seen her. She had decided that here was a case in which truth and a frank confession were the only possible way out.

'I . . . oh . . . you'd better come in . . . I'd like to talk to you,' she stammered.

Renwick strolled into the hall and shut the door behind him. For the moment he was bewildered. Here was a remarkably pretty girl

131

whom he had never seen before in his life. What was she doing here? A friend of Fiona's presumably, and yet it was queer that Mr. Standing had not mentioned that Fiona had a friend staying at the Manor.

Then Agnes came running down the stairs and the fat was in the fire, for immediately, out of breath, she exclaimed to Gilfred:

'Oh, you've found Miss Challis, Sir! I'm so glad, I was looking for her everywhere.'

Speechlessly Christine regarded the young airman. He stared back at her, frankly astonished now, and followed her into the library. Once there he said:

'Look here, am I cuckoo or did that girl say that I had "found Miss Challis?" But *you* aren't Fiona.'

Christine drew a deep breath and plunged into the battle.

'No. My real name's Christine Shaw. I was at school with Fiona. We're great friends.'

Young Renwick, fingering the forage cap which he had removed from his fair curly head, let his gaze travel over her. Damned pretty girl all right, but she looked scared as a rabbit and he couldn't for the life of him think what she was talking about.

'Delighted to meet you, Christine Shaw,' he said, with the ease and gallantry that Gilfred Renwick always displayed before attractive women. 'But what are you doing here, and where is Fiona?'

132

Christine's lips were visibly trembling.

'Please sit down and . . . have a drink and . . . I'll explain.'

'Never mind the drink.'

He balanced himself on the arm of the sofa, drew a cigarette case from his pocket and handed it to her. She shook her head, and before he could speak again, blurted out her story. The story of Fiona's crazy scheme . . . of her impersonation . . . of Fiona's secret marriage, and of the difficulties which attended the whole procedure.

And now when she actually recited the story aloud, it sounded crazy even to her ears. She ended wildly:

'I know I ought never to have done it. But Fiona persuaded me. She was so terribly in love and I was so afraid her father would prevent the marriage. I know what he feels about her . . . I'm sure he'd have flung up this American commission that he's on, and ruined his future if he thought Fiona meant to do anything stupid. But it wasn't stupid. Peter was right for her. I know it and that's why I did what she asked.'

Young Renwick had never taken his gaze off her during this recital. He was amazed, and frankly intrigued. So intrigued that he forgot to light his cigarette. He just stared at Christine and although his memories of Fiona were distinctly pleasant, he was very much a man to seize a moment when it presented itself. He had always been susceptible to feminine charm, and he thought Christine Shaw quite ravishing, especially with that wild-rose colour coming and going in her sensitive face.

'We-ell, we-ell,' he said, when at length she stopped talking. 'What a party! Has all the makings of a good exciting flick to me. Impersonations and so forth . . . Naughty of Fiona and rather naughty of you, don't you think?'

Christine, on the verge of tears, turned from him.

'You can joke about it, but I feel awful,' she said in a choked voice.

'Well, it *is* a bit of a joke,' he said, 'but I admit it has a serious side. Mr. Standing won't take very kindly to your story when you open up on him, and I daresay Poppa Challis will kick up the hell of a fuss.'

Christine played nervously with her sash.

'I don't mind how cross Mr. Challis is with me. But I'll be sorry to lose Uncle Bob's . . . Mr. Standing's . . . good opinion. Still what does any of it matter? Fiona has had her happiness.'

Gilfred Renwick lit his cigarette and tossed the match into the grate.

'Young woman with a romantic mind, aren't you? All for love and so on!'

His flippancy jarred on her although she realised that it was his way. Obviously Gilfred

Renwick was not a young man who took life very seriously, and perhaps, she thought, it was just as well. It would have made things more difficult for her if he had been shocked by what she had told him . . . as for instance Martin would be shocked. (Her heart missed a beat at the memory of Martin, who took life so *very* seriously.) Oh, it was a crazy world! Such a short while ago here in this very room she had been caught into Martin's arms and kissed as she had never been kissed in her life before. *And she had liked it.*

Renwick grinned at her.

'Well, Christine, alias Fiona, and where do we go from here?'

She dragged herself back to the problem of Pilot-Officer Renwick.

'Look here,' she said, 'is it too much to ask you to keep the secret for Fiona's sake, as you're fond of her?'

His grin widened.

'Tut-tut! I'm not the sort of chap to be fond of other fellows' wives. Fiona's lost to me. Snatched from my very bosom by the wicked machinations of a beautiful adventuress with lovely copper coloured hair and grey eyes . . . or are they blue?' He leaned nearer her and peered.

'Oh, how can you laugh about it like this?' she exclaimed.

'Do you want me to be serious?'

'I don't know,' she said lamely. She was

135

conscious that her sense of humour was somewhat dimmed tonight. She just could not laugh or joke with Gilfred Renwick. She was also very much aware of the fact that the good-looking young airman had not the slightest effect on her for all his efforts at flirtation. She could see only Martin's face, transfigured with emotion, and the look in his eyes just before his lips had claimed that kiss.

She shrugged her shoulders with a hopeless gesture.

'I'm afraid I'm rather upset by the whole thing. You must forgive me if I don't find much to laugh at. I just want you to keep quiet . . . if you will. It can't hurt you and it will help Fiona . . . and me.'

'I see,' said Gilfred, 'you wish me to let the family think you are the Fiona I knew in town. In other words, to be an accessory after the fact in this illegal game you are playing. It is illegal, you know, to impersonate anyone.'

Christine's eyes dilated.

'Oh! I never thought of it like that.'

He chuckled.

'You're like a babe in the wood, aren't you? You've just entered on this thing in a romantic mood without realising where it would lead you.'

Suddenly Christine's head drooped. Young Renwick was shaken to see two big tears roll down her cheeks while she mutely nodded her head. He sprang to his feet and touched her arm.

'Look here, Beautiful, you don't have to weep or be afraid of me. You don't think I can hurt anybody who looks the way *you* do! I'd be a cad if I did. I believe every word you've told me and Fiona and I were pals even if she preferred this other fellow. I don't want to hurt either of you, and I won't.'

Enormous relief flooded Christine. She looked up at him with wet shining eyes.

'Oh, it is sporting of you.'

The young airman struck an attitude.

'*Vive le sport!* (If I might use the Free French language).'

She had to laugh at him. He was really amusing and obviously not out to spoil the whole thing.

'Then you won't give me away?'

'No. You shall appear at my home and I shall address you as Fiona and join the Impersonation Gang.'

'It sounds so awful when you call it that.'

'Well, although I don't offer criticism, my child, you must surely realise you're playing a dangerous game, but if you don't care about anything except Fiona's romance, what matter?'

She looked away from him. She did care. She cared very much what Martin would say, for instance, when *he* found out. He would not take it so lightly. He was neither as young or irresponsible as this gay boy and he might place a wrong construction on the whole thing. He might even believe that she had done it for what she could get out of it. That would be awful.

Gilfred Renwick interrupted her thoughts.

'Don't look so tragic. It's all O.K. by me. You can give Fiona my best wishes, only tell her I'm not sending her a wedding present. Tell her I shall spend the money taking you out instead, and serve her right.'

Christine shook her head dumbly. The boy drew nearer to her.

'What about it . . . Fiona? (I'd better get into the habit of calling you that.) As a reward for my silence, will you lighten the hours of my leave and let me take you out?'

She felt that she would be churlish to refuse and yet she had not the slightest wish to spend a frivolous hour with young Renwick. She wanted to be with Martin. She wanted Martin to understand . . . and yet, when she thought about it, it seemed to her that the widest possible gulf yawned between them.

Gilfred would have stayed any length of time, talking, joking, trying to break through her reserve and make her less shy of him, but she was too tired and too worried to respond, and after a while he gave it up and took his departure. He was disappointed, too, that she would not take a day off from the farm and go sailing on Windermere with him. He had to be content with her promise to dine with him and

138

go on to a cinema.

'I've got the car and the petrol, and all I want is the girl,' he said.

She could not do otherwise than accept. He went away whistling, highly amused by the whole affair. Remembering Christine Shaw's exquisite colouring and perfect figure, he chuckled to himself as he drove away.

'Renwick, my lad, I think you've got something there!'

PART II

CHAPTER FOURTEEN

Daylight had just broken over the wild fens and fells of the countryside when Martin Farlong finished his breakfast and prepared to walk down to the milling sheds to see his men.

He had had a bad night, and slept badly, which was unusual for him. All through the hours he had been haunted by the thought of 'Fiona' and the intoxicating sweetness of that tempestuous embrace. And the more he thought about it . . . and her . . . the more crazily and unreasonably he wanted a repetition of last night. Of course, it was out of the question. The whole thing was mad. He, Robert Standing's factor, and the Challis heiress . . . could anything be more absurd?

Even if 'Fiona' cared for him (which, of course, she didn't) it was impossible. Maybe he would never see her again. She would stay away from the farm. Interest herself with men of her own type . . . Young Renwick, for instance.

These and a dozen other disquieting thoughts pursued Martin and robbed him of sleep. He had awakened to a stormy morning. During the night the fog had come down in heavy rain and now the wind had changed. It was driving from the North right across Cartmel Fell. The countryside was strewn with leaves and by the end of the day the creaking, tossing boughs of the trees would be ruthlessly stripped. It was cold, too . . . bitterly cold at this hour. There was a real taste of winter in the air this October morning, which Martin recognised. And while he ate his breakfast, unutterable depression seized him. He had always loved this place in all its weathers. All moods. But this morning it seemed to him the most desolate spot in the world. And all because he had held in his arms a girl with the most soft and alluring young body, and a maddening mouth.

He was in love. That was the answer. He who had forsworn the mere idea and avoided women all his life, was in love with 'Fiona Challis.' And Martin Farlong's world was upside down.

As he buttoned up his heavy mackintosh,

Susan Blythe came out into the hall with a thermos in her hand.

'Gran says you'll need a drop of hot tea later on,' she said, as she handed it to him.

'Thanks, Susan.'

She stayed near him, looking up at him with her bright sloe-black eyes.

'Will you be very busy this evening, Mr. Farlong?'

'I daresay,' he answered vaguely.

She bit her lip.

'There be an awful good picture in Ulverston. I thought maybe you'd take me.'

He concentrated on what she was saying, and realised with a sense of shock that the young girl's face bore a look of open invitation.

'My dear Susan, I'm sorry, but I shan't have time, nor can I waste the petrol!'

She pouted.

'I suppose it's only the likes of Miss Challis that gets taken to the pictures,' she said, before she could restrain herself.

Martin flushed darkly. His blue eyes were suddenly shot with a lightning look of anger which made Susan draw back.

'What utter nonsense!' he said roughly.

'I'm sorry,' she said with a whimper. 'I can't help being jealous of her, I'm that fond of you.'

That frank avowal and the ripe good looks of the girl left Martin Farlong cold. But it upset him all the same. Up to such a short time ago women had played so little a part in his life and now it seemed as though an avalanche of emotions . . . all going in the wrong direction . . . was threatening him.

And it secretly infuriated him to think that even this foolish child, Susan, should see into his heart. She had cause to be jealous of 'Fiona Challis.' Good cause!

He muttered a few noncommittal words to her and hastened out of the farmhouse.

The sudden howl of the wind in his ears drowned the sound of Susan Blythe's sobbing.

Through the grey cold of the stormy morning he hurried down to the cattle sheds. He was late. He had been late getting up and he felt exhausted even before the day's work had begun. This would never do, he told himself. He must pull himself together. And he must stop thinking about last night.

By the time he reached the byres, the milking was over and the cows had been let out. The door of the big barn, which he entered, crashed behind him in the wind and he stood with his back to it for a moment, wiping his eyes with the back of his hand. Then he saw the girl whom he believed to be Fiona Challis.

He had not for an instant expected to find her here this morning, but here she was in her familiar breeches, short tweed coat, and scarf. She was rummaging in a corner where there were some sets of rusty old harrows and scythes, evidently looking for something. She turned as she heard the door slam.

'Oh! Good morning,' she said.

He took off his hat.

'Good morning,' he repeated; but the simple words far from expressed what he felt. And his heart hammered as he had never known it to hammer before at the mere sight of that charming face.

'I lost a small silver cigarette case in here yesterday. It must have fallen out of my pocket,' she added in the same cool voice.

'I . . . can I help you find it?' he stammered.

She faced him again.

'I'm sure you're much too busy. What are my orders for today?'

He tried to answer but he was tongue-tied. Her coolness and unconcern floored him. He supposed that she was so contemptuous of what he had done last night that she had decided to ignore it completely. How could he know that Christine's own heart was plunging. And that as she looked up at him . . . at that thin brown face with the intensely blue eyes . . . she was thinking.

'He's marvellous. I've never known a man to touch him. He makes boys like Gilfred Renwick look nothing at all. And he's as strong as a lion!'

For an instant neither of them said anything but held each other's gaze. Above them on the great transverse beams the cobwebs hung like silver lace. Two or three chickens strutted over the floor, picking at the dust and chaff. It was dim and warmer in here than outside, but the rain beat against the dirty windowpanes which let in shafts of the grey morning light. It seemed curiously still in the barn with that wind raging outside.

But in the heart of Martin Farlong a storm was also raging. And it seemed to him that for the first time he recognised the deeper significance of these wild winds that swept across the fens and fells . . . these wild disturbances of Nature which he had heard and stood up to since his babyhood. They were like the disturbances in a man's soul. And, strong though he was, he could not stand up to them. He was shaking like a child.

And because he was a man unused to subtleties and disseminations, that hunger in his eyes was open for Christine to see, and she, too, felt the spinning of the world around her.

She had started off by being so cool . . . so casual . . . determined to do her day's work as usual and behave as though last night had not happened. But it did not work out that way. For both of them were remembering . . . *both of them*.

A rat suddenly appeared from behind a stack of linseed cakes and scuttled across the dusty floor, scattering the hens in all directions. Christine saw it and screamed.

'*Oh!*'

And the next moment, instinctively, she was close beside Martin gripping his arm. A rat was too much even for her courage.

Martin did not even see the avid little animal. His eyes were concentrated on the girl. The touch of her fingers was like fire to matchwood. He forgot his remorse for last night, his ridicule of himself and the situation. He did not even stop to wonder what she felt. He only knew that he was crazy for her . . . about her. And the next moment she was in his arms again, and his lips were hard against her mouth.

She surrendered to that embrace as she had surrendered last night, helplessly, knowing that here was the irresistible passion and the one man who had the power to stir her to the depths of her being. She hung in his arms, her feet barely touching the floor. One of his hands took off her hat and travelled feverishly through her hair.

'I love you! Fiona, Fiona. I love you!' He stammered the words, wildly, when that deep kiss ended.

She heard the words and was thrilled to the core of her being by them. She answered with a passion to equal his.

'I love you, too, Martin . . . Oh, *Martin*!'

For a moment he could not credit his ears.

'You can't love me—it isn't possible.'

'Why isn't it?'

For a moment he was speechless and, still

145

holding her hand, drew back from her a pace and looked her up and down. The slender beauty of her, the transformation of her face, radiant with love and with eyes so starry bright, so full of intense feeling, staggered him. He did not know much about women—but this much he knew . . . that no girl could look like that and feel indifferently toward a man. She must mean what she had just said.

Christine spoke again.

'Oh, Martin, Martin,' she murmured weakly. 'You don't know what you've done to me!'

'I know what you're doing to me,' he said hoarsely. 'You're bewitching me. All night I've been thinking of you . . . longing for you . . . yes, do you hear me? I've been mad with longing for you, and it's fantastic. You're Miss Challis. I'm just Mr. Standing's factor. I—'

He got no further. For Christine was back in his arms again. She seemed to melt into his embrace and he was no longer conscious of the difference in their social stations or of any barrier as he felt the fragrant softness of her once more in his arms. Against his lips were her lips, whispering:

'Martin, darling Martin, kiss me again.'

And he was showering her with kisses until her face burned under them and he was saying wild incoherent things which he had never imagined himself capable of saying. All the stored-up emotion, the repressions of long years of bitter loneliness, poured out into a torrent of feeling for this girl who so sweetly, so frankly, revealed her love for him.

She caught the sound of little phrases which enchanted her, and revealed this lover of hers as poet as well as farmer.

'You're magical . . . you're like Spring moonlight . . . you've got eyes as deep, as crystal clear, as the little pools of dew up in my beloved hills . . . And your hair, Fiona . . . have you ever smelled the hay with the sun on it . . . the warm ripe smell of it? It's like your hair . . . Have you ever put the petals of a wild rose against your cheek? It's like your skin, silky-soft, you lovely, lovely thing!'

Her hands wandered to his hair, smoothing it, caressing it.

'You're magical, too, Martin. You're all that I've ever wanted in a man. You're so strong, darling . . . so brown and strong and wonderful!'

He buried his face against her neck.

'I don't know what you see in me, I can't believe it yet. Fiona, believe me when I tell you, I've never loved any women except you.'

'I do believe it, and I've never loved any man except you.'

'Say that again.'

She gave an excited little laugh.

'I do say it. It's absolutely true.'

'And do you know I nearly went mad with jealousy when I saw Renwick's car going up to

147

the Manor House?'

'Oh, Martin, darling, you needn't be jealous of him or any one.'

'Listen,' he said fiercely, 'do you know that I couldn't bear it if I came to my senses now and found this was just a dream? You've got to swear that you do love me, swear it by everything you hold sacred.'

She raised her brilliant eyes and answered without hesitancy.

'I swear it.'

For a moment with his own passionate gaze he devoured her, then he said:

'Do you realise what this means to me, my dear? I've fought against you . . . a bitter fight, just as all my life I've fought against myself. You mustn't let me down, I couldn't stand *that*!'

For a moment her feverish ecstasy subsided and a cold little feeling of fear gripped her.

'How do you mean . . . let you down?'

'Just that you mustn't play with me, Fiona. You're sacred to me. Our love is sacred. If you've any doubts about that love, tell me now.'

Speechlessly, she looked up at him. There was silence in the great barn, broken only by the sighing of the wind outside, the rattle of the door, and the spatter of rain against the dusty panes, and it seemed to her that she could hear the beating of her own heart. Her whole body was weak, half-fainting in the close embrace of this man who had such amazing power to disturb her very being. Those deep blue eyes of his were asking her for truth and honesty, and yet, how could she tell him now that she was a living lie . . . that she had no right to the name of Fiona and that she was just a girl who had impersonated another . . .? It might drive him away from her . . . She couldn't . . . she couldn't bear to watch the look in his eyes change to one of contempt. She couldn't bear him to turn and walk away from her, out of her life, and break his own heart in consequence. She could see what a confession would bring about. Perhaps a revulsion of all his feelings. One half of her desired more than anything in the world a complete understanding between him and herself, but the other half avoided this issue. She was just a woman who loved him, needed him, and his love . . . this breath-taking wonderful emotion which had swept her so completely off her feet. She heard his voice again, pleading this time.

'You do really love me, don't you . . . darling, my darling, say it?'

And then she was dissolved again into an agony of love and longing for him. Once more both her arms went about his neck, and with her lips against his, she whispered:

'Yes, yes, Martin. I love you with all my heart, all my body, all my soul.'

CHAPTER FIFTEEN

Martin Farlong thrilled to the depth of his being as he heard that passionate declaration of love uttered by this marvellous girl who had swept aside with a single kiss all his old fears and prejudices against women. He looked down at her upturned face, so exquisitely tender and beseeching for tenderness from him. He was lost . . . just for a few moments lost to reason and sanity and the stern realities of life. The old grim Martin who had stood aloof from the opposite sex, remembering with bitterness his own mother's betrayal of him as a child, vanished. He was a boy, young, idealistic, desperately in love. And it was this new young Martin who caught Christine close to his heart again and showered her with kisses and caresses.

'Oh, my darling, darling love. My sweet Fiona . . . sweet, heavenly Fiona!' He almost groaned the words, his brown fingers playing with her hair, his lips drinking in the fragrance of her smooth skin, the irresistible temptation of her red young mouth. A mouth made for kisses. For *him*, he thought deliriously.

'Fiona, darling, angel, I adore you.' He kept repeating the name which he believed to be hers, and it seemed to Christine that he was insatiable for her lips . . . her response to his crazy, new-found passion. And with all the woman in her she responded. They stood there together in the dim old barn, locked in that feverish embrace, caring nothing for the world outside. Both of them learning for the first time in their lives the sweet and almost terrible power of passionate love.

It was the sound of a dray rumbling over the cobbles in the yard that sent them apart. Martin drew a deep breath, like a man who has been drowning and just come to the surface again. He flung a quick glance over his shoulder.

'That'll be Tom or Luke bringing in the pig-feed,' he said. 'They will want to see me. I . . . I ought to go.'

Christine—herself dazed, weak with emotion, nodded and tried to pat a stray silk lock of hair into place.

'Yes, and I . . . I must find my hat.'

He stooped and picked up the little felt hat which had fallen to the ground, a hat dear and familiar to him now.

'Here it is . . .'

Their fingers touched. Once more the fiery stream of passionate emotion flowed between them. With fast beating hearts they looked into each other's eyes. Then Martin said:

'My little love, I must go to Robert Standing tonight. I must be straight with him and tell him about this. He may think it crazy and impossible. There are serious barriers between us. But tell him I must . . . now that I know you truly love me.'

At that Christine's heart seemed to turn over. She caught his fingers in hers.

'No,' she said, before she could restrain her impulsive fears . . . 'don't go to him, Martin . . . please.'

Ecstasy fell away from Martin Farlong, leaving him suddenly cool and calm again. His pulse-beats slackened. It was as though the hot veil was torn from his eyes by that appeal from 'Fiona.' He looked at her gravely, questioningly.

'But why, my dear? Of course, I realise . . . believe me . . . the difficulties. I'm just a factor and you . . .'

'That isn't it,' she broke in confusedly. 'It wouldn't matter if I were a queen and you a thousand miles beneath me. I would still love you, and as far as I'm concerned I don't consider you beneath me at all. Just because you think of me as William Challis's heiress is of no account.'

'But it is true,' he reminded her.

She hung her head, twisting the brim of her felt hat in nervous little fingers. If only she could tell him the truth, she thought. But it would cause chaos . . . complete misunderstanding. Her only course was to steer him away as tactfully as she could from this inclination to go straight to Mr. Standing.

'Listen, darling,' she said. 'It isn't a question

152

of social barriers between us, but merely that I . . . this love is new to me . . . it's kind of swept me straight off my feet. I . . . I just want a little breathing space before we mention it to a soul.'

Some of Martin's old natural mistrust revived within him. The ecstatic boy became a suspicious man again:

'You are sure that you do love me, Fiona, and that the word love means to you what it does to me?' he asked.

'What does it mean to you?' she asked in a whisper.

'Everything,' was his solemn answer. 'I want you for my wife, Fiona . . . if that isn't too mad a dream.'

Words failed her. To be Martin's wife . . . oh, dear heaven she thought, what a miracle that would be. It made her whole body tremble to look up into those piercing blue eyes of his and hear him say those words, *I want you for my wife . . .*' She longed almost unbearably to hear her own name, '*Christine*,' from his lips. She hated . . . hated the 'Fiona' which she had taken upon herself.

'You must know,' added Martin, 'that there has never been anything like this before in my life. It is *everything*, my darling. Does it mean the same to you?'

'Oh, yes, yes.'

He caught her back in his embrace.

'It's all so incredible to me . . . that you, *you*,

153

Fiona Challis, should love *me*. And now you seem as though you are not anxious to acknowledge our love. I can't quite understand it. Aren't you sure of yourself yet, Fiona?'

She caught at that loophole desperately.

'Perhaps that's it. I . . . I'm not one hundred per cent sure that I want to get married just yet . . . I . . . I want to think it over. You see, Martin . . . my . . . my father is in America. I . . . I'd have to cable him . . . break the news . . . I . . . it's a big step. We've only known each other a few weeks. Let us both think it over before we announce it to the world.'

She finished that speech, her head drooping, not daring to meet the clear honest gaze of the man, and she felt utterly miserable. Every word she uttered was a lie . . . to cover the main lie, and she knew it. For she was one hundred per cent sure of her love for him. She *was* . . . and she wanted no time for thought. She would gladly, proudly have walked out of this barn this moment and married him here and now. But she must make time, she thought desperately. She must take action now, where Fiona was concerned. She must go down South and see her, tell her that the deception could not go on, and that the truth must be told. And then, with Fiona's cooperation she would clear up the tangle here and tell Martin the truth.

'God forgive me for lying now,' she thought. 'I'd cut off my right hand rather than do it ever again. Dear, *dear* Martin!'

154

But she realised that she was too deep in the morass now for immediate recovery. She could not unburden her story at this moment and bring this new, lovely world of illusion and romance crashing about his ears and her own.

He seemed to be thinking over what she had just said. Then he tightened his hold of her for a fleeting instant, touched her lips with his, and released her.

'It's all right, my little love,' he said in the deep, tender voice which thrilled her so. 'I understand. I mustn't be greedy and expect too much. Life has given me more this morning than I dared hope for in my wildest dreams. Just take your time, my sweet little Fiona, and think it well over. Then when you are sure . . . sure you do care enough to give up everything and marry me . . . I'll speak to Mr. Standing and you can cable your father.'

She marvelled a little at the honesty, the simple straightness of this man. She respected him so deeply for it. He was incapable of duplicity . . . of a light, thoughtless action. And he was fearless . . . adorably proud, she reflected He would face William Challis himself, if he could, and ask his permission to marry his daughter. That was his way. But it made Christine shrink all the more from exposing herself as a girl who had lied and impersonated another . . . even in an idealistic, romantic cause.

She was grateful for the respite offered,

however. She really must see Fiona now, at once, she reflected. And meanwhile she must keep Martin's love and trust.

'You are so grand to me,' she said with shining eyes, 'and I do adore you, Martin, honestly I do. I . . . I just want a few days.'

'You shall have it, my dearest,' he said, the sternness of his lips relaxed into that sweet, grave smile which made his brown face look less bitter and so much younger. He caught both her hands and kissed them, adding: 'And now I must get to work. You've had me right off my feet this morning, you little witch . . . I still feel under some kind of spell.'

'So do I, Martin darling.'

'We must both keep our heads,' he added, 'and my very dear, please . . . if you find after thinking things well over that you can't give up the old life and join yours and mine . . . tell me. I will bear it . . . I only want the truth.'

She writhed. His words made her feel horribly embarrassed.

'I shan't ever feel that,' she stammered. 'I don't want any life now . . . except with you.'

'Could Fiona Challis, the spoiled darling of fortune, bear to settle down as a farmer's wife?' he asked, smiling down at her. 'I daresay in the days ahead I shall have saved enough to buy a farm of my own . . . but so far, I'm just managing Stonehead and the rest of it for Mr. Standing . . . and you are used to being the lady of Wyckam Manor. Remember all that,

156

when you're thinking it over, my darling.'

Helplessly Christine looked up at Martin. She could not argue or protest, as she longed to do . . . could not tell him that she was in reality only Christine Shaw, a city typist . . . and that life as the factor's wife at Stonehead would be heaven to her.

He mistook her silence for some slight mental doubt and confusion. He longed to sweep her back into his arms and draw from her fiercely the passionate reassurance of her feeling for him. But he restrained himself. He was madly in love, but he must keep a tight rein on that madness, he thought grimly. She was right to ask for time . . . not to rush things. Quite right.

He turned and moved away from her. She followed him.

He turned back to her.

'What is it?' he asked eagerly.

She swallowed hard. She could not say what was in her mind and heart. It was a cruel strain on her. She just whispered:

'I love you . . . I always will.'

'Oh, my darling Fiona,' he said. 'Bless you.'

On the verge of weeping, she said: 'I may . . . have to go to London tomorrow . . . on business. I . . . I shall long to get back to you.'

'And I to see you,' he said. 'It means so much to me now to see you about the place. I realise now it always has meant a lot . . . ever since you first came. You've been so plucky . . .

so grand, doing a land-girl's job. I admire you for it more than I can say.'

'I've loved it, Martin.'

'Then come back soon,' he said. 'And while you're away in the South . . . weigh it all up in your mind . . . and give me your answer when you come back.'

'Darling Martin, I will,' she said, and determined there and then that she would never come back to Stonehead as an impersonator of Fiona Challis. Fiona *must* listen to her now.

Martin unlatched the door of the barn and it swung open. The wind tore in like a live thing, driving the rain against his face, swirling about Christine, almost lifting her off her feet.

'It's a rough morning!' exclaimed Martin, buttoning up his collar. 'You must do an inside job, Fiona . . . you'll get soaked outside.'

'I'm ready for orders,' she said, smiling up at him, and added softly: 'My *darling* Mr. Factor.'

His cheeks burned. He looked at her under his lashes, passionately.

'You sweet,' he whispered back.

In the yard one of the men had pulled up in a dray piled with turnips. He hailed the factor.

'Eh, Mr. Farlong . . . might I speak to thee, Sir . . .'

'Coming, Tom,' shouted Martin, then added in an undertone to Christine, 'I must see you later tonight. I'll come up after the evening meal to the Manor, about half-past eight, if you can slip out and see me for a moment. Till then . . . so long, darling girl.'

She watched the tall figure stride through the rain toward the dray. The rain slanted down, drenching her hair. She hardly noticed how cold it was. She could see nothing . . . nobody, but Martin. And her whole being was in confusion. She had not had time to tell Martin that she would not be up at the Manor House tonight. For, of course, she had promised to dine and go to a cinema with Gilfred Renwick. It was the last thing she wanted to do. It was Martin, her beloved, darling Martin whom she wished to see tonight. But she could not refuse young Renwick. He knew the truth. Nice though he was . . . he had the advantage of her in this.

And if Martin knew she was going out with Gilfred what would he think? Wouldn't he begin to wonder if she was fickle . . . not seriously in love with him?

A wretched little feeling replaced Christine's ardour. She watched Martin drive away on the dray beside Tom. Digging her hands in her coat pockets she battled her way through the violent storm down to the milk byres where she could, she knew, do a job that was waiting.

And as she worked, all that morning, she was torn between the glorious emotion of loving and being loved by Martin, and the terror of this deception which might eventually come between them.

CHAPTER SIXTEEN

The stormy day seemed endless to Christine.

Once or twice while she got through the tasks given her, she saw Martin. Once or twice spoke to him briefly. And always the flame of passionate longing darted between them, only to result for Christine in fresh confusion and anxiety.

Before sunset the rain stopped. The heavy dark clouds rolling behind the hills dissolved into the mists of night. The wind died down and a great silence came over the land. To the West, the sky was shot with red and orange light and the sodden earth lay quiet, brooding after the storm.

Christine went home, chilled and damp, and was glad of a hot bath and a change of clothes. She had a glass of sherry with 'Uncle Bob,' and informed him that young Renwick was calling for her that evening, and he seemed pleased.

'Renwick is a first-rate fellow. The sort your father would like you to associate with, my dear,' he said.

That made Christine feel miserably guilty. What would Mr. Standing say, she wondered, if he knew about Martin . . . to say nothing of the impersonation.

Perforce she had to scribble a note to Martin and send it by one of the servants, down to Stonehead.

'I have to go out tonight, so don't come,' she wrote. *'I love you. Always believe that.*

'Fiona.'

She hated signing that name. She hated everything and everyone except Martin tonight. Most of all she hated herself and thought ruefully of all that B.J. had said to her on the matter.

Christine rested her head on her hand for a moment and something suspiciously like a sob, mixed up with a laugh, escaped her.

'Oh, B.J., if you could see me now . . .' she thought . . . 'The complications have been ghastly. How could I ever have guessed that I was going to meet Martin or Gilfred . . . or get tied up in any of these hateful knots?'

When she was dressed and ready to go out with Gilfred, she reread a letter which she had received from B.J. that morning. It filled her with envy. Alan Torcross had come home. B.J., like Fiona, had married her man and was divinely happy. B.J. deserved that happiness . . . every inch of it, and Christine was glad for her. Dear B.J., who had always worked so hard and loved her Alan so faithfully. Now she was Mrs. Alan Torcross. They had had a week's honeymoon in a little inn in a remote village tucked away in the Cotswolds. This letter had been written from Plymouth, where Alan, for

161

the moment, had a shore job, and B.J. (Christine could never think of her as anything else) was living in a small hotel cherishing the days that were given to them although she knew that this could only be temporary happiness. Alan must eventually go back to sea.

Christine sighed as she put this letter back in her bag and stood by the fire smoking a cigarette, expecting at any moment to hear the sound of Gilfred Renwick's car.

She had a vivid imagination and she could picture quite clearly the life that B.J. was leading down in Plymouth with her Naval officer husband. How completely content two human beings could be when they loved each other, no matter how foul the food or cramped the space . . . no matter what discomforts or financial difficulties had to be faced. She put herself in B.J.'s place and Martin in Alan's, and at the mere thought an electric glow spread through her whole body. That was how she loved Martin—as B.J. loved Alan.

To be his wife . . . to live with him no matter how humbly, would be perfect. B.J. was right. Money didn't matter. Nothing mattered to a real woman except love . . . the right husband . . . and their home together.

How she hated the role of Fiona Challis now. How incredibly stupid and short-sighted it had been of her to let Fiona persuade her to do this thing.

Tomorrow she would write and tell B.J. about Martin. She must pour out her heart to someone. She couldn't tell Fiona . . . somehow she didn't want to. But B.J. she could tell, and B.J. would send her some good advice. In fact, she knew what her friend would write before the letter came. She would advise her to snap out of this situation quickly and tell both Martin and Mr. Standing the truth . . . even though it might let Fiona down. B.J. would say that she must consider herself and not sacrifice everything for Fiona.

The sound of a car coming up the drive diverted Christine's thoughts into another channel. She threw her cigarette into the fire and went out to meet Gilfred. She had not the least desire for this evening's entertainment. But young Renwick was in good spirits and threw an admiring glance at the lovely girl. Christine had put on a dark grey suit with a crisp organdie shirt, a short fur coat, and a yellow scarf tying up her curls.

'You look most attractive,' he greeted her, and opened the car door for her. Then as she climbed into the seat beside him, sniffed the air appreciatively and added: 'What divine scent. You take me right out of the country and into Paris. I'd like to be driving with you this moment down the Champs Elysées.'

Christine laughed shortly.

'Well, I wouldn't. I much prefer the countryside up here.'

163

Young Renwick started up the car and they moved off through the purple dusk. It was no night for a long drive, for although the wind had died down, it was very damp. In the grounds of Wyckam Manor the trees were sodden and the flowers were scattered upon their beds in ruined loveliness.

'The country is all right,' said Gilfred, 'on a fine hot day; but tonight I want Paris.'

'How absurd you are. What's the good of such a "want"?'

He gave her a sidelong glance.

'I believe in striving after the impossible.'

Christine smiled a little grimly.

Wasn't that what she, herself, was doing? In wanting Martin she was striving after the impossible. Somehow she could not conceive of him forgiving her for what she had done up here no matter how high the initial motive.

'Where shall we go?' Renwick asked her.

'Not too far. I'm rather tired and I don't want a late night.'

'Oh!' he exclaimed crestfallen. 'Aren't you out for a party?'

'Isn't it a bit difficult to have one in this wild countryside with the petrol ration?'

'Oh, my mamma has saved me a couple of gallons or so for my leave.'

She looked at the mist which was slowly descending upon the desolate fields, and shook her head.

'I don't want to go far, Gilfred.'

'You don't mean you only want a snack at a place like the King's Arms in Cartmel?'

'No,' she said. 'Not Cartmel.'

'Don't you like it?'

'I love Cartmel, but I don't want to go there tonight.'

She connected Martin with Cartmel. Martin who had been born and brought up there, and who might, at this very moment indeed, be found at the King's Arms. No—that was a place she wished to avoid. Martin must not see her out tonight with Gilfred Renwick.

Gilfred peered down at the girl's face.

'You're being much too serious,' he said. 'You disappoint me, Beautiful. Why won't you play?'

'Sorry. I'm just not in a playful mood.'

'Anything wrong?'

'Everything. You know that I regret being here—sailing under false colours.'

'I didn't know you regretted it that much.'

'Well, I do,' she said, glad to talk about it even to this boy. 'I'm not at all good at impersonation and I shall have to go down South and see Fiona and put an end to it.'

'Well, I told you when you first gave me the low-down that I thought you were playing a dangerous game,' he said, adopting a more serious tone.

'You were right.'

'Oh, well, never mind—don't think about it tonight,' said Gilfred. 'It was a mad sort of scheme but I don't suppose anything awful will come of it. And perhaps I can be of help.'

Christine sighed.

'It's nice of you but I don't quite know what you can do.'

'I might propose to you,' said Gilfred cheerfully. 'I had meant to ask Fiona to marry me but you're an ideal substitute. How about a special licence and changing your name from Christine Shaw *alias* Fiona Challis to Mrs. Gilfred Renwick? That'll get everyone so foxed, they won't know who you are in the long run.'

'Don't be ridiculous Gilfred, you must really be sensible. I . . . I need a friend. You know all about me and it's a relief for me to come out with you and feel that I can be myself.'

'Is there a boy friend lurking somewhere in your life?'

She turned her gaze from him.

'Possibly that's the answer.'

'And does he know that you're putting over the Fiona act up here?'

'No.'

'Isn't it going to worry him a bit when he finds out?'

Christine suddenly had to swallow very hard.

'Yes. In fact, it's going to be hellish,' she said in a low tone.

'Oh!' said Gilfred, nodding once or twice. 'So that's how the land lies. You're heading for the last round-up with the boy friend, who doesn't think you capable of being such a naughty girl. Is that it?'

She shot a look almost of anger at him.

'Yes, that's it. I've got myself into a tangle and possibly it will break my heart and his, too, and now you know, and perhaps you are satisfied, and oh, please leave me alone.'

Then to her horror Christine burst into tears and covered her face with her hands.

Young Renwick looked at her aghast, pulled out a blue silk handkerchief, and hastily pressed it into her fingers.

'Oh, I say! Don't do that. Oh, look here! I never meant to make you cry. Fiona . . . Christine . . . dash it all, I don't know what to call you. But don't cry. You're much too beautiful. I won't worry you any more. I'm sorry—honestly, I think you're marvellous and we're supposed to be having a party. *Please* don't cry. It will all come right. Go and see Fiona and tell her to get on with her own job. You've taken on far too much and it's not fair to you, you poor little thing.'

Christine wept helplessly while Gilfred rambled on. But she could see that he meant to be kind and in a way this little outbreak relieved her pent-up feelings. Eventually she found herself sitting there drying her eyes and attempting to make up her face, with young Renwick's arm about her shoulders in friendly fashion while he continued to give her good

167

advice mixed up with the boyish flippancies that poured so glibly from his lips.

In the end she agreed with him that she must abandon this role at once and go down south to see Fiona.

'And I don't know who this chap is that you're smitten with, but I suggest you tell him the facts and stop getting yourself tied in any more knots,' was Gilfred's final observation.

'You're right,' she nodded. 'You've never been more right.'

'And I,' said Gilfred, switching on the engine, 'have never before taken a lovely girl out for the evening and found her shedding tears over another fellow. My whole evening is spoilt.'

'I'm sorry—truly, Gilfred, I am. You've been very kind to me.'

'I could be a lot kinder, only it wouldn't be popular,' he said. 'So we'd better get on to Grange and have a spot of food at the Netherwood.'

The evening passed off rather more pleasantly than Christine had anticipated. Gilfred Renwick could not help flirting . . . he was made that way . . . but his behaviour toward Christine could not have been called offensive in any way. In fact, she went back to Wyckam Manor feeling that he was a truly nice boy and was rather regretful because she had not been able to play up to his mood and be more amusing for him. He heaped coals of fire on her head when he said 'good night' and told her that he had thoroughly enjoyed their 'party' and would take her out again any time she wanted while he was there on leave.

She felt that it was more than she deserved, but at least she meant to follow his advice and put an end to this ridiculous situation immediately.

She must tell Mr. Standing that it was imperative that she should go down to London at once. She could say that she had received an urgent letter from a friend living in the West of England who needed her help. After all, Mr. Standing could not stop her going south and would not try to. But see Fiona she must—and without further delay.

Then she remembered Mr. Standing's birthday party. It was all arranged for Saturday—and she knew that the old man would be bitterly disappointed, if not hurt, if she left Wyckam before then. So she decided that she must contain herself and stay up here until after the week-end. On Sunday she would break it to Mr. Standing that she must go away the next morning. She would write to Fiona and tell her to expect her down south on the Monday. As for Martin . . . Martin had given her a few days in which to think things over . . . so he was not expecting any immediate decision from her. Until Mr. Standing's birthday party was over, she must go on playing the part which had become so irksome and difficult. She must go on with the deception and the lies. It was all hateful. And she loved Martin so much that she could hardly bear it.

CHAPTER SEVENTEEN

Martin Farlong stood before the tall mahogany dressing chest in his little bedroom, staring into the small mirror, trying desperately to tie a small black bow. He had been struggling with it for the last ten minutes. Standing before that mirror was not a pastime in which Martin often indulged, and he hated the feel of the crisp white shirt which Emmy had specially ironed for him, and the idea of putting on the dinner jacket which hung unused in his wardrobe for months on end. Since the war there had been no evening parties to attend, and even before the war, Martin, the farmer, rarely got out of his old clothes unless to wear grey flannels or tweeds when he was not working.

Gritting his teeth, his brown face red, he pulled the little tie this way and that. The light was bad. Emmy had tied a piece of brown paper over the glove of the oil lamp which stood on his dressing-chest, drilled by himself into the habit of safeguarding the black-out from all angles. As Emmy said, if those 'vile

Germans' could drop a bomb on lovely Cartmel Fell, they could drop one on Stonehead Farm—so the more careful they all were, the better.

Martin gave an almost irritable look at his smooth-brushed head and freshly shaven cheeks. He disliked this 'dolling up.' He dreaded the thought of going up to the Manor to mix with all Mr. Standing's friends in celebration of his birthday. But, as Mr. Standing had issued the invitation, Martin, the factor, could scarcely refuse. Besides, a little note had come down to the farm from 'Fiona' begging him to come.

I'll teach you how to dance, she had written. *Don't be worried, we can keep our lovely secret a little longer, but the party won't be a party for me if you aren't there, my darling Martin.*

Martin had read that note a dozen times today before he had torn it into pieces. It thrilled him inexpressibly to know that she wanted him like that, and it was the first note of the kind which he had ever received. It seemed to him so dear and womanly . . . a real love-letter expressing her feelings for him. She was not afraid to show them and he liked that. He wanted to sit down and write to her, too— he who hardly ever put pen to paper these days. Yet as a boy he had loved poetry. The man was a poet in his soul. He could have written pages to *her.* The artist was there under the shell which for years had encased the Martin of deep emotions, the lover of beauty.

Ever since the first hour he had held the woman whom he believed to be Fiona Challis in his arms, he had been a changed being. It was as though the ice around his heart had thawed and his love and longing raced now like a mighty torrent which he held in check only because she wished it so. He loved her crazily. He wanted to go straight to Mr. Standing and admit to his love for her proudly and candidly. Mr. Standing might think it a crazy presumption on his part, and, since he stood in Mr. Challis's place, might even try to prevent her from seeing him again. But Martin did not care. There was a pride in his soul not to be defeated by the small barriers of social position. And if 'Fiona' loved him enough, then he would go on loving her and striving to marry her and nothing should prevent him.

He was sure of himself. He was almost as sure of her. But that was one thing he wanted to test a little further. He wanted to make quite sure that this lovely girl who had bewitched him so completely was not just temporarily infatuated with him and would not regret it. He felt that there were so many attractive, wealthy, clever men in the world from whom 'Fiona Challis' could choose. He was still lost in wonder and bewilderment that she had chosen him, the plain unvarnished factor of these farms. But if that was her choice and he could be convinced that she meant it, he asked for nothing more of life than to remain at her side for ever.

He smiled a little wryly as he went on fiddling with the tie.

'Only for you, my adorable Fiona, would I bother with this party tonight,' he murmured.

Jess, the spaniel, sat on her haunches looking up at him with puzzled golden eyes. He prodded her gently with the toe of the patent leather shoe which he found most uncomfortable after his big boots or his house slippers.

'You might well look astonished, old girl,' he said. 'I'm stepping out of character tonight. I'm going to dance, Jess. What do you think of that? I'm going to tread on the dainty slippers of some unfortunate girl. But if I can hold *her* in my arms even for a few moments, it'll be worth it.'

Jess's tail thumped on the floor as though in agreement. She lay down with her muzzle between her paws, keeping her eyes on the beloved master, who, in the black trousers and white shirt, was an unfamiliar figure to her.

Somebody knocked on the door.

'What is it?' asked Martin.

'It's Susan, Sir. Gran has sent me up with this . . .'

The door opened and Susan's black curly head appeared, and then a hand proffered a white silk handkerchief.

173

Martin smiled and took the handkerchief.

'Thanks, Sue. My! I'm going to be a howling swell tonight.'

Susan opened the door a little wider. She had never before seen Mr. Farlong in a dinner jacket and she thought he looked 'beautiful.' She sighed audibly.

'Eeh, but I'd like to be going up to the dance with you, Mr. Farlong.'

'Poor Susan. I wish you could come,' he said kindly. 'I know you'd enjoy it more than I shall.'

She pouted.

'Reckon Miss Challis will look beautiful tonight.'

'I daresay,' said Martin carelessly; but his heart slipped a beat at the mere thought of how his love might look.

'Anything I can do for you?' persisted Susan, who was enjoying the novelty of hanging around her beloved Mr. Farlong's bedroom. And a very untidy room it was, too, with his clothes lying all over the bed and the floor, and drawers half-open, ransacked. Martin dressing for a party had no sense of method or tidiness. That was obvious.

Martin approached the girl.

'Here's something you can do, Susan. Tie this darned thing for me.'

The girl was thrilled and anxious to do so. With deft little fingers she tied a neat bow which seemed to him a miracle after all his

174

struggles.'

'Ah!' he exclaimed. 'That's better.'

The girl eyed him covertly through her lashes. She felt a passionate wish to draw nearer him—tempt him if she could—into giving her just one kiss. But Martin seemed to have no interest in her. He was putting on his coat now, brushing his sleeve, tucking the handkerchief in his pocket, searching for his one and only white scarf and the grey tweed coat which hung behind the door.

'Now I'm ready,' he said, 'and I'm late, too. Turn Jess out for me before you go to bed, Sue. Good night.'

'Good night,' she said forlornly, and thought with passionate envy of 'Miss Challis' up at the Manor House waiting to receive Mr. Farlong. She went down to the kitchen and told Gran that she wagered there wouldn't be a gentleman at the dance to touch their Mr. Farlong for looks.

Martin drove up to the Manor House thankful it was a dry night, although cold, and with a bright moon to silver the wild countryside which he loved so well. He concentrated on the thought of 'Fiona.' He hoped he would not give himself away by a look or a gesture which might tell the world what he felt about her. He was sure to know everybody at the party. After living so long in the district there were no residents whom he did not know. It had never worried him that he

175

was not a regular visitor at the houses of the wealthy landowners about here. Why should they ask him? He was only a farmer, after all. But he had played cricket with most of the young fellows from the big houses, and he drank with them at the King's Arms, and he had always been treated as an equal by Mr. Standing. Tonight, because 'Fiona' had accepted him as the man she loved, he felt princely—more than the equal of any man he would meet.

When at length he entered the house and gave his coat and scarf to one of the maids, he looked around him feeling slightly out of his depth, but with a burning anxiety to find 'Fiona' or speak to her. He was sure that he would be clumsy at dancing, and that he would have little to say to the ladies. He was not really a man for a party. He alternated between the inclination to turn and fly back to his solitary farmhouse and the desire to walk up to all these people and tell them he was going to marry 'Fiona Challis.'

At length he stood at the door of the big reception-room, finding it a distinct contrast to the quiet night outside. It was a glitter of lights, a kaleidoscope of colours from the women's dresses, a symphony of dance music, gay chatter, laughter and the slipping of feet over a polished floor.

The big electric chandeliers glittered with lights. The beautiful reception-room was decorated with multi-coloured plants from the Standing hot-houses. Mr. Standing had made up his mind to make this a 'pre-war' affair, as far as it was possible, and to give all the young things in the district a real treat in the midst of the rigours and sacrifices of the war.

At first Martin stood unnoticed, hiding his nervousness by lighting and smoking a cigarette while he searched the room for familiar faces. Ah! There was young Renwick in his Air Force uniform . . . Mrs. Renwick and her husband dancing together . . . old General Whiteley from Windermere sitting next to Miss Youngton who owned big property up here. Representatives of well-known families from Ulverston and Grange . . . two pretty girls from Longlands, which was one of the loveliest houses in Cartmel. Fortunately for Mr. Standing's birthday party, there were quite a number of young men up on leave . . . all of them in uniform. Martin was the youngest man there in a dinner jacket, which he was quick to note and dislike. Once again it gave him an inferiority complex which he resented.

Then Martin saw *her*. Christine was dancing with Mr. Standing. It was a waltz and Robert Standing prided himself on being an exponent of the art. With a fast-beating heart Martin followed his 'Fiona' with his gaze. Susan had said that 'Miss Challis' would be beautiful tonight and how right she was! More beautiful than any other woman in the world, Martin

177

thought, with ardent appreciation. It was the first time he had seen her in full evening dress. She wore a Victorian gown, with a corsage of mist-blue flowers, drooping a little off sloping shoulders, and tight at the waist. Such an incredibly small waist, Martin thought . . . and he looked enraptured at the long skirt of mist-blue gauzy material floating, as she waltzed, down to the small feet in blue satin slippers which had high silver heels. Her chestnut curls were bunched high on the top of her head and into the curls at one side was pinned a diamond star. One of Fiona Challis's model frocks . . . one of Fiona's jewels. Christine Shaw, who had no right to be wearing either, looked her loveliest with a soft pink flush on her sun-browned cheeks and her eyes full of light and laughter.

Then she, too, saw Martin. Across Mr. Standing's shoulder she flung a quick deep look at the tall young man whose face looked so darkly brown against the white of his collar, and whose eyes were so vividly blue. Darling Martin! She had been afraid he might not come. For the last half hour she had been watching and waiting for him. She had been paid a dozen compliments by a dozen men. She had just danced with Gilfred, who had told her that she looked exquisite tonight. But only now that Martin was here was her soul satisfied. In her eyes he stood out above all these other men and she adored him.

The waltz came to an end. Christine disengaged herself from Mr. Standing's arm and hastened to greet Martin. Because General Whiteley was within earshot and the eyes of the world upon her, she could only offer her hand and say formally:

'How do you do, Mr. Farlong—it is so nice of you to come.'

His hard brown fingers gripped hers so tightly that she winced, but she went on smiling. She knew from the way that he looked down at her how he, too, was feeling and all the things he wanted to say but dared not. She knew, too, that she had made no mistake the other day when she told him she loved him. She wanted to tell him so again. She would before this evening ended. She took a little oath to herself.

Mr. Standing came up.

'Evening, Martin, my boy. Glad you were able to come.'

'Many happy returns of the day, sir,' said Martin stiffly.

Robert Standing gave a hearty laugh.

'I've no right to be celebrating my birthday—an old josser like myself—but it was just an excuse to give the young things a party.'

Martin's eyes turned again to Christine—a burning look. He longed to say:

'You are a goddess and I worship you. I want to kneel at your feet and pour out my heart to you.'

But he was tongue-tied, and as he stood there Gilfred Renwick came up and caught Christine by the arm.

'Come on, Beautiful, it's a rhumba. Let's show them how London does it.'

Nothing could have annoyed Christine more, but with Mr. Standing so near, she dared not show her annoyance nor her wish to stay with Martin. She moved away with Gilfred and Mr. Standing, who loved to 'talk shop' at any time, began to discuss sheep with his factor. Martin answered his employer mechanically but his gaze was wandering round the room, following that fairy figure in gossamer blue . . . watching the little swift-moving feet . . . envying the slick fashion in which Gilfred was able to dance with 'Fiona.' The two looked well together. Martin was conscious of absurd jealousy. He wondered if all his aspirations toward marriage with a girl like this were not ridiculous and doomed to failure. 'Miss Challis' came from London. She liked this sort of atmosphere. She would never be content to settle down on a farm in Lancashire with a dull fellow like himself.

If he had only known it, Christine was disliking every instant of that dance with young Renwick—wishing with all her heart that she could take Martin's hand and lead him out of this room and away to some quiet spot where they could be alone. She did enjoy dancing but she was not pleasure-mad like the real Fiona.

Her love of the country and of simple things far exceeded any desires which she might have for 'a good time' as understood by the average girl.

It seemed to her ages before she could, without provoking comment, attach herself to Martin Farlong again and give him the opportunity to ask her for a dance. Before then she had seen him dancing with one or two women—a little clumsily it was true—but, oh, how she loved him! And it gave her a distinct thrill to hear old Miss Youngton say to the General:

'That young factor of Mr. Standing's is a very good-looking boy. So intelligent-looking, too.'

'Of course, he is intelligent,' Christine laughed softly to herself. 'Hasn't he shown it by falling in love with little me!'

And then the moment came which she had longed for and planned all through the evening. At last she and Martin were dancing together. He held her very tightly. She could feel his heart pounding against her breast.

'Are you enjoying the party?' she murmured.

He looked down into her eyes.

'No. I want to run away with you. I hate all these people. Oh, Fiona, my dear, I wonder if you know how heavenly you look tonight.'

'Do you like my dress?'

'It's ravishing.'

'Shall I tell you something, Martin?'

181

'What?' His lips touched her ear for the fraction of a second.

'I'd rather be in my old breeches and pullover, walking over the fields with you.'

He pressed her hand convulsively.

'I hope that's true. I'd like to think it.'

'It is. Parties don't mean anything to me. I just want to be with you down at Stonehead.'

'I want to think that's true,' he repeated.

'You can. I swear it.'

'Can I see you alone at all tonight?'

She looked quickly around the room.

'Yes. In a minute, guide me toward the door and then walk with me to the dining-room. I'll pretend that I want to see about supper.'

'What have you been doing since I last saw you?'

'Just looking forward to seeing you again.'

His blue eyes half-closed.

'You say such wonderful things to me—I can hardly believe them.'

'But they are true, Martin, true.'

'Well, I don't know what you've done to me but nothing's the same now without you. The hours drag. I can't concentrate on my work. You've gone completely to my head, Fiona.'

She was silent a moment. How that name jarred on her, as usual. She got out of step and he trod on her toe and apologised profusely, but she did not care.

'Let's get out of this,' she whispered.

Then they were in the quiet hall. The door

of the reception-room closed behind them. Christine, with all her emotions keyed up, knew that she must be alone with Martin for a few seconds or find the rest of the evening unbearable.

This, then, was love, she thought . . . this aching for close contact with the person one loved . . . this desire to creep away from the rest of the world . . . this utter concentration upon one person in the world and one only. Oh, she could feel for Fiona now! She could understand why Fiona was ready to do any crazy thing in order to get her Peter. She could even be glad that she had helped her gain her heart's desire. But Fiona must be counted out of it now. Love made an egotist of one. She, Christine, would think only of herself now and of Martin.

There was a little lobby between the hall and the big oaken doors of the Manor House.

'Follow me,' said Christine breathlessly. And the next moment Martin found himself alone with her in the darkness, hidden from the rest of the world. Two slim arms wound around his neck. The softness of her was in his arms in intoxicating sweetness. The perfume of her hair brushed his chin. A little voice said:

'Oh, Martin, *Martin!*'

He lost his head completely then and gathered her up in a fierce embrace, heedless that he crushed her flowers, bruising her lips with the violence of his kiss. She yielded completely to that wild embrace and for Martin it set the seal upon all the emotions that had been tearing him to pieces these last few days. In the delirium of that kiss, he knew that nothing could keep him from her now and that he must have her for his own one day, or life would mean nothing . . . nothing at all.

When at last he raised his head he gave a little smothered groan.

'Fiona, my darling . . . my angel . . .'

'Oh, darling, I'm not an angel at all but I love you,' she whispered back.

'Forgive me for loving you so much,' he stammered.

'I want you to. I love you the same way.'

'I can't go on like this. I must tell Mr. Standing. We both must tell him.'

'Not yet, Martin.'

He put his hands under her elbows and held her a little apart from him, searching her face.

'Aren't you certain yet that you really love me? Surely you wouldn't have kissed me like that just now if you were not.'

She felt miserable and afraid.

'Oh, Martin, I am sure. But I still want . . . a few days more.'

'I don't understand you.'

'Oh, Martin, don't try to. Just have faith in me, please.'

'I'll do anything you ask. I'd die for you.'

She flung herself back into his arms.

'And I for you. Dearest, beloved Martin,

don't misunderstand me . . . I just want a few days more. I'm going to London tomorrow. When I come back . . . everything will be different. We'll tell Uncle Bob and everyone else how much we love each other.'

He was bewildered by her. He felt intuitively that she was hiding something from him and that within herself she was not altogether happy. Yet when she had abandoned herself just now to that long close embrace, he could have sworn that she was utterly his.

Christine saw the puzzled look in his eyes and hated herself because she knew she must continue to practise deception upon him. She had only one wish now—to get down to Fiona and tell her that this farce must come to an end.

'Why must you go to London?' he asked.

She resorted to the lie she had told Mr. Standing.

'I have had an urgent letter from a friend who needs my help.'

'Darling, there are raids on. I hate you taking risks . . . In fact, I don't want you to go away from me, and . . .'

'I know,' she broke in. 'And I don't want to leave you but I must tomorrow, just for a few days. Will you drive me to Grange tomorrow morning, so that we can have a little time together before I catch my train?'

'I'll do anything you ask.'

She drew back from his embrace and searched in her bag for a powder puff and a comb.

'Oh, darling,' she said with a little shaky laugh. 'I expect you've made an awful mess of my face. Listen, I'm going to fly upstairs. You go on back to the others, will you? But ask me to dance again before the party ends, won't you?'

He took both her hands and covered them with kisses.

'If you'll put up with my clumsiness. I adore you, Fiona. Come back from the south as quickly as you can, my dearest, and I shall pray that when you make your final decision about me, it will be the right one for us both.'

She remembered those words all through the rest of the evening and later the next day as she sat in the train speeding down to London. She remembered his burning farewell kiss, his tender passion. And she knew how completely she was in love with this man. And now for Fiona . . . and some arrangement whereby the hopeless deception must come to an end.

She did not stay in London. It seemed queer to her even to pass through it on her way to Paddington, after the weeks up at the farm . . . the peace and glory of Martin's beloved countryside. She knew now she had always hated cities and city life. She was saddened by the sight of fresh scars on the buildings she passed, great gaps where German bombs had fallen since she left. Last night, according to the morning paper, there had been a 'blitz' on a town in the West. It had made Christine a bit anxious. Peter was stationed in Bremhaven, a town on the Bristol Channel. Fiona lived in an hotel not far from the barracks. Christine worried about them both during that second journey, although she did not feel nervous for herself. In a measure she had always been a fatalist. If she was to be killed in a raid . . . she was to be killed. She did not anticipate danger. Mr. Standing had cautioned her not to spend more time than she need 'in a danger zone.'

It was dusk by the time she reached Bremhaven. She felt tired after the all-day travelling from Grange and with so much on her mind.

But thank God now she would see Fiona and clear up the whole trouble. At least, *begin* to clear it up . . . she had yet to make her confession to Martin, she reminded herself.

She found the town of Bremhaven in a sorry state. Last night's blitz had been severe. Taxis were scarce and a portion of the main station was still a smouldering ruin. But the porter who took Christine's suitcase was still smiling.

'We can take it, miss,' he said, 'and we'll give 'em worse than they give us. But we caught it good and proper in the centre of the town last night.'

Again Christine felt a twinge of uneasiness

about Peter and Fiona.

'Is the Kingsway Hotel all right?' she asked.

The porter shook his head.

'That and the Plaza Cinema both got direct hits, miss.'

Christine changed colour.

'Oh, heavens!' she said under her breath.

'Anyone you know there?' he asked with a sympathetic glance at her ashen cheeks.

Her heart was pounding.

'Get me that taxi and take me to . . . what is left of the Kingsway,' she said.

Ten minutes later Christine stood on the pavement staring with horrified eyes at the shell of the Kingsway Private Hotel where Fiona had lived since she returned from her brief honeymoon, and to which address Christine had been regularly writing.

It had not been a big building, and as Christine was informed by an A.F.S, man who was there with his colleagues, still playing hoses on the smouldering ruins—it had received a direct hit from a high-explosive bomb. Twenty-three people had been killed and many more injured.

Christine—sick with anxiety—looked at the twisted girders, the heap of rubble and masonry, the blackened window frames . . . the tragic skeleton of an electric lift. On either side were buildings with pitted walls and smashed windows.

She thought of Fiona . . . so young, so

188

lovely, so full of *joie-de-vivre*, and love for her Peter. Where was Fiona now? Was she alive or dead? Had Peter been with her last night? Had those two who had married in secret, madly in love, perished together in that dreadful raid?

Half stunned with horror, Christine turned back to the taxi.

'I must find out what has happened to my friend, Mrs. Hollis, who, so far as I know, was in this hotel last night,' she told the taxi-driver tersely.

The man opened the door for her in silent pity. He had seen many cases of heartbreak and human despair after last night . . . natural emotions even while courage and patriotism ran high. He suggested a tour of the local hospitals, and Christine agreed. She was shivering with nerves and worry as she got back into that taxi. Dry-eyed she looked at the wrecked streets and re-echoed what the station porter had said:

'We'll give them worse than they give us . . .'

But she was mortally afraid for Fiona. What . . . what would she do if she found Fiona in some hospital, dying . . . or, worse still, in some mortuary . . . already dead?

Christine tried to drag her thoughts from this 'blitzed,' suffering town to the memory of Stonehead. What heaven it seemed . . . the picture she could so vividly conjure up of the green pastures . . . the rolling hills . . . the silver, tranquil lakes. The brown ploughed earth and the grazing cattle. Up there it was as God had meant it to be in this world, she thought. This havoc of war was terrible and cruel, and Fiona . . . dear little Fiona *must* be still alive. She *could not* be dead.

'Oh, Martin!' thought Christine . . . 'if only you were here with me now!'

She would have given much for the strength of his arms and the comfort of his lips. She concentrated on the memory of him with passionate intensity. But even as she drove through the bombed streets, she thought:

'I understand why he would rather fight than be a farmer. He is every inch a man . . . he wants to hit back . . . because of *this* sort of thing. I would like to hit back, too!'

The first two hospitals she visited brought no news of Fiona. There were casualties in the wards, but Mrs. Hollis was not amongst them.

Those less seriously injured had been taken by ambulance straight out of the town and into outlying rural districts, Christine was told; when finally she had exhausted the local hospitals, and ended up at an A.R.P. centre to ask advice. Mrs. Hollis might be at any of these, but they could not tell her which.

In despair, Christine ended the search for that evening. She must get to an hotel before dark. The town might even be 'blitzed' again tonight, she was told. Well, she had no particular fears for herself, but she was distracted with worry about Fiona. And she had given Mr. Standing the Kingsway Hotel address. She had been forced to. He had asked where he could get her if necessary and she had not been able to refuse. If he heard, by any chance, that the Kingsway had been bombed, he might come down to Bremhaven in person. Not that that was likely. But the possibility all added to Christine's mental stress.

She took a room in an hotel as far out of the town as she could get, and then set to work to find out where Captain Hollis was, through his barracks.

When eventually she succeeded in getting into touch with military headquarters it was only to be told that Peter and his regiment were no longer in Bremhaven. They had gone abroad two days ago. That, at least, meant that Peter was alive. But the mystery of Fiona's whereabouts remained unsolved. Alone in her hotel bedroom, thoroughly exhausted and dispirited, Christine faced the oncoming night . . . and a possible return of the raiders to the 'blitzed' town.

Just before midnight the sirens sounded and she heard the dread familiar zoom . . . zoom . . . zoom . . . of enemy bombers and the sharp bark of anti-aircraft guns.

Within ten minutes of that warning, the hotel wherein Christine had taken refuge out of the town, was shaken to its foundations, and it seemed to the horrified girl that the very floor on which she stood, opened and that she fell, screaming, into darkness and oblivion.

CHAPTER EIGHTEEN

Martin Farlong stood by the shepherd's hut near Stonehead Cross, watching old Matthew drive the sheep up the rugged crags overlooking the broad acres of the Standing farms.

It was a fine morning, brisk and cold with a wind that sent the clouds scudding across a pale blue sky. But there had been a frost last night. The first of the year. Summer was over. Martin knew his country. This was the beginning of autumn in earnest and quickly enough it would drift into the wild white winter: the short bitter days and the long dark nights.

Martin, pipe in his mouth, his faithful spaniel at his heels, watched the grey, moving mass of sheep climbing the hillside. Two well-trained collies raced from left to right, in pursuit of the silly animals that went astray. The sharp barking of the dogs and the incessant bleating of the sheep were the only sounds to pierce the stillness of the October morning. Occasionally there came the long harsh warning note from a pheasant, disturbed back there in the thick spinney.

This was a scene that Martin had witnessed often during his life as Robert Standing's factor. A scene he loved. As a rule it never failed to give him a thrill of pride and pleasure. He was reputed to raise the finest sheep in the district.

But today his thoughts were not really on his work. His senses were unresponsive even to the beauty of the keen breezy morning; the glorious red and gold of the beech-trees, and the rich brown acres of ploughed land in which the winter wheat was already fertilising.

Martin's mind was not on his job. Martin's spirit was not in his beloved countryside. He was thinking of 'Fiona'. Of the last long kiss they had exchanged and the fierce exhilaration of loving her, the first woman in his life . . . the pride of being loved by her. He had never known hours to drag as slowly as they had done since she left Stonehead. He craved for her return, for her decision to marry him. He had tried, mentally, to follow her in her journey South and to picture her with her friends. Somehow he had failed. She seemed lost to him now that she was no longer with or near him, and he found that intolerable. He was almost afraid of this new burning passion which rent him. He was a slave to it . . . he who had thought himself the most independent and impregnable of men. He was obsessed by the thought of 'Fiona' and the almost crazy longing to see her again.

When would she come back? Would she wire, as she had promised, so that he could meet her train? Would she decide to link her life with his . . . or would she find, once she got away, that she did not love him enough?

A sound of car-wheels on the rough road running past Stonehead Cross, disturbed Martin's thoughts and made him turn around. He was surprised to see his employer's big car. Taking his pipe from his mouth, he slipped it into his pocket and walked to meet Mr. Standing.

Robert Standing pulled up. Martin thought he looked pale and worried.

'Good-morning, Mr. Standing . . .' began Martin. But the older man interrupted unceremoniously:

'Look here, Martin . . . bad news, my boy . . . they told me you were out here so I came up to look for you.'

'Bad news?' repeated Martin. 'I'm sorry to hear that.'

'It's about Fiona . . . Miss Challis,' said Mr. Standing. 'My God . . . I don't know what her father will say. I ought never to have let her go down to the danger-areas alone.'

Martin changed colour. That name 'Fiona Challis' sent an electric shock through him.

'What has happened, Mr. Standing?' he asked tensely.

'Have you heard this morning's news?'

'I listened to a bit of the seven o'clock.'

'Then you must have heard they raided a town in the West of England again . . . the same place they attacked the night before.'

'Yes, but . . .'

'I have found out that is where Miss Challis has gone,' continued Mr. Standing. 'I didn't realise it myself until this morning I looked at the address she gave me. She went to Bremhaven. Her friends, Mr. and Mrs. Peter Hollis are there at a place called the Kingsway Hotel.'

'But, Mr. Standing,' exclaimed Martin, his heart thumping. 'She need not necessarily have got the worst of it.'

'My boy, she may well be lying dead or seriously injured at this very moment,' said Robert Standing gloomily. 'I have a certain amount of influence, as you know. I managed to get a priority call . . . and I got on to Sir James Turnbell who has one of the biggest dairy-farms in the West Country . . . not twenty miles from Bremhaven. He tells me there was considerable damage done in Bremhaven on both nights and that amongst the buildings which received direct hits from high-explosive bombs, was the Kingsway Hotel.'

'Good God!' said Martin. And he stood there, staring at his employer, the healthy brown of his cheeks ashen, his eyes full of horror. Then Mr. Standing added:

'Of course, I am not sure Fiona was *staying* there. That was merely the address of her friend, Mrs. Hollis. Fiona may be elsewhere. But it is the only address I know, and I feel I should go down to Bremhaven at once. At *once*. But I'm in a quandary, Martin. Dr. Riley has forbidden me to go south while these raids are on. You know my heart is rocky and . . .'

He stopped, shaking his head, his brows knitted with worry.

Martin, his pulses still racing madly, stared at the older man. Yes, he knew Robert Standing had a 'heart' and ought not to expose himself to the possible shock of an air-raid. But the thought of Fiona alone in a 'blitzed' city . . . Fiona dead or dying . . . completely unnerved Martin. He forgot the necessity for tact or discretion. He said:

'Let me go, Mr. Standing. I can go straight down to Bremhaven on the next train. I'll find Miss Challis for you, and bring her home.'

Robert Standing's brow cleared.

'That's the very idea, Martin. I never thought of sending you. But, of course, my boy. You're the person. I can rely on you. Go straight down and bring her back. No matter what she says . . . tell her that she must come back to Wyckam Manor at once and stay here, till her father returns. It's too big a responsibility for me.'

Already Martin was in the car beside his employer. He felt excitement and fear. He was afraid of what he might find when he got to Bremhaven. Yet he was wild with delight at the thought of seeing that lovely face again . . . of bringing 'Fiona' back here, himself.

Mr. Standing turned the car and drove back to the Manor.

'I'll give you money and you can just tell me if there is anything important for me to see to here while you are away.'

The two men talked of the farm as they drove back to the Manor House. Neither referred to the raid on Bremhaven. Both harboured their secret fears, scarcely daring to express them.

Agnes met them, whimpering, holding out the piece of paper.

'A telegram has just been telephoned through, sir,' she said in an agitated voice. 'About Miss Fiona, sir . . . and she's been bombed.'

Martin's heart sank like a stone. He was white to the lips as he looked over Robert Standing's shoulder at that message.

'From the Matron at the Lady Margaret Hospital, Tollbath, near Bremhaven. Miss Fiona Challis was injured in last night's raid and is in the Lady Margaret Hospital. She wishes Mr. Standing to know she is all right except for minor injuries and he is not to worry.'

Mr. Standing dropped into a chair, took out a handkerchief and wiped his forehead.

'Not to worry, indeed! Good heavens, I don't know what I'm going to say to Challis!' he groaned.

Martin swallowed hard. He scarcely knew what to say or think, or how to conceal his feelings about Fiona. The words *'minor injuries'* in that message relieved his greatest anxiety. At the same time it was shattering to him to think that she had been exposed at all to the terrors of a bad air-raid and that she was in the hospital.

'With your permission, Mr. Standing, I'll still go down to Bremhaven,' he said. 'I'd like to go to the hospital and make sure Miss Challis is all right, and bring her back if I can.'

'Quite, quite. I'd feel less worried if you'd go at once, Martin.'

'I can catch the twelve o'clock train if I hurry.'

Mr. Standing went to his desk, unlocked a drawer, and drew out a ten-pound note which he handed to his factor.

'Take this for the time being. Telephone me as soon as you've seen her, and try to find her friends, the Hollises, and let me know everything.'

'And God grant you'll find the poor child is all right. What a terrible thing, Martin . . . this bombing of women and children!'

For a moment Martin pictured the slender, lovely figure of the girl whom he had so recently held in his arms . . . the sweet, passionate young face . . . all the exquisite tenderness and allure of her. And at the mere thought of her lying injured in a hospital bed,

198

the man in him revolted. Rage against the common enemy gripped his very vitals.

'By God,' he said under his breath, 'I want a crack at those—Germans myself, Mr. Standing. You'll have to let me go, sir. I can't stand it much longer.'

The older man gave him a sympathetic look.

'I understand, Martin. I'd feel the same at your age, my boy. We'll talk it over. But, cut along now. I want you to get down to Bremhaven and look after Miss Challis, and the sooner the better.'

Martin nodded, turned, and walked quickly out of the room.

CHAPTER NINETEEN

Christine had just been washed and made ready for the night, and was waiting for her supper tray when Martin arrived at the Lady Margaret Hospital, on the outskirts of the twice-raided town of Bremhaven. Christine lay quiet, helpless, a bandage over her eyes. They ached incessantly. She could do nothing but think and think. And it must be confessed that her thoughts were slightly depressed and confused.

It seemed a century to her since she had left the North and come down to the West Country to see Fiona. Yet it was only a mere twenty-four hours. But in that one day and night so much had happened. Her failure to find her friend. Her own shattering experiences in her hotel last night. It seemed to Christine that an evil star must have followed her. She shuddered at the mere memory. It was all like a nightmare. The wail of the warning sirens . . . the guns . . . the bombs . . . then the awful explosion when the hotel had been struck. An instant of horror . . . of falling plaster and masonry . . . of brief, sharp pain before she lost consciousness.

When she recovered, she had found herself with bandaged eyes in an ambulance travelling to this hospital and she had been told that she was lucky to have escaped with her life. Several other people in the hotel had lost theirs.

For a few hours she had suffered the agonising dread of permanent injury to her eyes. Fear of blindness . . . a fear second to none. But the opthalmic specialist at the Lady Margaret had assured her that her eyes were not seriously hurt. In a few days the bandages could be removed. The injuries were small.

For the rest of it, Christine was bruised in every limb, but whole . . . and, indeed, thankful to God for her escape.

She had been forced to send that telephone message to Mr. Standing. But what would be the outcome of this disaster, she dared not think. Fiona was still missing. Mr. Standing

200

was bound to discover the truth now . . .

And what about Martin?

With all her heart and soul, Christine longed for Martin. In this shocked state, and with her temporary blindness, she was 'down and out.' She needed him desperately. His love. His strength. *Him.* And because she was Christine Shaw and not the real Fiona, she dared not send for him.

A nurse came to her bedside and gently touched her wrist.

'Miss Challis . . . a gentleman to see you. He is being allowed in, although it is long past visiting hours. But matron makes concessions for those who have been bombed.'

Christine's heart slipped a beat. She sat upright.

'Who is it, please, nurse?'

'A Mr. Farlong, my dear, from the North.'

A burning wave of colour darted across Christine's face. And now her heart pounded in earnest. *Martin.* Martin, himself, had come. She felt a wild thrill of joy, followed by an equal anxiety. Now she must lie again . . . she *must* until she could find Fiona. The secret was not hers alone. It was Fiona's, and she, Christine, must not give it away without Fiona's permission. But under these new circumstances, the whole thing was going to be terribly difficult.

The next moment she felt warm strong fingers gripping hers. She heard a well-remembered, beloved voice:

'Fiona . . . my poor little darling . . . my poor sweet child!'

She gave a smothered sob.

'Oh, Martin . . . darling, darling Martin . . .'

And then she was in his arms and her bandaged face was pressed tenderly against his shoulder. Unseen by her, a kindly nurse had placed screens around her bed. Christine clung to Martin desperately. And he held her, every fibre of his being aching with pity . . . with hatred against the Nazi evil that had done this thing to her. Only yesterday he had seen her off from Grange . . . brown, starry-eyed, full of radiant health. He was shocked by the sight of this pitiful little figure . . . the tender cheeks cut and bruised . . . the eyes bandaged . . . the slim figure trembling with nerves.

'Oh, my darling, my little love,' he murmured, 'never mind. I'm here. Here to look after you and take you home again. Thank God you're alive my sweet. Thank God.'

'It was awful,' she said in a smothered voice. 'But it's over now. Everything's all right, now you're with me.'

'You do still love me, then?'

'I adore you,' she said, almost in despair.

Martin, however, knew no despair. His heart was singing again. The nurse had assured him that those beautiful eyes were not seriously injured and that 'Fiona' could leave

202

the hospital in a few days. And she loved him . . . her clinging arms and lips told him that. As well as her words. He thanked God again and again that her life had been spared.

He said:

'Mr. Standing is in an awful way, my darling. I'll phone him tonight and tell him I'm going to take you back as soon as they'll let you travel.'

'Yes, get me out of here,' said Christine feverishly. 'I want to go back to the farm. I'm quite all right . . . a corner of a falling beam caught my eyes, but I shall be able to use them again quite soon. Oh, I *want* to go back to the farm, Martin.'

'You shall, my darling,' he soothed her, stroking the brown tumbled curls. 'You shall.'

She lay still against his heart, trying not to remember the shadow that lay between them. But when her thoughts returned to the real Fiona, she felt desperate. Then Martin mentioned the fatal name.

'What has happened to your friend, Mrs. Hollis?'

'I don't know. I think she was hit at the Kingsway in the first blitz . . . the night before last. I . . . haven't seen her.'

'I'll find her for you,' said Martin cheerily. 'I can spend tomorrow making enquiries. You must be very worried about her. And her husband.'

Christine drew away from him.

'Peter has gone abroad. I did find that out.'

'Then we must certainly find your poor little friend and do what we can for her.'

'Y-yes,' whispered Christine miserably.

Martin stayed with her for a while, caressing her, trying to give her what happiness and comfort he could. He loved her more than ever. This tender little creature who had been hurt in an air-raid was doubly precious and beloved to him. He had not known it possible that he, Martin Farlong, could feel such acute love and tenderness for any human being.

By reiterating his intentions of finding Mrs. Hollis for her, he thought he was cheering her up. He little knew the despair he caused her. For Christine knew that if Martin found the real Fiona . . . the game would be up. The harm done. And that harm might be irrevocable.

After Martin had left her, she ate a poor supper and had a restless night. In the early hours of the morning, the night-sister, thinking that her eyes were troubling Christine, gave her a drug which helped her to sleep.

In the morning she still felt ill—worse than she had felt at first after the raid. She had been rather numbed then. Now reaction was setting in, and her whole body ached. Her nerves were jumping. When the doctor examined her, he advised her to keep as quiet as possible and not to be in too much of a hurry to leave the hospital. She would not be fit to travel just yet, he told her, and she need not be afraid of raids out here. The Lady Margaret Hospital lay in a secluded valley in which the village of Tollbath nestled, fringed with woodlands. They might get German planes flying overhead, but it was most unlikely bombs would be dropped on Tollbath.

'You must try not to be nervous,' the doctor said.

Christine did not answer him. She could not tell him that her nervous condition had nothing to do with bombs or fear of raids. It was her own private affairs that were worrying her.

Martin, apparently, was doing Mr. Standing's job for him thoroughly. He had given orders for Christine to be moved into a private room. A huge bunch of flowers came— and a basket of grapes.

The nurse read to her the card that came with the flowers:

'You cannot see them, but you can smell them, and they will remind you of the country. Keep smiling, darling. I love you. Martin.'

'There!' said the nurse. 'How romantic. Is he your fiancé?'

'Yes . . . at least, no . . . not officially,' stammered Christine.

The nurse smiled and gave Christine one of the roses which she put against her lips. She inhaled the fragrance of it and it thrilled and soothed her . . . just as though she felt the touch of her lover's lips. She thought:

'Oh, my darling, I love you so . . . what will be the end of it all?'

Later in the morning Martin came.

Christine was still a pathetic little figure, sitting up in her narrow, white, hospital bed, with her eyes hidden in bandages. But he assured her she looked more 'herself' in her private room surrounded by flowers.

She sighed, leaned luxuriously in his arms.

'Darling Martin . . . it's marvellous to have you here. How will the farms get on without you and your land-girl?'

'Go to the dogs, I daresay,' he laughed, 'particularly without my hard-working little land-girl. But I spoke to Mr. Standing on the phone and he said I was to stay here and take you home, myself.'

'I must hurry up and get well,' sighed Christine.

Then Martin—without realising that he was so doing—gave her a considerable shock.

'By the way, darlingest, I went into Bremhaven early this morning and made enquiries about Mrs. Hollis. At last I've traced her for you.'

Christine stiffened in his embrace.

'You've traced her . . . ?'

'Yes. She was injured, as you thought, in the Kingsway and brought to this hospital. Without your knowing it, darling, your girl friend is here under this very roof. Only you were put into the Ophthalmic wing because of your eyes, and Mrs. Hollis had injuries to one leg and is in another wing. I thought I'd go and look her up for you when I leave you.'

Silence. Christine felt drained of her strength, her resources. Her brain was in a whirl. Fiona here . . . in the Lady Margaret Hospital. Good heavens, what a coincidence! Yet not really . . . it was one of the receiving hospitals for casualties from raids in Bremhaven. Fiona must have been brought here on that night of the first 'blitz' and here she had been ever since.

While Christine was foundering mentally for a suitable reply to make to Martin, he added:

'I'll do whatever I can for her, darling. You'd like me to take her some flowers, wouldn't you?'

'Y-yes,' stammered Christine.

'Would you like to dictate a message and I'll write it?'

Christine pulled away from his arms. She felt sick and faint. Her nerves were really not in a condition to cope with a crisis of this kind. And to go on lying to this man who loved and believed in her, was sheer agony to her.

Martin bent over her.

'Darling . . . are you ill? You've turned so white.'

'No, I'm quite all right . . .' she whispered.

He looked out of the window. It was a dull,

close day. The gloom of Autumn lay over the village of Tollbath. He himself had been feeling suffocated all the morning, longing for the fresh keen air of his native country. He said:

'You'd like that window opened wider, wouldn't you?'

Christine put her hands up to her bandaged eyes. Oh, if only she could see, she thought desperately . . . if only she were capable of doing something about Fiona without having to have the medium of Martin or anyone else. At length she said:

'Listen, Martin. I . . . don't want you to see Mrs . . . Mrs. Hollis for me. She . . . she's desperately shy. I . . . I'll get nurse to find out if I could be wheeled along in a chair to her ward. That's that idea.'

He was puzzled. Something was worrying his 'Fiona' unduly, and he could not think what. She did not seem at all pleased that he had discovered her friend.

He said:

'Oh, very well. If you'd rather I didn't go to see Mrs. Hollis, of course I won't.'

Christine groped for his hand, seized it, laid her cheek against it, kissed it passionately.

'Darling, you're so kind . . . you've been so wonderful. I'm grateful, truly. But don't worry about Mrs. Hollis. I . . . I'll see to her myself.'

'Just as you wish, darling. And now about cabling your father. Mr. Standing said on the

208

phone last night that he was anxious you should cable, personally, to relieve Mr. Challis's mind. Would you care to dictate that?'

Christine would much rather have consulted Fiona about the cable, but she saw no way of getting out of this, without offending Martin. He would think she could not trust him with any commissions.

In despair, she dictated a cable to Mr. Challis. It was noncommittal enough, and applied as much to the real Fiona as to herself, she thought.

'Don't worry. Stop. Rapidly recovering. Stop. Returning Wyckam Manor soon. Stop. All Love Fiona.'

'I'll send that off at once,' said Martin.

Christine thanked him humbly. But she felt, after he had gone, wretchedly guilty of a long series of falsehoods to him which he might never understand or forgive, once he found out.

As soon as she was alone again, she demanded to see the doctor.

'I must be allowed to walk, or be wheeled to the ward where Mrs. Peter Hollis is lying,' she said feverishly. 'She is my dearest friend and it is essential I see her. She has no one else but me.'

At first the permission was denied. It was essential Miss Challis should lie quiet, Christine was told. But she created such a 'scene' then, that they gave way. Wrapped in dressing-gown and blanket, she was wheeled along the rubber-tiled corridor to the Hope Ward, in which Fiona was lying.

At the glass doors of the Hope Ward, the sister-in-charge met Christine and spoke to her.

'Mrs. Hollis is not really fit for visitors. You must only stay a few minutes.'

Christine's heart sank.

'Is she . . . very bad, then?'

'Her leg is not doing as well as we hoped. She is to undergo another operation on it this evening. Doctor says she must on no account be worried.'

Christine said:

'I understand, sister. I . . . won't worry her.'

A moment later her chair had been pushed up to the bed in which Peter Hollis's unfortunate young wife was lying. The only injury Fiona had sustained was to her left leg. But it was a bad one and she was feverish with pain and loss of blood. She stared at the girl with the bandaged eyes.

'Who are you? Why do you want to see me?' she asked.

Christine held out a hand.

'Fiona,' she said huskily. 'My dear, it's Christine.'

Fiona gasped and stared afresh.

'Christine . . . *Christine Shaw* . . . good heavens above, what are you doing here? I

210

thought you were safely in Stonehead. What has happened to *you*?'

Christine clung to her friend's hand.

'Darling, I came down to Bremhaven to see you. I couldn't find you, and I, myself, was blitzed . . . last night. My eyes were hurt. Not seriously. There is nothing to worry about. Just superficial bruises.'

'Oh, my God,' said Fiona. 'How mad of you! What did you want to do this for?'

'I had to see you. There are complications up North . . .' began Christine.

Fiona interrupted on a hysterical note:

'There can't be. There mustn't be. You've got to carry on a bit longer, Christine. You should never have come here.'

'But, Fiona, you promised you would take your rightful place as soon as Peter went abroad.'

'I can't be bothered with it all now. I've had a terrible time and I'm hanged if I want a lot of fuss from father and Uncle Bob. Wait until I'm fit again,' said Fiona.

'But, darling . . . your father knows that you've been blitzed. That is . . . he knows about me. Mr. Standing cabled him . . . I had to cable again today to say I'm quite all right and going back to Stonehead.'

'All the better. You can go back.'

'But why won't you tell Mr. Standing the truth now?'

'Because I don't want to go up there and be

buried alive while Peter is away, nor do I want father to be fed up with me and Peter. He'll be back in England soon, himself. I've decided to wait and meet father and tell him the truth personally. It's far better than writing and creating all that fuss and upset.'

Christine let go her friend's hand.

'It's all very well . . . but it's landing me in for difficulties you don't understand. I've fallen in love with Martin Farlong and . . .'

'Oh, what does that matter! Get engaged to him . . . do anything you want . . . only don't ask me to unburden the whole tale now. I'm ill, I tell you. I can't be bothered with it, Christine.'

For a moment Christine was tempted to tell the other girl that she was being utterly selfish now. Then she remembered that poor Fiona was undergoing another operation tonight, and must not be worried. In despair, Christine said:

'Well, we'll wait until you're out of here, then we'll discuss it again.'

Fiona gave a miserable laugh.

'Sometimes I feel I won't leave here alive. My leg is hellish. I don't think I'll ever stand another operation.'

'You mustn't talk like this,' exclaimed Christine.

'Well, if I do die . . . you'll have to tell father the truth yourself. Tell him I loved Peter and my weeks with Peter were utterly happy. My darling Peter . . .'

Fiona's voice broke. She was crying now. Christine groped for her hand and pressed it, thinking only of Fiona now, not of herself.

'Darling, don't! Cheer up. Keep smiling! Of course you'll get over this . . . and you'll see your Peter again. Oh, Fiona, my poor dear . . . what can I do for you?'

'Nothing . . . but carry on. Don't give me away . . . yet. Promise you won't Christine.'

For a moment Christine was silent. Fiona repeated feverishly.

'Christine, Christine . . . please promise you won't give me away. I want to tell father what I've done, myself. Promise you'll keep on in my place . . . till he comes back.'

CHAPTER TWENTY

Christine put both hands up to her bandaged eyes. She had never felt more helpless. She wished that she could see Fiona. She wished that she could make her understand how impossible her position was up in the North these days. At length she said:

'Fiona, I don't understand your point of view. Surely the matter has reached a point when you can tell the truth. If Mr. Challis knows you are actually married to Peter, and that you have been blitzed, he'll forgive you.

213

He'll forgive anything. Let me send a long cable to him explaining everything.'

'No, I tell you!' exclaimed Fiona. 'I know exactly what will happen. Daddy will rush straight back by air even if his job in America is not finished, and then when he finds out what I've done, he may forgive me, but not Peter. He'll say Peter has gone behind his back, and there'll be endless trouble.'

'But there'll be trouble anyhow,' said Christine weakly.

'Not if I let Daddy get his job through successfully and see him and tell him myself. I can handle him. No one else can, and I tell you it won't do to spring this on him by cable.'

Christine shrugged her shoulders helplessly.

'Fiona, darling, there is *my* side of it. I hate this deception . . . all these lies . . . I ought never to have taken your place. I admit that I regret it now, and, as I have told you, I have fallen in love with Martin Farlong . . .'

'Then stay in love with him,' interrupted Fiona. 'Carry it off somehow. Do anything you like, but don't give me away for the moment. Oh . . .!'

She started to cry now in earnest. Christine, always soft-hearted, and knowing that her friend was facing an operation, could not bear to hear that sobbing. She gave way.

'All right, all right, darling. Anything you want. I'll manage somehow; but for heaven's sake don't let it be too long, as I'm getting myself tied up in knots, and I loathe all these lies.'

A nurse came up to Fiona's bedside.

'Now, now, what's all this about?' she asked in her bright, professional voice. 'We can't have our patient being upset.'

'I'm sorry,' said Christine; 'perhaps I'd better go back to my own room.'

'I'll get someone to wheel you,' said the nurse, and departed.

Christine, her heart sinking even lower than it had been when she had first come to her friend's bedside, groped for and caught one of Fiona's hands in hers.

'Don't worry, darling. I won't give you away, I promise. But Fiona, you oughtn't to be in this ward. You ought to have a private room like mine. I must arrange it.'

'Oh, it's not too uncomfortable in here,' said Fiona; 'but you can arrange anything you like. I'm too miserable to think. It's *hell* without Peter.'

'Poor darling! You still love him so much?'

'Yes. But he's gone. I don't even know where. Out to the Middle East, I suppose. He said I might not hear from him for weeks. Thank goodness for his sake he doesn't know what has happened to me.'

'And here we are, both of us blitzed,' said Christine with a little laugh. 'What a nightmare!'

Fiona was drying her tears.

215

'Darling, I've had a long letter from Daddy which you'll find in my bag, just inside the cupboard to my bed. You can dictate an answer to it. Say you came down here to see a friend and got caught in a blitz, but that you're perfectly all right except you can't use your eyes or hands. Any tale you like to trump up, only make the letter sound cheery so it won't bring him back in a panic.'

'More lies,' said Christine gloomily.

Before Fiona could answer, a nurse came to wheel Christine back to her room. Christine found the letter which Fiona wished her to answer and then, after kissing Fiona and wishing her the best of luck, she found herself back in her own part of the hospital.

The nurse helped her into bed. Once there, Christine collapsed and putting her hands up to her face burst into tears.

'Oh, I don't want to go on with this! I don't want to go on with it!' she sobbed aloud.

She did not hear the door of her room open or see Martin come into the room with a great bunch of roses in his hands. But Martin took one look at the forlorn young figure, put the roses down, and hastened to the bedside.

'Why, my *darling*, what is it? What don't you want to go on with?' he exclaimed in deep concern.

She surrendered to the clasp of his arms and the touch of his lips against her hair. She had never wanted more ardently to unburden the whole truth to Martin. Yet she had given her word to Fiona, so she must keep it.

She did not answer Martin's question, but just sobbed out her frustration and unhappiness in his embrace.

Martin frowned over the pretty brown head which lay against his heart. He felt decidedly perplexed. It was obvious that 'Fiona' was worrying. He had guessed for some time that she had had something on her mind. Yet he could not discover what it was. He felt an immense love and tenderness for her.

'What is wrong, my own darling?' he asked. 'I can't bear to see you unhappy or ill. You mean so much to me now that anything that affects you affects me. Your troubles have got to be mine. Do have faith in me. Tell me if there is anything upsetting you.'

She shook her head dumbly, But she wished to God that she could do as he asked.

'You mean everything to me, too, Martin,' she said.

He stroked her hair.

'When you left home, you told me that you were going to think things over and give me a final decision,' he said. 'Is it to be "yes" then, Fiona?'

Despite her dislike of hearing that name from Martin, she answered recklessly:

'Yes, yes, I know that I love you better than anybody in the world.'

He bent and kissed her passionately on the

lips.

'I'll never let you regret it, darling. I'll spend the rest of my life trying to make you happy and trying to be worthy of you.'

She gave a little shiver.

'Oh, don't use the word "worthy".'

'But I've got a lot to live up to, my sweetest,' he said with a wry smile, 'for, after all, it's a bit ambitious of Martin Farlong proposing marriage to Fiona Challis.'

She made no answer. Her tears had dried. Quiet and comforted, she lay in his arms trying to shut her mind to the desire for truth. After a pause, Martin added:

'We must tell Mr. Standing as soon as I get you home.'

Again she made no answer, but bit hard at her lips. 'Home' . . . that sounded good. Yes, she longed for the wild wind-swept fens and the quiet pastureland of the farms and the smell of hay and heather and of twigs and dry leaves burning in the frosty air. She longed for *Martin's home.* And it struck terror into her heart lest he should turn from her once he knew of her impersonation of Fiona, and all hopes of sharing that home with him would be lost beyond recall.

That night when Martin had gone and the night-nurses were on duty in the dimly lit wards, Christine lay awake, unable to sleep in her quiet little room. There was too much on her mind. And her first question, when her night-nurse brought her some tea, in the early morning, was:

'Can you find out how Mrs. Hollis is—Mrs. Hollis who is in Hope Ward?'

The nurse came back shortly afterwards with the news that Mrs. Hollis had had her operation, was not yet out of the anaesthetic but that Mr. Farnley, the surgeon, hoped that it had been a complete success.

That made Christine feel a little less anxious. But there was still plenty of trouble ahead of her and she knew it. To begin with the Eye man, who examined her in the morning, was sufficiently pleased with her to allow the bandages to be removed, and to tell Martin that Miss Challis would be allowed out of the hospital tomorrow. Owing to the numbers of casualties in recent raids, her bed was wanted.

Christine could see again. Her eyes were very sore and she had to wear smoked glasses, but she was, at least, less helpless and bodily stronger and Martin was delighted.

'I had a chat with Mr. Standing on the phone last night,' he told her. 'He has instructed me to get you back to Wyckam Manor as soon as you're fit enough to be taken to the train. He says he won't feel happy about you until you're safely back in Stonehead.'

Christine considered this somewhat miserably. There was nothing she wanted more than to go back to Stonehead. But how could she leave Fiona down here, ill and alone? It seemed unthinkable.

Martin looked searchingly at the small pale face of the girl who meant so much to him these days.

'Something still worrying you, darling?'

'Just my . . . my friend . . . Mrs. Hollis . . .' Christine stammered.

'Well, when she's better won't you ask her to join you up at the farm? I'm sure Mr. Standing would welcome her if she's a friend of yours.'

Christine positively blushed for shame as she heard this invitation. If only Martin knew who 'Mrs. Hollis' was, she thought wretchedly.

That evening, she was allowed to see Fiona for a few moments. Fiona was still a bit drowsy with dope, but more cheerful than she had been yesterday.

'They tell me my leg is going to be all right this time,' she whispered.

'Good, darling, and I've got to go back to Stonehead tomorrow,' Christine whispered back. 'They're insisting on it. I can't avoid it. But who will look after you?'

'I'll manage. And when they let me out I think I'd better come up and stay with you,' said Fiona with a twisted smile.

'That's exactly what Martin Farlong suggested,' Christine said. 'But, of course, it's impossible.'

'I'm not at all sure it isn't a good plan. After all, none of them up there know who Mrs.

Peter Hollis is, and we can convalesce together.'

'Fiona, you're quite mad,' said Christine in a tone of despair. 'It would cause the most endless complications.'

Fiona eyed her friend a trifle resentfully.

'I thought you didn't want me to stay down here alone and miserable.'

Christine opened her mouth to protest, but Fiona looked so white and pinched and was such a pathetic picture lying there in the narrow hospital bed with a cradle over her wounded leg, that she had not the heart to argue with her further.

Fiona would have to stay in bed for at least another fortnight. After that, Christine hoped devoutly that Mr. Challis would have returned to England, and put an end to this crazy venture.

That next day, a cold bleak morning with a touch of winter's austerity in the air, Christine left the town of Bremhaven and the blitzed areas and returned to Stonehead with Martin.

She felt weak and unlike herself and she looked ill, having lost some of her healthy sunburn and with those dark glasses hiding her eyes. And she was not a particularly smart Christine, either; for she had lost all the clothes she had taken to her hotel on the night it was bombed. The warm coat that Martin had bought for her to travel in was too big, and her hair needed attention, and was wrapped in a scarf lent by one of the nurses.

But to Martin she was the most beautiful and desirable woman in the world. She found his care of her, his solicitude, most touching. He wrapped her up in a rug in a corner of a first-class carriage, brought a flask of brandy with him, a thermos of hot coffee and a cushion for her back. Everything that he could think of for her comfort. And as the train moved out of the station he gave a sigh of relief which he expressed also in words.

'My lord! I was never more glad to see the last of the South. You know they raided London again last night. You're well out of it, my darling, and you ought never to have been allowed to go down to Bremhaven.'

She smiled and touched his crisp dark hair with her hand.

'Darling Martin! You're so sweet to me. But I'm all right now.'

'We'll have to take good care of you. No more work on the farm.'

'But I shall miss it, and I shall soon get fit again. The doctor said I mustn't read too much or strain my eyes, but it won't take me long to recover my strength.'

'Nevertheless, you won't be allowed to do hard farm work, darling. Don't you realise that you belong to me now?'

'Oh, Martin, darling.'

'I don't know what Mr. Standing's going to say,' he added, 'and still less do I know how

I'm going to have the nerve to ask Mr. Challis to accept me as a son-in-law. But I am!'

Her heart raced. There was nothing weak or vacillating about Martin. There never had been. She realised now that it was his strength of character, his pride and self-assurance that had always attracted her. She said:

'What would you do if . . . if my father refused his consent?'

He looked at her solemnly with his vivid blue eyes.

'Then it would be up to you, I suppose, my darling. I should be sorry to cause any trouble, but I think every man and woman alive have the right to choose whom they wish to marry.'

She held up her arms to him.

'I shall always choose *you*,' she said under her breath.

Their lips met and clung in a passionate kiss as the train gathered speed and rushed across the countryside towards the North.

CHAPTER TWENTY-ONE

It was impossible for Christine to be depressed or even worried about the future when she first returned to Wyckam Manor. Her homecoming was so very pleasant. The Manor House was filled with flowers to welcome her. Mr. Standing seemed overjoyed to get her back.

'I've been in a cold sweat ever since that blitz,' he told her. 'My goodness, child, you had a narrow escape! You might have been killed.'

'Yes, I have a lot to be thankful for,' she admitted. 'Quite a number of people in my hotel were killed. The bomb got us at an angle and exploded in the vestibule. Fortunately for me I had dressed, but was sitting on my bed and had not gone down. The next thing I knew was that the floor collapsed and I was pinned by a beam and the A.F.S. men were digging me out.'

'Well, it's grand to know you're safe and almost well again,' said Robert Standing. 'I don't know how I would have faced your father. And what about this poor friend you went to see?'

Christine hung her head.

'Oh, yes . . . she was wounded, too.'

Mr. Standing looked at Martin, who was in the library with them.

'I'm glad we managed to send Martin down to bring you home,' he said.

'Martin has been very kind,' said Christine in a low voice.

Martin caught her gaze. She knew that, like herself, he was remembering the close passion of that embrace which they had exchanged in the train, and the tremendous thrill that each one had for the other. But it did not seem to

224

Martin the right time to break the news to Robert Standing. Christine was almost relieved when he made an excuse that he must get down to the farm.

'There's plenty of leeway to make up, I'm sure,' he said.

The two men walked together to the door talking about the farm. Christine, lying on the sofa, looked at the leaping log-fire in the big open grate. Darkness had fallen outside. There had been a storm of wind and rain to greet her as she drove over Cartmel Fell with Martin, but she had gloried in it. The air had smelt so fresh and keen. She adored this place.

When she was alone with Mr. Standing, she hoped that he would not ask too many questions which closely concerned her private affairs. He did not. He seemed to have no inkling that there was any kind of an 'affair' between his factor and herself. And he was mainly interested in her story of the bombing and the conditions in general down south. Then the name of Gilfred Renwick came up. Christine had hoped that Renwick's leave would be up by the time she had returned and that he would have gone back to his squadron. But fate had yet another surprise in store for Christine. Gilfred, who was the only one up here to know the truth about her, was still at Lingford. He had caught a chill, apparently, out shooting in the week-end, and had developed jaundice.

'Of course,' said Mr. Standing, 'the poor young fellow's leave has been definitely prolonged. He isn't seriously ill, but he feels mighty bad with jaundice. He sent you a message of condolence about your bad luck at Bremhaven and is extremely glad to know you're safe and well and asks that you go and see him as soon as you can. That is provided you won't mind him being a beautiful shade of yellow!'

Christine gave a faint smile.

'I shan't mind at all, Uncle Bob. I'm very sorry for him. I know jaundice can be rotten.'

'Then you two convalescents must cheer each other up,' said Mr. Standing heartily.

Christine nodded. The last thing she wished to do really was to see much of Gilfred. She was afraid of him and his knowledge. And Martin was jealous of him, too. It was all very awkward.

And now the next thing on her mind was what Martin was going to say to Mr. Standing . . . and when . . . and how she could cope with the complications that were bound to follow. For, of course, Mr. Standing would insist that she wrote at once to 'her father' and asked for his permission. And it seemed to Christine so absurd and futile since she was *not* Fiona Challis. Added to which it would only make things much more muddled and complex, when Mr. Challis arrived home, heard the truth, and found that he had been told so many unpardonable lies.

All through that night of her homecoming, glad though she was to be back at the Manor and not to hear those awful sirens or feel the dread of raids, Christine worried about her affairs. When morning came she had made up her mind definitely that Martin must not tell Uncle Bob how things were between them. She must persuade him to keep their love a secret, and so mark time until the situation became slightly more elucidated.

After breakfast she wandered slowly down to Stonehead Farm. During the night there had been a sharp frost and this morning it was clear and bright. A white, wonderful world with every little blade of grass, every twig, every bush blanched by the frost. The sun shone down bravely from the pale blue sky. A keen wind blew across the Fells. Everything sparkled. The tranquil silence was broken only by the bleating of the sheep from the hillside, the lowing of a cow, or the sound of a tractor working in the fields.

A glorious place, she thought, and little wonder that Martin loved it. Heaven, after that grim city which she had left, with its shattered streets, its weary citizens who were still standing at their posts, and would have given much, she was sure, to enjoy such peace and beauty as this.

She stopped to speak to old Tom and Luke and one or two of the land-girls whom she

227

knew, all of whom greeted her eagerly and congratulated her on her lucky escape from death.

Eventually she found Martin in one of the sheds giving his aid to a man who was mending the engine which worked the slicer through which they put the mangels for winter feed. As he saw the girl Martin's brown face lit up with pleasure. With an arm through hers he walked with her through the sunlit yard and down a quiet lane.

'How marvellous to see you, my darling. But are you fit enough to walk?'

'I'm absolutely fit again except for my eyes and a few bruises,' she said.

He stood still a moment, removed the smoked glasses and looked into the lovely hazel-gold eyes.

'Still a bit bloodshot,' he said anxiously.

She laughed and put the glasses on again.

'Nothing to worry about,' she said.

'Well, it was dear of you to come and see me.'

Her heart shook a little as she thought of the decision that she had formed during the night. She prayed desperately that he would understand. She said:

'Martin, I . . . I know you must be awfully busy this morning, but I must speak to you.'

'I can always make time for you, my Fiona.'

She winced. Before she could speak he added:

'But you're not to stand about in this wind. There's a touch of east in it. Come along to the farm, and I'll get Emmy to make you a cup of coffee.'

She walked with him to the farmhouse.

'Is Susan still there?'

'Susan!' he echoed in astonishment. 'Why?'

'I think I'm rather jealous of her.'

'What nonsense.'

'She's rather pretty, Martin.'

He pressed her arm to his side.

'I don't notice any woman in the world except you. No other woman exists for me.'

Those words gave her courage. And once they were sitting by his fire in his oak-beamed sitting-room, she came straight out with what she had to say.

'Martin, I love you. I think you know that. I love you and I want to marry you. I shall never marry anybody else. But for the moment I feel that it would be better for us to keep our engagement a secret.'

The eager light died from his face. He looked at her gravely, and with obvious disappointment.

'You mean you don't want me to tell Mr. Standing. I was going to see him tonight.'

'I'd rather you didn't,' she said, her lashes fluttering nervously. 'The fact is . . . I know there's going to be some trouble . . . I mean . . . Uncle Bob won't do anything about it until . . . until Mr. Challis comes back and it would be so much better . . . to wait until then.'

He stared at her. It struck him as being odd that she should call her father 'Mr. Challis' when speaking of him. And it was not to be wondered at that he mistook her meaning. 'Fiona' believed that both her father and Mr. Standing would oppose this marriage because of the difference in their social standings, and she was afraid of that opposition. Yes, he told himself, that was it. She loved him but she was not strong enough to stand up to difficulties and so she was putting off the evil day.

So intense was his disappointment . . . indeed, his momentary disillusionment in her, because he had thought her braver than that . . . he could scarcely speak. This new love that had come into his life was to him such a tremendous thing that he was ready to fight the world for it. He had hoped that Fiona felt the same about him.

She looked anxiously at him. She could see the old Martin now whom she had first met, in those tightening lips and that resentful jaw.

'Oh, Martin,' she said, 'don't be angry with me. Try to understand that it's best to wait until . . . my . . . my father comes back. Nothing can be done now. We couldn't even announce our engagement, so why not keep it our secret? It'll be less . . . less embarrassing for everyone at the moment.'

He drew his pipe from his pocket and knocked it against the grate.

230

'Very well, if that's how you feel.'

She swallowed hard.

'I've disappointed you.'

'Frankly yes, my dear. You see I'm a proud man. Perhaps I've been too much of an egotist . . . too self-confident over our affair. I thought you loved me as much as I loved you and that you had no qualms about it.'

'I have none, I assure you,' she said miserably.

'Are you sure? It seems to me that you must have many. You must be putting off the announcement that we love each other because you're afraid that Mr. Standing or your father will try to separate us.'

'No, but . . .'

She broke off and shrugged her shoulders in despair. The whole thing was so hopeless. She could not be frank with him, and the more she said the deeper she sank into the morass into which her impersonation of Fiona Challis had led her.

After a pause Martin took his pipe from his mouth, came up and laid a gentle hand on her shoulder.

'All right, my dear,' he said, 'don't worry. I shan't make any announcement until you wish it. And perhaps you're right. Perhaps it was foolish of me to expect so much. Wait until your father comes home. If that is your wish, it is mine.'

She felt near to tears. She could see that she

had driven him a long way away from her and she was losing his confidence. There was little left of the exhilaration, the tremendous thrill of mutual passionate love and understanding which had flowed between them yesterday.

'Oh, Martin!' she whispered, 'have I made you love me less?'

A wave of the strongest feeling . . . something almost approaching resentment . . . surged through him. She was so utterly feminine and appealing in that moment with her dark glasses, her chestnut hair blown into untidy curls about her uncovered head; something so defenceless about the slim figure in the Jaeger coat. She seemed to love him and yet to be afraid of her love. It perplexed and infuriated him. Before he could restrain himself he had caught her in his arms and almost savagely kissed her on the mouth . . . a kiss that held less of tenderness than passion. She went limp in that fierce caress. She abandoned herself to it knowing that she was utterly his, and yet helpless to explain away her actions, her apparent weakness.

When at length he lifted his head, he was strained and breathless.

'You have no right to be so lovely or so tempting,' he said hoarsely, 'no right to make a man love you if you don't want to love him in return openly and honestly in the eyes of the world.'

'But Martin, I do,' she said with a sob.

Then both of them heard a door open and close.

Martin released Christine. He walked to the window and saw the figure of his employer walking rapidly away from the farmhouse.

Martin turned back to the girl with a grim smile.

'Well, that's done it, my dear. That was Mr. Standing. He must have come here to see me about something.'

Christine put a hand to her trembling lips.

'You mean he saw *us*?'

'Yes,' said Martin, 'quite obviously he did.'

CHAPTER TWENTY-TWO

'What are we going to do about it?' asked Christine.

Her heart was sinking low. The exhilaration of Martin's embrace had left her and she foresaw ahead of her nothing but fresh entanglements and difficulties.

Martin said:

'Don't you think we had better tell Mr. Standing exactly how things are between us, Fiona?'

The very sound of that name (she felt that she would hate it for the rest of her life) made Christine all the stronger in her resolve not to carry this thing any farther than she could possibly avoid. One day, both Mr. Standing and Martin must hear the truth. Please God that day would soon arrive and Fiona would release her from her promise to keep silent. But meanwhile she would not go through the farce of announcing her engagement to Martin as the daughter of William Challis. As Christine Shaw she would only too gladly tell the world.

Martin, watching the girl closely, felt his own heart sinking. He could not understand the hopeless muddle of her thoughts. He could only judge for himself by appearances and it seemed to him that Fiona was just weak and uncertain of herself. A girl without character or grit to acknowledge her love because she was afraid of the consequences.

'All right. Leave it. I don't blame you,' he said with a sudden, harsh laugh. 'I can see that you don't want to tell Mr. Standing that you wish to marry his factor. You would rather let him think you are having a little amusement on the side.'

That brought the hot blood stinging to Chris's cheeks and sent a thrust of real pain into her heart. She could not bear Martin to look at, and think of her so contemptuously.

'Oh!' she gasped. 'How *can* you?'

Martin set his teeth.

'I'm sorry, my dear, but you leave me no alternative.'

She swallowed hard.

'Then if you think me like that . . . you can't love me.'

He looked up from the pipe which he was holding in his fingers. The brilliant blue of his eyes was ice-hard.

'Yes, I love you, Fiona,' he said quietly. 'I think you know exactly how much. You're the only woman I have ever wanted for my wife. But love should never be one-sided. I'm not going to give you everything that's in me to give, just for a half-hearted response.'

She felt maddened. Why must she stand here and listen to such words from Martin? She wanted to run to him, fling herself into his arms and tell him everything . . . how her hands were tied, how her lips were sealed. She wanted to show him how wrong he was . . . how much she loved him. And she could do nothing but stand staring at him in helpless misery.

He was not blind to the anguish on her face but he mistook its meaning. He thought it was just that this spoiled, pampered girl, heiress to a large fortune, was struggling between her love for him and her desire to retain her position and her reputation in John Standing's eyes. He acknowledged the fact that she was having a fight with herself but he misunderstood the nature of that fight. He pitied her but he was himself too proud and too forceful a character to allow any woman, even this one, to play havoc with his feelings.

'Listen, my dear,' he said gently. 'I repeat

235

that I don't blame you, and in actual fact I am going to offer you a piece of advice. Forget that you ever told me that you were in love with me. My love may thrill or excite you a little but cut it out. Do without it. Just go back to our former relationship. You are Miss Challis and I am Mr. Standing's employee. You're not ready or willing to acknowledge our love. Well, I'm not going to squeal about it. We'll just call it a day, shall we?'

She went on looking at him, speechless and unhappy. She could find no arguments against what he was saying. With a sense of despair she realised that until she could tell him the truth she could not convince him of her love. Neither could she even reproach him for misunderstanding her.

Martin spoke again:

'Don't look so worried. Go back to the Manor and explain away what Mr. Standing saw as best you can. Put the blame on me if you like. Tell him I insulted you!' He gave a brief hard laugh.

That laugh seemed to tear Christine's heart in two. White to the lips, she picked up the scarf which had fallen from her neck. Her eyes were so blinded by tears that she could hardly see what she was doing. In a muffled voice she said:

'You don't understand. I do love you. I do . . . I *do* . . . but you don't understand . . .'

Then she rushed out of the room past him,

and shut the door behind her. He put away his pipe, went quickly to the window and looked after the slender figure walking away from the farm, head bowed to the wind. There was something so abject, so defenceless about her thus . . . fighting her way through the gale . . . it brought compunction to him. It made him sorry that he had said hard things to hurt her and that he had let her go in such a spirit. He wanted to run after her and bring her back here to his quiet firelit room, gather her into his arms and kiss the tears from her soft cheeks. He wanted to pour out his soul to her . . . the first woman he had loved in his life. He adored every hair of her head. And yet . . . pride held him back. Let her go. She could not love him. If she loved him she would not be so reluctant to acknowledge her love to others.

Jess, the spaniel, jumped up on him, whining. He turned and automatically patted the little dog. But looking down into the faithful eyes he remembered with a pang how he had once likened those eyes to *hers*.

'Oh, hell,' he said savagely, and turned and walked out of the farmhouse, followed by the spaniel. The sooner he got back to work the better. Work was the only thing that mattered in a man's life. He had always said so. Women were the devil . . . inconsistent, incomprehensible, best left alone.

Up at the Manor House, Christine faced her kind friend, John Standing. Her mind and heart were in a turmoil. Mr. Standing had at once opened the subject of what he had just seen down at Stonehead.

'I was rather shocked, my dear, and I admit it,' he said, his weather-beaten face sterner than she had ever seen it. 'After all, you are Miss Challis and Martin . . . fine lad though he is . . . is my factor. I don't think it is quite "done" for you . . . for him . . .' he broke off with an expressive shrug of the shoulders.

Christine, both hands clenched in the pockets of her coat, strove in vain to find words to say. But it was as hopeless up here as it had been down there at the farm. She could not explain. Because of her vow to Fiona, who was still lying ill in hospital, she could not unburden the whole story to Mr. Standing as she wished to do. So she allowed him to think her a light, feckless sort of creature who was content to amuse herself with a man whom she had no intention of marrying.

Mr. Standing looked rather sadly at the girl's pretty, downcast face. He was frankly disappointed in the daughter of his old friend. He had thought her so sweet and so lovely. He had admired her. In fact he had begun to wonder why Bill Challis could have been so anxious about her. She had seemed to him a steady, reliable child, keen on hard work Now he knew why Bill Challis had sent her up here 'to keep her out of mischief.' He supposed that she found life boring here and was ready to flirt with the first available man. But why she couldn't have chosen a fellow like Renwick instead of Martin Farlong . . .

'You know, my dear,' he said after a pause. 'It's none of my business and I don't believe in interfering. I think you young things of the present generation know how to take care of yourselves. At the same time I wish you hadn't chosen to fool around with Martin. He's a serious young man and you might hurt him. I fully realise that you have no serious intentions toward *him*. But that's hardly fair, is it?'

Christine was trembling. So acute was the nervous strain to which she was being subjected that she felt that if it continued she would break down and pour out the whole story, despite Fiona. It wasn't fair that she should be thought so badly of. And she couldn't *bear* to stand here and listen to what Uncle Bob said and not cry aloud from the housetops her love for Martin. She would have given half her life to say:

'You're making a mistake. I *am* serious about Martin. I'd go to the ends of the earth with him. I want to live with him, cook his food, bear his children, *worship him* . . .!'

And instead, she behaved as she had behaved down at the farm. In tears she rushed out of the room and left Mr. Standing in a state of complete perplexity, wondering what had come over her.

Really, these young girls of today were

239

beyond him. He had witnessed a very passionate embrace between those two down at Stonehead. And come to that, young Martin deserved a ticking off. Even if he could say 'The woman tempted me' he ought to know his place and keep away from Fiona Challis. Obviously, thought Bob Standing, he had made a mistake in letting the girl work on the land and come in close contact with Farlong all the time. He was a good-looking fellow and only human, and so was she. But an affair between them would never do.

During lunch neither Mr. Standing nor Christine made any further mention of the matter. Christine had regained her equilibrium and decided there was nothing to be done but to brave the thing out and wait for Fiona to release her from her obligations. If Martin thought the worse of her, then he must think it. She must just break her heart in secret.

And for the next two weeks in secret that young heart of hers continued to break, for she did not set eyes on Martin. She was not strong enough to resume her job on the land and Martin did not come up to the Manor. Several friends came to see her. Once or twice Mr. Standing took her to Tanleigh to see Gilfred Renwick, who was only too anxious to talk to her and hear all about Fiona. But she fretted unceasingly for Martin . . . wondered how she could go on like this without him.

Then one afternoon Bob Standing came in

for tea and for the first time for over a week mentioned Martin's name to her.

The afternoon was wild and stormy. Rain had set in again, driving across the fells. It looked as though sky and earth were meeting in a thick grey veil. It was the coldest, wettest, windiest day that Christine had ever known. Feeling most dejected . . . ill in body and mind . . . she crouched by the big log-fire in the library. Then Mr. Standing came in and gave her the news.

'It might interest you to know that young Farlong has chucked in his hand and is joining up,' he said.

Christine's heart seemed to turn over.

'Joining up!' she repeated.

'Yes. When I saw him this afternoon he said that he couldn't possibly go on running the farms. He said that his heart and soul were in the idea of fighting for his country, and he begged me to let him go.'

Christine clung weakly to the sides of the stool on which she was sitting. Her face looked drained of colour.

'And you said . . . yes?'

Mr. Standing put his hands behind his back, letting the heat of the fire seep into his cold limbs. He had got wet through walking round the farm with Martin just now.

'I had to. I've held out against him for months, but in the circumstances I felt it my duty to let the boy go. He's restless and his heart isn't in his job any more. It's no good keeping a man when he's like that.'

Christine's brown curly head sank low.

'Is it . . . Is it my fault? I mean . . . is it because I . . .' She broke off and looked up at Mr. Standing with beseeching eyes.

He avoided her gaze.

'My dear Fiona, you certainly can't take all the blame. Martin has been military-minded for a long time. But I think his . . . shall we call it his interest in you . . . has helped him to make the final decision. He didn't mention your name to me. He merely said that he thought it as well for him to get away as soon as possible.'

'Oh,' said Christine, 'I see.'

During tea she hardly said a word. She ate nothing and the slim hand holding the cup to her lips trembled slightly. Every nerve in her body was quivering. She felt suffocated by her thoughts. Martin leaving Stonehead and joining the Army . . . Martin going to be a soldier . . . to wear uniform . . . perhaps to be sent away out East somewhere to fight . . . to be killed . . . her thoughts would carry her no farther than that. She sat mute and aghast at the turn events had taken. And she was filled with self-reproach, with all kinds of misgivings. For it seemed to her that *she* had driven him away. She had made it impossible for him to stay here.

Her mind was made up. She must see him.

She must speak to him again and without betraying Fiona she *must* pull down the barrier which had arisen between them. She could not allow him to leave Stonehead and join up without being sure that she loved him.

Her nervous agitation was acute by the time that tea ended, but fortunately for her Mr. Standing did not notice it. He was too concerned with business; beginning to wonder anxiously whom he could put in charge of his farms in Martin's place. Nobody who would serve him as well. He knew it.

After tea he drove into Ulverston. The moment he had gone, Christine telephoned down to the farm. She must see Martin, and at once. It might be crazy to summon him up here in Uncle Bob's absence and give rise to talk. But she didn't care. Still feeling unfit after her recent blitzing and with her eyes more than ordinarily sore tonight, she did not want to go out in this wild, wet weather.

Martin was not in the house. Old Emmy who answered the phone said that he was still working. Christine left a message for him to ring her as soon as he came in. Then she walked feverishly up and down the library waiting for the telephone to go, terrified that Mr. Standing would come back before she could get Martin up here. At the end of half an hour she phoned Stonehead farm again. Emmy, cross at being disturbed from her cooking, snapped at her: No, Mr. Martin was *not* in and *not* coming in for tea at all. Luke had just come along with some eggs and said that the factor had gone into Cartmel.

A little further questioning and Christine deduced that Martin had an appointment at the King's Arms with a member of the Lancashire Egg Market, and Em had no idea what time he would be back.

Then Christine went a little crazy. All week, ever since that scene with Martin, she had been in a state of nerves and depression, frantically in love, and maddened by the difficulties of her position. Now, knowing that he was leaving Stonehead and joining up, she felt that she must see him before this day ended or break down altogether.

With a complete disregard for what anybody said or thought, she telephoned to Windermere and asked for a car to be sent at once to the Manor House.

'I want to get into Cartmel before the black-out. Can you manage it?'

The garage proprietor said that he could just manage it, grumbled about the petrol shortage, and hung up.

Trembling with nerves, Christine hurried to her room, put on her coat and tied her hair up in a dark blue scarf. The sight of her own face in the mirror appalled her. It was so white. Her eyes looked blood-shot and miserable. She touched her lips and cheeks with colour, put on her smoked glasses and then went downstairs and waited for the car.

CHAPTER TWENTY-THREE

At the King's Arms at Cartmel, in the low, oak-beamed lounge which was already thick with smoke and full of men, both soldiers and civilians, drinking beer, Martin Farlong stood talking to his business friend.

The friend was discussing the new system of egg-control. Martin was hardly listening. One hand holding a mug of beer, the other his pipe, he stared out of the window at the gathering dusk. And his thoughts were all of the girl whom he believed to be Fiona Challis.

Having made up his mind to quit his job and join the Army, he felt as though there was a load off his mind. He had been on the edge of it for months and this affair with 'Fiona' had just pitched him over, he thought. He did not want to leave Mr. Standing in the lurch. He did not intend to. He had promised to stay until a suitable factor could be found to take his place. But any excitement or pleasure which he might have felt now that he had made the decision to join up was swallowed up by his desire for 'Fiona'. He was going through all the wretchedness of a man deeply in love with a girl who did not seem to love him in quite the same way. He had told himself a

245

hundred times all this week that he must get over it, and put 'Fiona' out of his mind. But day and night she haunted him . . . the memory of her soft lips, her little hands, her bright brown head, pursued him wherever he went. 'Fiona' in her land-girl's attire, bravely performing the tasks he had given her. 'Fiona' lying in hospital with bandaged eyes. 'Fiona' in that train coming home clasped in his arms. Always *that* 'Fiona' pursued him . . . not the one who had disappointed and hurt him. And he wished to heaven that he could get rid of her memory.

Through the little casement-window he looked gloomily at the village of Cartmel . . . the charming old square, the historic Gatehouse . . . all the places which he had known from his boyhood and loved. He had never felt more depressed or uncertain of himself. At one moment he had the strongest desire to turn his back on it and get into uniform and fight. At the next, he experienced an intense wish to remain among his native hills and fens, to go on tilling the soil, to watch the snows come and then the snows melt in the spring, and the brown earth grow golden with grain. His heart lay here . . . but only if 'Fiona' could be at his side.

The rain still beat against the window-panes. It was a melancholy evening and shortly it would be dark.

Martin drained his beer-mug and set it

down.

'Well, I must be off,' he said to his friend. 'The lights of my old Ford are none too good and I'd like to get back before total darkness.'

A moment later he was outside the warm comfortable atmosphere of the bar, standing in the rain, buttoning up his mackintosh.

A man wearing a peaked cap touched him on the shoulder.

'Are you Mr. Farlong, sir?'

'I am, yes.'

'A lady would speak to you in that car over there, sir.'

Martin peered through the dusk and he saw a closed car . . . a biggish saloon . . . a feminine figure sitting well back in it. Surprised, and not knowing what to expect, he walked up and opened the car door. The next moment he saw 'Fiona' . . . the 'Fiona' of his dreams . . in the Jaeger coat she had worn when last he had seen her . . . Fiona with a pale troubled young face and a pair of most unhappy eyes.

He said:

'Good God! What are you doing here?'

'Oh, Martin, I know you'll think me mad,' said Christine in a shaky voice, 'but I had to come. Mr. Standing's told me about you leaving here and joining up. I couldn't bear it. I had to see you.'

His whole body went hot. His heart jerked and his voice had a rough edge to it as he answered her. But every fibre of his being was

247

leaping with joy because she had come to him . . . because she seemed to care what happened to him, despite the apparent weakness of her love.

'Is this a hired car?' he asked.

'Yes.'

'I'll pay the man and dismiss him. I'll take you back to Stonehead in my old bus.'

Meekly Christine got out of the car. She was so pleased to see him that she hadn't the strength to argue or protest. A few moments later she was driving away from the King's Arms in the familiar old Ford, and despite the fact that it was draughty and that the springs were bad and that it had been much more comfortable in the big Austin which had brought her here, she was much happier now.

Martin drove in silence until they were out of the village, away out on Cartmel Fell, driving slowly and carefully through the purple dusk. Every moment it was growing darker. With unrelenting violence the wind continued to howl and the rain to batter against the windows.

Christine did not care. All feelings of fatigue and depression had fallen from her. She felt in tune with the storm. A wild, crazy feeling surged through her because of the warm presence of this man at her side . . . the familiar odour of his tweed coat and tobacco.

After he had driven for twenty minutes, Martin drew up the car with a jerk of the brakes and switched off the engine. Then he turned to Christine and said:

'Why did you come?'

She did not answer. She could not. With a quick gesture the man drew off her glasses and peered down into her eyes.

'Why did you come?' he repeated violently. 'Was it just to torture me further? To have another hour's amusement at my expense?'

Then Christine, with a gathering violence within herself and a resentment to match his, flared up:

'No, you fool, *you fool*, Martin! I came because I love you and I had to tell you so. You've got to believe me, no matter how much you think the opposite. You've *got to*.'

Breathing hard and fast he looked down at her. Her face was a pale anguished blur in the dim dusk. The faint sweet scent emanating from her drove him crazy. He caught her in his arms and set his lips to hers in a kiss that answered all unspoken questions and swept them both into a passionate oblivion.

With a little sob Christine surrendered to that embrace, giving him back kiss for kiss, her hands locked feverishly about his neck. The tears pelted down her cheeks.

'I do love you, Martin . . . I do. Oh, be patient and try to understand me!' she implored him.

His senses swam. He drank in her tears with fresh kisses.

'My little darling. Fiona, my beloved darling, don't cry, I can't bear it,' he said.

'Martin, tell me you believe in my love.'

He hesitated for a moment and then gave way to her.

'Very well. I'll believe anything you tell me. I don't understand you, but you must like me a little bit or you wouldn't have come to me tonight.'

She gave a choked laugh.

'Like you!' she repeated. 'Oh, my dear, that hardly describes what I feel for you.'

'But you're still afraid of telling the world, eh?'

'Only for the moment. Till . . . till my father . . .' she choked over that lie . . . 'comes home.'

He gave way again.

'Very well. Anything that you say. I only know that I can't go on without you.'

'And I can't go on without you, Martin.'

He held her closer, smoothing the damp curls back from her hot forehead. His body was shaking and she could feel his hands burning against her throat.

'You're in my blood now, Fiona,' he muttered. 'I'm a fool, but you've made a slave of me.'

'I don't want you to be one. I'd rather be *yours*.'

'It doesn't make sense, but I'll give you credit for telling the truth when you say that you love me.'

'Thank God,' she whispered, and hid her face against his shoulder. Then she remembered the news that Mr. Standing had broken to her.

'Oh, Martin,' she added in a tone of fear, 'is it true that you're going to join up?'

'Yes, as soon as Mr. Standing can get a factor in my place.'

She tightened her clasp of him.

'Oh, Martin, I don't want to lose you.'

'Don't worry, darling,' he said. 'It's all for the best, really. But I daresay it'll make things more difficult for you. By the time Mr. Challis gets back from America I shall be a private with a long number and a badly fitting battle-dress and you'll have some difficulty in persuading him that that's the right fellow for his heiress to marry.'

Christine did not answer. There was nothing she could say just now. She felt almost a fierce pleasure in that moment in the knowledge that she was not Fiona Challis. She was just a girl who typed for her living, and there was nobody to say 'yea' or 'nay' to her if she wished to marry a private in a badly fitting battle-dress.

She felt an enormous relief and satisfaction because Martin's arms were around her again and the awful barrier which had been between them all the week seemed to have lifted. Now her only wish was to get out of her present position and tell Martin the truth. And the next anxiety would be in case he turned against

her because of the thing she had done for
Fiona.

She could only pray dumbly that he would
understand when that time came.

They did not stay long together out on the
fells. Martin was practical and he saw the
necessity of getting her back before it grew
much later. Added to which, as he grimly told
her, she would have another explanation to
make to Mr. Standing.

'I don't care,' she said recklessly. 'I don't
care what he or anybody feels so long as you
believe that I love you.'

Martin sighed, gave her a last kiss, and then
started up the car.

'Strange little thing,' he said. 'You've got me
beat, but I adore you and there's an end of it.'

Her heart was still singing when she said
'good night' to him and walked into the Manor
House. But the radiance on her face was wiped
off suddenly as if by an invisible hand when
she opened the door of the library and saw the
figure of a girl sitting on the sofa with her legs
up and a rug over them. A girl who looked
pale and ill, with a mink wrap over her
shoulders.

Aghast, Christine stared at her. The name
Fiona died on her lips. Somehow or other she
managed to restrain it. For Bob Standing was
there, too. It was Mr. Standing who broke the
silence.

'Ah, my dear,' he said. 'Glad you've come in.

Where have you been? I was in Ulverston and luckily I dropped into the station for a paper. I found your friend Mrs. Hollis. She had arrived without warning us and was trying to get hold of a car. She couldn't stand the hospital a moment longer, she tells me. Came up to us. We're only too pleased to put her up. I told her it would be excellent company for you.'

Christine, still speechless, stared at Fiona. Fiona looked back at her defiantly.

'Hullo, my dear,' she said. 'Have I given you a shock?'

'Yes,' said Christine in a low tone. 'You have.'

Fiona smiled.

'I was just telling Mr. Standing when you came in that we're old school friends and it's so funny . . . we've both got the same Christian name . . . Fiona . . . haven't we?'

CHAPTER TWENTY-FOUR

Christine set her lips, turned her gaze from Fiona and began to take off her things. Her heart was beating rapidly and her cheeks were flushed with the tumult of her feelings. She was still under the spell of Martin's last long kiss but much of the enchantment had gone now that she found Fiona here. She ought not to have come. It was mad and dangerous and meant that a fresh tissue of lies must be uttered on all sides.

Fiona spoke again.

'How are you, dear? You look better in spite of the glasses.'

Christine said:

'My eyes are much better, thank you. How are you?'

Fiona held out her hand.

'All the better for being here and seeing you. Come and give me a kiss darling. I think it is so perfectly sweet of Mr. Standing to let me stay.'

'Not at all,' said Robert Standing, heartily. 'Any friend of "Fiona's" is welcome here. But . . . er . . . this business of the same name will be very awkward. Can't we find another one for you?'

Fiona gave a mischievous smile at Christine.

'I have only got one . . . but you . . .' she nodded towards Christine. 'You are Christine as well, aren't you? We'll have to call you "Chris".'

Christine went positively scarlet. This was carrying the whole thing too far and she began to feel furious with Fiona. She could hardly speak when Mr. Standing turned to her and started to question her as to where she had been. She stuttered some explanation . . . how she had wanted to do some shopping . . . she had thought of something important and hired a car . . . more lies . . . lies that made her grit her teeth. And Mr. Standing swallowed them as usual, for why should he see anything wrong, or even guess at the farce that was being played under his very roof? But as soon as he had gone out of the room and left the two girls together, Christine marched up to the sofa and looked down at her friend with blazing eyes.

'How dared you do this, Fiona . . . what right had you to come and create such havoc?' she asked in a low, furious voice.

Fiona took a comb from her bag and ran it carelessly through her fair curly hair.

'My dear,' she protested. 'No need to fly off the handle.'

'But there is,' said Christine, trembling. 'It was bad enough before you came but now it is a thousand times worse. All this deception and having to trump up one fabrication after another . . . All this nonsense about our names! It is just sheer idiocy. There is no excuse for it any more. When I consented to come in the first place I came to give you and Peter a chance but now it is all quite unnecessary and . . .'

'Ssh!' Fiona broke in, and pouted at her. 'Don't broadcast the whole story, darling. And do calm down. No harm is going to come of this at all. But I didn't see why I should languish in a hospital or convalescent home when I could come up and be with you in this lovely country place and have some peace. I have been through hell with my leg and I am

255

still frightfully lame.'

The hot colour faded from Christine's cheeks. Her temper cooled. With a sigh she sat down beside Fiona. How could she go on being furious with her? The poor little thing did look thin and pale and she *had* been through a dreadful experience in that raid and with two operations on her leg.

'Well, really, Fiona,' she said, 'I don't know what to say. I quite see that you didn't want to stay down in the hospital. But you needn't have come up here, need you? You must admit that it complicates matters for me terribly.'

'But, Christine darling, it needn't. There is no reason why you shouldn't have your girl friend to stay and nobody up here will dream that Mrs. Peter Hollis is . . .' her voice sank to a whisper . . . 'Fiona Challis.'

Christine shook her head.

'It is all hopelessly wrong and has been from the start.'

'Darling, I know you think so, but you *have* given me the greatest happiness with Peter. It was wonderful while it lasted, and please God he will come back safe and sound one day and we can go on being happy. And as I told you when we last met, as soon as Daddy gets back, I'll own up and soothe him down. But I just don't want to raise hell with Mr. Standing while Daddy is still in America.'

Christine nodded.

'I know all your arguments. And having let

myself in for this mess I suppose there is no way of escape until you say the word.'

Fiona gripped her hand.

'Don't regret it, darling. You have been an angel, and somehow, some day, I'll repay it.'

'I don't want payment. I only want peace of mind,' said Christine.

'Now, now,' said Fiona, 'you've quite enjoyed it really. What about this man you are in love with up here?'

Christine's face flooded with colour again.

'You are bound to meet Martin sooner or later and that is one of my main difficulties . . . having to tell Martin who I really am. He isn't the sort of man who will easily condone an offence like this.'

'Darling, it's not an offence . . . it is just an act of friendship which you were asked to do.'

Christine gave a short laugh.

'Martin mightn't see it that way. It has been an impersonation and a packet of lies from start to finish, and he may even refuse to believe that I love him by the time it is finished.'

'I'll make him believe in you,' said Fiona grandly.

Christine looked at her friend with some admiration.

'I must say I wish I had your mental make-up, my dear. You always were a wild little thing . . . always determined to get your own way at any cost.'

Fiona made a grimace.

'Poor little me! Blitzed, homeless and lonely.'

She knew that would win immediate sympathy from Christine.

'Oh, darling, is the leg still very bad? I don't know why they let you out of hospital so soon.'

'Wanting the beds, my dear. But the wound hasn't healed and I shall have to get the local doctor to dress it every morning. I warned Mr. Standing. I can only walk slowly and am not supposed to move off my couch more than I can help.'

'Oh dear, if there is anything I can do to help get you well, I will,' said Christine, 'but do let's tell as few lies as possible. You seem to take a mischievous delight in making up fresh ones but it worries me to death.'

'I'll be good,' promised Fiona. 'Now tell me more about your Martin.'

'He is going away,' said Christine. 'He is joining up, and he can't understand why I don't wish to announce my engagement to him before he goes. Uncle Bob wouldn't hear of it. I am still supposed to be Miss Challis, and the other day he saw Martin kissing me . . .'

She proceeded to tell Fiona the story and the complications that had arisen.

Fiona was genuinely distressed for her friend.

'I do see how involved it all is. Really ironical that you should now be in the position

258

I was in with Peter . . . but don't despair, Christine. Daddy will soon be back and then you can tell your Martin everything and get married to him.'

Christine rose to her feet, walked to the fireplace and looked into the fire uneasily. If only she could be sure that Martin would understand and forgive . . . but Martin was a man of the utmost integrity, of truth, of simplicity. And her actions would take more than a bit of explaining.

Mr. Standing returned to the room and the two girls discreetly changed the conversation. Mr. Standing, always the kindest and most generous of hosts, had already arranged for the little morning-room with a south aspect, down on the ground floor, to be converted into a bedroom for Mrs. Hollis, so that she should not have to worry about stairs. The maids were busy now with the arrangements.

'You two girls will have to look after each other,' he said smiling. 'Poor little "blitzed" pair. By jove! It makes me wish I were twenty years younger so that I could get back at those Nazi devils.'

'Oh, we aren't down-hearted, are we, Christine?' murmured Fiona.

'Funny to hear her called "Christine",' laughed Mr. Standing.

Christine coloured and hastily suggested that Fiona should come to her room and that she would unpack for her and get her ready for dinner.

Dinner was a pleasant meal. Mr. Standing was in good spirits and seemed to like the presence of the pretty, fair girl, who made light of her sufferings from the raid, and spoke with such love and longing of her young husband who had recently sailed for the Middle East.

'I admire the courage of all you young people today,' he remarked.

Dinner over, they were all drinking coffee by the drawing-room fire when the telephone bell rang. Mr. Standing answered it and then returned to the two girls.

'I thought you two wouldn't object,' he said. 'Young Renwick has just rung up and asked if he could come over with a friend . . . another fellow in the R.A.F., who is staying at Tanleigh for the night. Renwick seems much better . . . a bit yellow he says, but you must forgive him that.'

Fiona and Christine exchanged looks. Christine was thinking:

'Oh lord! Another awkward moment when Gilfred recognises Fiona.'

Her consternation grew when Mr. Standing added that he was now going to get a call through to Stonehead and ask Martin up to the Manor.

'When the R.A.F. lads come, I'll leave you young things alone and take Martin into my study for a business chat. Then I'll bring him in here for a last drink. You . .' he indicated

Fiona . . . 'must meet our Martin. He is a very good fellow and shortly going off to join the Army.'

Fiona made a suitable reply. Christine was speechless. But it was only a matter of minutes before the front-door bell rang and the two visitors were shown into the drawing-room. Gilfred in mufti, looking thin and still bearing the signs of his jaundice, and with him a short, good-looking man, wearing the uniform of a Flight Lieutenant and with a D.F.C. ribbon on his tunic.

Gilfred came straight across the room to Christine.

'Hello! How are you? We haven't met for weeks, thanks to my wretched illness and you getting yourself bombed. This is my friend, Jack Filby. Jack, this is Miss Challis . . .'

He broke off, for suddenly, over Christine's shoulder he had seen the girl on the sofa. A girl in a black dinner dress with a mink cape over her shoulders and a little black ribbon in her fair curls. He blinked with sheer astonishment, then before he could restrain himself, he exclaimed:

'*Fiona!*'

'Oh, do you know Mrs. Hollis?' asked Mr. Standing.

Gilfred got his bearings. Caution returned to him. He was amazed to find Fiona actually in this house, but it was easy to see that the truth was still being kept from Robert

Standing.

'Yes, I know Mrs. Hollis,' he said slowly, and then introduced Flight Lieutenant Filby.

Mr. Standing brought out cigars and liqueur brandy. The conversation became general but Gilfred managed to whisper a few words to Christine. He thought that she looked ill and unhappy. Her dark glasses gave her an added air of fragility but he found her as attractive as ever.

'What *is* all this about?' he whispered to her. 'A bit dashing of Fiona to come up here, isn't it?'

In an agony of nervousness Christine whispered back:

'It was outrageous of her to come but I couldn't stop it. *Do* be careful.'

'Count on me,' Renwick whispered back. 'It appeals to my sense of humour. In another moment I'll begin to wonder if I'm really me.'

Christine had no answering smile. She disliked the whole situation. After Mr. Standing had left them and gone to his study, she was even more miserable. She wanted to go with him. To sit in that study with Martin. Feel Martin's firm reassuring touch on her hand, his thrilling embrace. She was so completely in love with him. It was agony to keep away and pretend she didn't care and make a lot of silly conversation with two young men in whom she was not interested. Gilfred had gone across to the sofa to renew his old acquaintanceship with Fiona. They were talking and laughing together. Fiona didn't seem to care. She could share a joke with Renwick, but Christine could hardly answer the questions that Jack Filby was putting to her about the direct hit on the hotel where she had been injured. She kept looking at the door, waiting for it to open . . . waiting for Uncle Bob to bring Martin in here . . . dreading it . . . yet wanting it. She was in a state of hopeless confusion in her mind.

CHAPTER TWENTY-FIVE

It was about half an hour later that Mr. Standing put his head in the door and said:

'All you young people all right? Got plenty of drinks?'

Christine, who had been living for this moment, in a state of nervous excitement and anticipation in the hope of seeing the man she loved so desperately, moved quickly to the door.

'Isn't Martin coming in for a drink?' she asked, trying to appear casual.

Mr. Standing looked at her a trifle reproachfully.

'Now, young woman, you have plenty of admirers in here, and Martin doesn't like parties. He is going home to his bed.'

That was too much for Christine. She had only stood listening to all the nonsense, the idle flattery from the two young men in the Air Force, with the utmost difficulty. It had bored her. She wanted to see Martin more than anything in the world. The force of her feelings made her fling caution to the winds. With a heightened colour and a nervous laugh, she said:

'Oh, we can't allow that! Fiona wants to meet him . . . I'll make him come in . . .' And she slid past Mr. Standing and walked rapidly into the library. She found Martin there putting on his coat, the ever-faithful Jess at his heels wagging her tail, looking forward to her nightly walk.

Martin looked pale and tired. But his whole face changed when he saw the girl. She had taken off her glasses. Her eyes looked clearer and brighter than he had seen them for some time. Her face was flushed, her hair combed in sleek, bronze waves high up from her ears. She wore a tightly-fitting wine coloured dress which suited her. He had never seen her look so lovely or so alluring.

'Fiona!' he murmured and moved toward her.

She shut the door behind her and flung herself into his arms.

'Martin, Martin, it's heaven to see you again. You can't go away without saying good night to me.'

His lips met her hungry ones in a passionate kiss, then he released her.

'Little idiot! Mr. Standing will see us.'

'Oh, I don't care,' she cried recklessly, 'I'm fed up with lies and deception and everything but you.'

He looked at her with perplexity.

'Why lies and deception, darling?'

She calmed down, remembering the part she still had to play.

'Oh, never mind. Perhaps I'm a little mad. I really *am* a little crazy with my love for you, Martin.'

His heart beat rapidly. He thought it was wonderful that this glorious girl should be moved to such feelings toward him but her whole behaviour was quite beyond his understanding . . . never the less he allowed her to take his hand and lead him out of the study toward the drawing-room whence came the gay chatter of voices.

Mr. Standing had told him that Gilfred Renwick and a friend in the R.A.F. were here, and that Mrs Hollis, 'Fiona's' friend, had arrived from the south. He had no real wish to meet any of them. Mainly because of the present position in which he found himself. If there was one thing he disliked it was being 'Fiona's' lover in secret. It would have been different if she had been willing to announce their love for each other to the whole world. But Christine had her way and introduced

Martin to everybody. Mr. Standing stood by with a somewhat disapproving air. She knew what he was thinking. He did not like the idea that she was just 'amusing' herself with Martin.

Martin and young Renwick greeted each other with some reserve. They had played games together in the village as boys but since then their lives and ways had lain apart. Jack Filby had no particular interest in 'the farmer'. But Fiona kept Martin a moment beside the sofa and made him talk to her. She was interested to see the famous factor who had won Christine's heart. And she had to admit that Martin was extraordinarily good to look at with his brown healthy skin, those vivid blue eyes of his, and that rather secret brooding air that sat upon him. He was attractive all right, she thought, but not easy to know. And possibly Christine was right in thinking that he would not easily forgive the part that she had recently played up here.

'He might be difficult,' she thought, 'poor old Christine! I hope I haven't ruined her one big romance.'

'I hear you are joining up soon, Mr. Farlong,' she murmured to Martin.

'Yes, as soon as I can get things fixed up at the farm,' he replied.

'Then you'll leave this district I suppose and be sent right away.'

'No doubt.'

'Christine will miss you.'

He stared at the fair, delicate-looking girl who, in his opinion, bore the 'society stamp' on her far more than the other girl who had come up here and helped on his farm. He couldn't imagine Mrs. Hollis working on any farm.

'Who is Christine?' he asked.

Christine, herself, who was standing nearby, listening nervously, looked from one to the other, realising what dangerous ground they were treading. Fiona flung her a mischievous look.

'I call *her* Christine . . .' she indicated the girl whom Martin knew as Fiona.

'Oh, why?' asked Martin.

'It's her other name,' said Fiona.

'Don't you like it?' asked Christine anxiously.

Martin, somewhat embarrassed, sought refuge in the whisky and soda which had been given to him.

'It is very nice,' he said politely.

Christine thought:

'Oh, my darling, one day you will have to know that that's the only name I've got and you'll have to get used to it—that is if you ever speak to me again!'

The telephone bell could now be heard through the hubbub of voices. Mr. Standing excused himself and left the room. When he came back a few minutes later, his whole bearing had changed and his genial face looked grey under its tan. He wore the expression of a man who had received a great shock.

He stood a moment looking agitatedly round the room, listening to the flippant conversation and the laughter between the young people. Then he passed a hand over his forehead as though trying to make up his mind what to do. At that moment Christine moved across the room to the radio-gramophone and put on a record.

'I must play you my favourite tune,' she said gaily. ' "*All The Things You Are*" . . .' she looked at Martin from under her lashes. 'It's most attractive, even if it's an old one.'

The lilting melody began to filter through the room. Gilfred Renwick immediately put an arm around Christine and danced a few steps with her on the polished wood floor.

'Good work,' said Jack Filby, and began to roll up rugs.

Then Mr. Standing seized his opportunity. He walked quickly to the couch on which Fiona was lying. Martin had seated himself on the arm and was watching Christine's slim figure moving so gracefully in Gilfred's arms . . . admiring her . . . hating the man who held her.

'My dear,' said Mr. Standing in a low voice, addressing Fiona. 'I have just had terrible news. Terrible news which we have got to break to poor little Fiona and I don't know how to do it. I want you to help me.'

Martin stood up.

'I'm sorry to hear that, sir. Is there anything I can do?'

The real Fiona stared at Mr. Standing. She had grown suddenly white and a look of fear had come into her large blue eyes.

'What sort of news?' she asked breathlessly.

'It is about Fiona's father. My poor old friend, Challis.'

Fiona shrank as though he had struck her. She stubbed the end of the cigarette she had been smoking into an ashtray beside her.

'What has happened? What news have you just had?'

Mr. Standing took out a handkerchief and wiped his face. He cast a look at Christine. She was dancing beautifully with Gilfred Renwick. Young Filby was standing by the gramophone now beating time to the music, urging the couple on.

'Oh dear!' groaned Mr. Standing. 'What a shock it will be to the poor child. I would give anything for this not to have happened.'

Fiona seized his hand with ice cold fingers.

'What has happened? What have you heard? Tell me quickly.'

He was so agitated himself that he hardly noticed the extent of her agitation.

'You will be the best one to break it to her, my dear, after these people have gone. We must break it to her gently.'

'*What?*' Fiona asked between her teeth.

269

'News has just been received in London . . . it was telephoned to me by William's secretary . . . that poor Challis was coming back today from New York as a passenger on one of these new transport planes. It crashed when they were taking off. Poor old William is dead. The poor little girl will never see her father again.'

There was silence. The record had just finished. Filby was turning it over on the other side. Christine and Gilfred were solemnly thanking each other for the dance.

'This will do my jaundice a lot of good,' came Gilfred's voice.

Then across the room came another voice . . . the voice of the girl on the sofa . . . in a piercing cry which those who were present did not forget for a long while . . . it was so heartrending.

'Daddy!' she screamed. *'Daddy!'*

Christine swung round, the blood draining from her face. Renwick stopped the record just as it began. And Mr. Standing stared in complete confusion as Fiona fell back on the sofa in a dead faint.

'Good God!' he exclaimed. 'What is this?'

Christine rushed forward.

'Fiona! Fiona, darling, what's happened?'

Martin, forgetting the need for personal restraint, took her arm.

'My dear, Mr. Standing has had bad news . . .'

'What?' demanded Christine, a hand against her throbbing heart.

270

'It is about your father, my dear,' said Mr. Standing in a shaken voice. 'He was on his way home and there has been a terrible accident . . . I told Mrs. Hollis . . . but I can't understand why she has taken it like this. She seems to have fainted . . . did she know your father very well? She called out "Daddy!"'

Christine stood stock still. For a moment she felt as though she were in a whirlpool . . . that she was going round and round and didn't quite know where she was going to land. It did not take her many seconds to guess that Mr. Challis had been killed and to realise the effect it must have had on poor little Fiona . . . At the same time she saw that her role of Fiona Challis was played out. There was no further need for impersonation now.

Gilfred Renwick and his friend discreetly left the room, and wandered into the library. Only Gilfred, knowing what he did, had a vague idea of what had happened. Martin poured out some neat whisky and gave it to Christine who knelt down and moistened her friend's colourless lips with the alcohol.

Mr. Standing stood by helplessly.

Then Fiona opened her eyes.

'Daddy!' she said again, in a kind of wail.

'Darling, it's all right, I'm here with you,' murmured Christine, holding on to her hands.

'Daddy's dead,' cried Fiona in an anguished voice. 'His plane crashed this morning just as he was coming back. I shall never see him

271

again. He will never know about Peter and me. I have lied to him and I'll never be able to tell him that I'm sorry. Oh, Daddy, *Daddy*!'

She broke off and turned her face to the cushion in a passion of tears, all self-control broken. Martin Farlong stood like a figure of stone staring at the two girls, trying to comprehend what he had just heard, and for the moment, failing.

Then Robert Standing faced Christine squarely.

'What does she mean?' he asked. 'She talks as though she is William's daughter. But he hadn't got two daughters. Only one. Tell me what this means, Fiona.'

Then Christine, without daring to look at Martin although she felt his piercing gaze, flung back her head and answered:

'I am very glad to be able to tell the truth at last. I have loathed the whole of this impersonation ever since it started. You see I am not Fiona Challis at all. I am Christine Shaw and she . . .' Christine touched the sobbing girl . . .' is Fiona, William Challis's daughter.'

CHAPTER TWENTY-SIX

Complete silence followed Christine's confession. Mr. Standing was a simple man

272

and such an astounding revelation reduced him for a few moments to utter perplexity. Second by second the fact penetrated his consciousness. He looked from Christine to the girl on the sofa and then back again slowly as though trying to convince himself that he had heard aright.

Martin Farlong was equally quiet. But the words that Christine had just spoken had a deeper psychological effect upon him than upon his employer. He grasped the basic facts of what Christine had told them quickly, and quickly it went down to the very bottom of his consciousness, leaving him more angered than astonished. If there was one thing in the world that Martin loathed it was deception. Lies and duplicities were abhorrent to him. He could forgive worse crimes but he demanded the truth. In his own line of life, he had always found it hard to accept deliberate falsehood, while he was Robert Standing's factor, from any servant that he had employed. He dismissed such people. He looked now at Christine, and realised that she stood there a self-confessed liar of the first order. In fact her whole life since she had lived at Stonehead had been a lie. She was not Fiona Challis. She was some strange girl, unknown to him, whose real name was Christine Shaw.

Christine turned her head and met Martin's full gaze. In her eyes he read a touching humility; a plea for pardon. But those blue eyes of his were like ice. Her heart sank at the remorseless severity in them. He was as a man turned to stone.

There was no sound in that room except Fiona's sobbing. And then at last Robert Standing pulled himself together and spoke again.

'Good God,' he said, in an almost feeble voice. 'This is . . . this is *terrible*! I just don't understand.'

'I am sorry,' said Christine. 'More sorry than I can say because you have been so good to me. But I'll try to explain . . . perhaps you'll understand a bit better when I tell you why I came here in Fiona's place. Only now we ought to see to *her* oughtn't we?'

Mr. Standing passed a hand across his forehead.

'Yes, yes, of course.'

'Could we ring for one of the maids and help Fiona to her room,' suggested Christine.

Yes, of course,' repeated Mr. Standing, and moved to the bell and pressed it. His face looked lined and a little shrunken. He was not a young man and these were two severe blows which had been delivered to him tonight. For in his way he had grown fond of this girl whom he had thought to be his friend's daughter, and he did not like what he had just heard. He did not like it at all.

Then the figure of stone which was Martin came to life. He began to walk to the door.

'If I won't be wanted any more,' he said in a queer strained voice, 'I'll get along home.'

Christine's heart began to thump. She moved after him.

'Martin, Martin, wait a moment, and talk to me,' she began.

He turned and gave her a look which cut her to the quick; it was so full of icy scorn.

'I am sorry,' he said, 'but I don't think you and I have anything to say to each other.'

Her face flushed a scorching red.

'Oh, but, Martin, we have. You must let me explain . . . really.'

'I don't really want any explanation. I thought you were Fiona Challis, but you're not . . . and I just don't know you . . . that's all.'

She fell back as though he had struck her. The colour faded from her face. Before she could speak again he had walked out of the room.

She heard the front door close and knew that he had left the Manor House. Left it and left her, despising her, thinking the very worst. And for a moment her little world crashed to ruins about her. Then Fiona's wailing voice drove away thoughts of herself.

'Christine, Christine, I want you. Christine, tell me that Daddy isn't dead!'

Christine made an effort to forget Martin and that awful contempt with which he had looked at her, spoken to her. She went back to her friend. That next half hour was a nightmare. Mr. Standing made some excuse to get the two young airmen out of the house. They drove away, neither of them having spoken to the girls again. But at the front door, Mr. Standing put a hand on Gilfred's shoulder and said:

'Don't say too much about this in Cartmel, as a favour to me, my boy. It will be all round the district soon enough.'

'I assure you I shall say nothing to anyone,' Gilfred replied.

And after that it was a question of looking after Fiona and Fiona alone. She was not in the state of health to stand the sudden shock of her father's tragic end. It was a sick girl whom they carried to her bed and shortly afterwards Mr. Standing's doctor drove in from Grange to see her. Christine had no time to think of herself. There was so much to be done for Fiona and not until a sedative had quietened her down and got her to sleep at last, did Christine turn her thoughts to her own affairs.

She was on the verge of exhaustion. It was past eleven o'clock by the time the house was quiet again and she faced Mr. Standing, knowing that he would not go to bed until he had heard a fuller explanation of the whole affair.

She sat with him by the dying fire in the drawing-room, sipping the strong drink he had insisted on giving her for she looked, herself, as though she might collapse at any moment. And angry, disappointed, whatever he might feel about her, he felt no malice toward this girl whom he must come to know as Christine Shaw. He was a humane man and a kindly one, never ready to judge too harshly or be too quick to condemn.

'You have done a very serious thing, my dear,' he told Christine. 'It is against the law, you know, to impersonate someone else. You took great risks and you did a great wrong to poor old Challis. Do you realise that?'

The girl bit her lip.

'I can't feel that I have done any harm to him. He didn't know . . . he will never know now. So I can't, I *won't* feel that I have hurt *him*.'

Mr. Standing drew a heavy sigh.

'Well, perhaps you have hurt yourself more than anyone, young woman. That's rather the way I look at it.'

Her head drooped.

'I am quite sure of that,' she said.

The thought of Martin stabbed her like a knife.

'Why did you do it, Fiona . . . forgive me, I can't quite remember yet that that isn't your name,' said the old man wearily.

She poured out the explanation . . . the story of how Fiona had begged her to come up here in her place so that she could marry Peter Hollis and escape all the trouble which would have followed had William Challis known about the marriage.

'There is nothing more to it than that,' she assured Mr. Standing earnestly. 'Fiona was going to tell her father when he got back. But she was so deeply in love with Peter, she couldn't bear the thought of parting from him and I was stupid enough to think there would be no harm in aiding and abetting her romance. I knew it was the real thing with her at last and would be best for her in the end, even though Peter Hollis wasn't quite in the position that Mr. Challis wanted.'

Standing shook his head.

'It was all wrong. Both you girls made a grave mistake. Honesty is the best policy, no matter to what it applies.'

'I agree with you now. I regret it bitterly.'

'Besides,' added Mr. Standing, 'it was cowardly of Fiona. If she loved the young man as much as all that, she should have been prepared to over-ride her father's wishes openly and stand by the consequences.'

Christine put her face in her hands.

'Oh, yes, it was a mad thing and it has led to all kinds of complications I never anticipated,' she said in a muffled voice. 'I can see now how crazy it was. Oh, Uncle Bob . . . don't think too hardly of me. It wasn't that I wanted to gain anything for myself. Do please believe that.'

'I do, my dear. You have just been a sentimental little idiot, and landed yourself in for more than you could cope with.'

She raised streaming eyes to him.

'You are being terribly kind. I wonder you don't feel like turning me out of the house. I am just an impostor, and . . .'

'Oh, come,' broke in Mr. Standing, with an embarrassed cough. 'No tears, my dear child. We've had enough trouble for tonight with that other young woman. She is being punished now for her foolishness. Naturally her conscience is smiting her, now she knows she'll never see her father again.'

'My conscience is smiting me too,' said Christine huskily.

'Well, we must just do our best to put things right, but it is going to take a bit of explaining in the village, isn't it?'

'Oh, I don't want it to be a source of misery to you. Fiona and I must both go away at once. Perhaps they need never know around here. No one need ever see us again, and . . .'

Mr. Standing interrupted.

'And what about Martin?' he asked, with a queer look at her.

Christine drew a deep breath and her white young face burned with sudden unhappy colour.

'He won't forgive me. He's gone away without even waiting for an explanation.'

Mr. Standing bent forward and, picking up the bellows, blew a little flame into life at the charred end of the log.

'What you have done to Martin is one of the worst things of all,' he said. 'I have known him all his life and he's not an ordinary fellow . . . he couldn't just take a thing like this with a laugh the way young Renwick might have done. He is serious-minded and a stickler for honesty. And I think I am right in saying, my dear, he is very much in love with you.'

'But I am in love with him!' Christine exclaimed. 'I am crazy about him. I haven't been playing with him, as you think. I'd go to the ends of the earth with Martin if he wanted me to.'

Mr. Standing looked at her with some surprise. There was such sincerity in those large, lovely eyes. He could not fail to believe what he heard.

'Well, of course, if you feel like that it puts rather a different complexion on the whole matter.'

'I do feel like that, only Martin will never believe me.'

'I know Martin is a difficult man,' said Mr. Standing, 'but if you talk to him as you have done to me perhaps you'll be able to convince him that you haven't done such a very dreadful thing after all.'

Tears welled into Christine's eyes.

'He thinks it dreadful. Oh if you knew the way he looked at me . . . the way he spoke to me as though I were a stranger to him . . . I can't bear it!'

'Naturally the fellow has received a shock. You couldn't expect him to take it too well. It shook me, my dear, and you must remember that Martin loved you, and a man in love always thinks the particular object of his devotion is perfect.'

A sob shook Christine's whole body.

'Well, he knows now how imperfect I am, and as you say he can't bear lies, he will never never forgive me for lying to him.'

Mr. Standing drew a sigh.

'Well, well, we'll have to see what we can do in the morning. I'll have a few words with him. We're all a bit dazed tonight, and you must admit that we all have to readjust our feelings . . . our thoughts. You are not what we thought you were. We've got to get used to thinking of you as Miss Christine Shaw instead of Fiona Challis. It is a bit of a poser for us, my dear, and especially for the young man who was in love with you.'

'I've lost Martin. I know I have,' said Christine in a tone of despair.

'On the other hand,' said Mr. Standing thoughtfully, 'there were many more barriers between Martin Farlong and Miss Challis than there are between you two. You say you have no ties and no money. There is nothing whatsoever to prevent Farlong marrying you if he wishes to.'

'Except the fact that he will have fallen out of love with me by now,' said Christine bitterly.

281

Mr. Standing rose.

'Now, my dear, you had better go to bed. You are worn out and we shall only talk in circles. Get some sleep and we'll all review the whole thing in the morning. You've got that poor girl to look after. Better send a cable to her husband and let him know what's happened. Challis put his daughter in my care, you know, and I feel responsible for her. But you've all had me nicely by the nose, haven't you?'

Christine put a hand on his arm.

'Please do forgive me for my share in it.'

He gave a half-smile.

'I'll try to forgive you . . . Christine.'

She gave a sigh.

'It's good to hear that name. It's mine. I've never heard the other without being miserable.'

'You are a good child at heart, I'm sure. You have just been misguided over this affair, but I will say you played your part very nicely, young woman, and it's all most reprehensible.'

She went up to her bedroom in a stupor of weariness and misery. How right Mr. Standing was! Honesty was the best policy indeed. And the thing that she had done for Fiona had merely led from one mistake to another, ending in *this* . . . breaking her own heart and Martin's faith. She could not sleep for thinking of Martin and how he must feel about the whole matter. He was an idealist and integrity

282

meant so much to him. Looking at things from his point of view, it must have hurt him so badly. And, loving him as much as she did, that was now her most bitter regret.

She must see him tomorrow. She must *make* him see her.

In bed that night she felt for the first time since she had slept under this roof that she was no longer an impostor. She had regained her own identity and with it her soul. Fiona Challis no longer had a father. But she had Peter and her fortune. And Christine Shaw had nothing. She was the loneliest girl in the world.

CHAPTER TWENTY-SEVEN

There was no sleep for Martin Farlong that night. Once he got back to the farmhouse he busied himself in a great many ways, for he had made up his mind to leave Stonehead early the next morning. He must get away from this place . . . from that girl, Fiona, Christine, whatever her name was . . . from everything connected with her. He must get away at once even if it meant leaving Mr. Standing to control the farm until his new factor arrived. He felt that if he stayed on here he would go mad.

For an hour he worked like a man possessed, turning out papers, putting account books and documents connected with the farms in order, packing his own personal belongings.

His state of mind was unenviable. He was like a man in the grip of a fever . . . a fury. He could hardly tolerate the thought of the girl he had loved. The first, the only woman to whom he had given his heart's devotion and his faith.

'I might have known,' he told himself again and again. 'I might have known that I was a fool to give way to my feelings in the first place. I should have learned my lesson from my mother and known that no woman is to be trusted.'

He did not care why Christine Shaw had come here in Fiona Challis's place. He knew nothing about her, nor did he intend to enquire. She was an impostor and that was enough. If he thought about it at all he supposed she had done it for money . . . for *fun*. Equally could he suppose that she had indulged in the same *fun* with him, and now, of course, he knew why she would not become engaged to him. She hadn't dared. She had known that he must eventually discover the trick she had practised upon everybody up here.

When he looked back on these weeks and months . . . remembered how wonderful he had thought her . . . how far out of his reach she had seemed . . . William Challis's daughter and heiress . . . it made him writhe. She was

284

just a little adventuress . . . in all probability one of the real Fiona Challis's Mayfair playgirls, who had found it amusing to impersonate her friend.

He worked himself up into a state of indignation and resentment which drove reason from his mind. Yet whenever he remembered the sweetness and dearness of her . . . how he had thrilled to her lips and caresses . . . how utterly and completely in his imagination he had been possessed by her, he could hardly bear it. It was as well, he told himself, that she did not appear down here at this moment. He would have hurt her . . . he would have taken her in his arms and kissed her savagely until she begged for mercy, would have taught her that she could not toy with a man's heart and soul like that and get away with it.

In the next instant he swung to icy contempt and felt that he could not bear to touch her again. But never once during those nocturnal hours of battling with himself did he feel indifference toward her. To one of his intense and reserved nature it could be love or hatred, but never indifference.

Tomorrow he would take the first train to Manchester. He would strip off his civilian clothes, get into uniform, and serve as a soldier. Yes, that was what he craved to do now. To forget all the tension and emotional disturbance that this girl had brought into his life . . . lose his individuality . . . himself . . . in the service of his country. He would hope to be sent abroad soon and get into the thick of a fight. The sooner the better. He would no longer concern himself with the love of women or any personal matters. He would become a cog driving the vast national wheel toward victory. He would direct all his hatreds and emotions against the common enemy— Germany.

His brain went round in circles. He exhausted himself with too much analysing. When the dawn came he had not gone to bed. He was still walking round the farmhouse. Jess, the spaniel, sat on the hearthrug staring at him with puzzled, patient eyes. She could not understand why her master had not gone upstairs as usual. She wanted her basket and yawned in a bored way. It was getting cold as the night drifted into the early morning. The fire had gone out. Man and dog were both shivering, but Martin did not notice it.

He had finished his sorting and packing. Opening the front door he walked out into the little garden. The air struck chill. The light was still a dim, uncertain thing. The outlying farmhouses were shrouded in a white mist that curled from the fell. All was quiet with that unearthly stillness of the dawn, broken only by the faint plaintive piping of wakening birds . . . the crowing of a cock . . . the lowing of a cow from the byre. All passionate feeling was spent in Martin Farlong. His face looked grey and gaunt in the dawn light. He was conscious of a great weariness and depression as he looked around him. He loved this place. Cartmel . . . the old Gatehouse, the Priory churchyard, where his father lay buried . . . the wild, beautiful fells, where, as a boy, he had picked flowers in the spring, blackberries in the autumn . . . where, as a man, he had gloried in the hills and valleys so familiar to him . . . the earth which he had sown and reaped . . . all of nature to which he had felt akin. It would be like the sharpness of death wrenching himself from it all. And back came the searing memory of the girl he had known as Fiona, and whose hair he had likened to the ripeness of chestnuts, whose eyes had seemed to him as clear and beautiful as the lakes, whose skin was softer than flower petals, and whose mouth was like red fruit offered up for his kisses.

Despair suddenly seized him.

'I shall never see her again,' he thought. 'And I may never see Stonehead or Cartmel or the Lakes again. I may be killed. I don't mind if I am. There is nothing left!'

He turned back into the farmhouse, numb with cold, shaking. Jess whined and wagged her tail at him, and the sight of her added to his heartache.

He would have to leave her too . . . his dear little spaniel. Old Emmy would have to take care of her. But he feared that she might lie down on an old coat of his and stay there; refuse to eat or drink.

And once he had thought of giving her to *that* girl to take care of . . . God, how the memory of her hurt!

A slight figure came down the stairs, and met him. It was Susan, Emily's granddaughter. He had almost forgotten Susan was still here. He had seen little of her lately. She came toward him rubbing her cold hands, peering at him in the dimness of the hall.

'Are you up already, Mr. Farlong?'

He gave a curt laugh.

'I haven't been to bed.'

'Eeh!' she said. 'You do look queer. Are you ill, sir? Shall I call Granny?'

'No. Certainly not.'

'She's got a bit of rheumatism. I was coming down to light the fire for her. Shall I get you a cup of tea?'

'Yes, and some hot water to wash in as soon as you can, Susan. I want to catch the first possible train to Manchester.'

'Will you be away long, Mr. Farlong?' she asked, drawing nearer him. 'I do hope not.'

He looked down into her pert young face. He knew that this child had a very warm corner for him, but it left him unmoved, and in his present state of mind the last thing he wanted was to be sentimentalised over by anybody.

'I am not coming back. I am joining up.'

'Oh,' she said, and bit her lip. *'Are you? Today?'*

'Yes, today. Now hurry up with that tea.'

Puzzled and a bit hurt, Susan ran into the kitchen to see to the fire.

Martin went up to his room, threw himself as he was, fully dressed, on to his bed and slept for an hour, exhausted.

Up at the Manor, Christine slept until late that morning. After a wretched night she had closed her eyes just about the time that Martin was drinking the cup of tea that Susan had made for him, and she opened them again to find that it was nearly eleven and the sun was streaming into her bedroom. She sprang out of bed, walked to the window, and looked down upon a white world. Last night there had been the first severe frost of the year. The gardens glittered as though with a thousand diamonds. The sky was a clear pale blue and a keen north wind blew from the fells. The warning breath of approaching winter.

But the beauty of the grounds and of the countryside failed to move Christine. She only knew that she had overslept and terror struck in her heart at the idea that she might not see Martin.

She slipped on a dressing-gown and putting on her smoked glasses, for the glare still hurt her eyes, hurried down to Fiona's bedroom.

Fiona was awake. She looked very ill and

dejected, and her eyes were swollen from weeping. A breakfast tray, barely touched, lay on the table beside her. With a block on her knees she was writing rapidly. As Christine entered the room she looked up and said:

'I am writing to Peter. You'll send a cable to him for me about poor dear Daddy, won't you?'

'Yes, of course, darling.'

'There will be so much to do. Uncle Bob says that Daddy's secretary will be coming up to see me and there will be lots of letters about Daddy which must be answered. You must help me, Christine.'

'Yes, darling, but . . .'

'I can't think of anything else but Daddy,' interrupted Fiona, thoroughly egotistical in her own personal suffering, and hardly noticing that Christine looked almost as ill as she felt herself.

Christine said:

'Fiona darling, we ought really to leave Wyckam Manor at once. We must find somewhere else to go. We can't stay in London because of the raids, but we must both get away from here. All the scandal and talk will be too much for poor Uncle Bob.'

'I don't feel well enough to travel today,' said Fiona morosely, and putting down her fountain pen burst into tears.

Christine had to forget herself once more in the effort to comfort Fiona.

'Darling, you've still got your beloved Peter. He'll come back to you. You've got that to look forward to,' she kept reminding her.

When at last Fiona dried her tears and continued with her letter, Christine went in search of Mr. Standing. She was very perplexed and unhappy. She knew that Fiona was ill and should not be left here alone, and yet she, Christine, longed to get away from this place. The district would soon be humming with scandal about the 'impersonation,' and it didn't seem fair on Uncle Bob. What ought she to do for the best? And what was Martin thinking and feeling this morning? She ached with longing to see him.

Just as she was about to walk into Mr. Standing's study the front door opened and the owner of the Manor House, himself, came in. He looked cold and tired.

'Oh, hello, my dear,' he said as he saw her, 'I have just been down to Stonehead. I went down to have a word with Martin.'

Christine turned an eager, hopeful face to him.

'Oh, what did he say?'

Mr. Standing looked with some pity at the slim girl in the violet blue house-gown. With her tumbled brown curls and no make-up on her face she looked to him so pathetically young . . .

'I am afraid it's no use, my dear. Martin doesn't want to see you again, and in any case

. . . he's gone now.'

Christine's heart seemed to leap to her throat, then sink to the very depths.

'Gone where?'

'To Manchester. He's catching a train which leaves Grange in a short while. He is going to join up at once. Of course, I wanted him to stay for my own sake . . . it means a lot of extra work and worry for me until my new factor arrives . . . but I've had to let him go. He's in a pretty bad state of mind, and I think being in the Army will be the best thing for him.'

White and cold, Christine stared at him.

'You mean he . . . refused to see me?'

'He is obstinate, my dear. He's got it into his head that you led him a dance and deceived us all; you see he made an idol of you, and there you are . . . he just told me to tell you he bears no malice, but he thinks it much better not to have a meeting which could only be painful for the pair of you.'

Christine put the back of her hand against her lips.

'Oh!' she said, in a little whimpering voice.

Mr. Standing started to say something more, but she did not wait to hear it. She turned and ran up the stairs, shut herself in her room, and flung herself down on the bed, a torrent of tears shaking her.

'Oh, Martin,' she moaned. 'Oh, *Martin*, how could you be so cruel?'

She wept passionately, heart-brokenly. She

felt that this punishment that Martin was inflicting upon her far exceeded the crime she had committed. He had taken his love, his belief, and himself from her, and all she had done was to try to help Fiona. It had been mistaken kindness, she knew that now. But she hadn't meant any harm.

In an anguish of weeping she lay there, realising that she was not to be given the chance to see Martin or make her explanations to him personally. He despised her so much that he had walked out on her. He couldn't have loved her, she told herself vehemently. He called himself an idealist, but he was a prig . . . a cold-blooded, hard brute. He wasn't worth her loving. She didn't care if she never saw him again. She wished she could die. Prig, brute, whatever he was, she still loved him with all her heart and soul. That was the worst of it.

When she had cried herself sick and blind, Christine went slowly into the bathroom and began to dress. She moved like an automaton. Violent emotion had died down to a complete numbness. And when at length she was dressed, she looked at her grief-stricken young face in the mirror and sought desperately to regain a sense of humour.

'You've just asked for this, my girl,' she said to herself. 'You would allow yourself to be drawn into other people's muddles and now you've muddled up your own life, good and proper. You've lost the only man you ever loved and the only man you ever will love in your life.'

The more she thought about Martin, the more she began to resent his conduct. What right had he to judge another human being so harshly? Why couldn't he have been human and understanding like Uncle Bob? True, the sex element made a difference, and he was disappointed in her. She had shocked and horrified him. But surely if he had really loved her he would have given her a chance?

She felt that she had no fight left. And, indeed, no mental or physical energy to give to Fiona and her particular troubles. She felt the need for fresh air in order to recover her equilibrium before turning her attention to Fiona again.

With a tweed coat over her shoulders and her hair tied up in a scarf, she walked through the frost-whitened gardens and down the hill which led to Stonehead. Something impelled her to go down there to the place where she had worked as a land-girl and where she had been so completely happy when she first came up here in Fiona's place.

She stood a moment in the yard watching old Tom turn the cows out of the sheds. She saw the familiar black and white collie chasing across the field after the sheep. She saw in the distance the grey drift of smoke curling up from Stonehead farmhouse, and the pain of remembrance caught her by the throat.

How could she bear life without Martin? How she had loved him! Here they had walked together many times. There, in that empty barn he had taken her in his arms and she had known all the swooning ecstasy of his new and rapturous love for her. She could almost see his tall figure in the loose tweed coat, the corduroy breeches, the polished gaiters, cap on the side of his handsome head, swinging through that gateway followed by Jess, his little spaniel. She could see those blue eyes of his blaze with the pleasure of meeting her, and it smote her like a physical blow to realise that she would never meet him here again. She had driven him away from this place which he had loved. She had driven him away from *herself*.

She had thought she had no more tears to shed but they came smarting to her eyes again. One of the farm hands saw her and touched his cap.

'Marning, miss! Eeh, but it's a fine marning. It is that!'

She murmured an answer and made her way into the barn, afraid that the man might speak to her. She closed the door, shutting out the frosty sunlit world. As her eyes grew accustomed to the darkness she looked about her with a feeling of hopeless misery. Why had she come . . . to this very place sacred to the memory of their love? A shaft of light slanted through the high dusty window panes and showed up the thick cobwebs on the rafters.

She remembered that day when a gale had been blowing and the rain driving in torrents and she had stood here with Martin in the shelter of this atmosphere of dry hay and oats and corn and the musty odour of old harness.

She saw a bundle of hay in the corner and suddenly threw herself upon it and lay very still in a kind of choking misery.

'Forgive me, Martin,' she whispered, 'I did love you. I swear I did!'

If she had been still standing out there in the yard, she would no doubt have been amazed to see a car drive up outside the gate and the ex-factor of Mr. Standing's farms, himself, walk up to old Luke to whom she had just avoided speaking.

Martin Farlong, not as Christine would have remembered him, but in a dark lounge suit and with a soft grey hat on his head. Martin looking like a city gentleman instead of a farmer.

He greeted old Luke.

'Is the boss down here?'

'No, Mr. Farlong, sir, I haven't seen him this marning.'

Martin frowned.

'That's funny. And he wasn't up at the Manor. He must have gone into Ulverston.'

Luke scratched his ear.

'Eeh now, Mr. Farlong, I've heard that tha's leaving us and going for a soldier.'

'That's right, Luke,' said Martin shortly.

'We shall miss thee,' said old Luke with a sincerity that could not fail to touch the man who had employed him for many years.

'Thanks, Luke,' he said. 'But you'll soon get used to a new factor.'

'And tha'll get used to drilling and fighting for tha country, no doubt.'

'No doubt,' said Martin grimly. 'As a matter of fact I ought to be on my way to Manchester now, but like a fool I took myself off to Grange without looking at my petrol, ran out and of course missed the train. There isn't another fast one till the afternoon so I thought I might as well come back and do a bit of work until it's time to leave.'

Luke turned his head in the direction of the barn, and pulled at the red handkerchief which was tied about his weather-beaten neck.

'Reckon young lady that used to work here might be looking for thee, Mr. Farlong. She's in yonder . . .' he nodded in the direction of the barn, and then passed on with his barrow-load of manure.

Martin stood irresolute, frowning at the barn. *The young lady who used to work here?* Did Luke mean Fiona? (Damnation! That wasn't her name at all. It was Christine . . . Christine Shaw.) Well, if she was there he didn't want to see her. Yet if she was, what was she doing in there? Why shut herself in the barn? What the devil did old Luke mean?

For an instant Martin was on the verge of

297

turning around and walking back to his car. Then a stronger instinct, for which he was to be thankful for the rest of his life, urged him to walk towards the barn and push the door open.

The sunlight streamed in and showed up the figure of a girl in a tweed coat lying huddled on a bed of hay. She lay still, almost like one asleep, her head buried on her folded arms.

Martin knew that slim figure, that chestnut head well enough. He knew that he was moved to the very foundations by the sight of her. Like one fascinated he stood staring. Then Christine turned her head and saw him. With a little gasp she sprang to her feet, wisps of hay sticking to her hair and the soft blue woollen jumper which she was wearing.

'Oh,' she exclaimed. *'You!'*

Martin did not speak. He looked at her dismayed by the change in her face. It was so white, so much older. And it was smudged, like a child's, with tears.

It was in no way the face of a heartless adventuress who did not care what she had done and who was pleased with herself for the reprehensible part she had recently played.

Indeed the sight of that tear-stained pathetic face took the wind right out of Martin's sails. He could not say one of the hard and bitter things which he had imagined last night he would say to 'Christine Shaw' if he ever saw her again. He just looked at her speechlessly and waited for her to speak.

Christine having recovered from the first shock of seeing Martin, found her voice.

'I . . . I thought you had gone.'

'I missed my train,' he said, feeling stupid.

'Oh, did you?' she said, equally stupidly.

'I . . . er . . . am going later,' he added.

She put up a hand and smoothed back her hair nervously.

'I see.'

The door swung behind him, caught by a sudden gust of wind. They were alone in the dim, old barn. Shut out from the rest of the world. They were both looking at each other as if they could not tear their gaze away, and in both of them was a wild tumult of feeling which sought in vain an outlet for expression.

Then Christine burst out:

'Oh, I know what you think of me. Mr. Standing told me. You think everything that's awful. And you never meant to see me again.'

'I don't think everything that's awful,' he said with difficulty. 'But you must admit that your admission last night was a shock.'

She tilted her head back with sudden defiance.

'Why should *you* be so shocked? Uncle Bob was, too, but he did try to listen to me and understand. You did nothing but walk out. You just judged me without a hearing.'

His tanned face reddened.

'I have no right to judge any one. I admit it.

299

But I loathed all those lies you told me and everyone else.'

'You think I enjoyed telling them?'

He gave her an almost angry look.

'You did it remarkably well.'

'I had to carry it off to do it at all. I gave Fiona my word that I'd come here in her place and stick to it until Mr. Challis came back.'

'Oh, yes, Mr. Standing told me the whole story. Do you think you were justified in taking her place just because she was afraid to go openly to the man she was supposed to love?'

'She did love him.'

'I don't call it love. It was cowardly and it involved a lot of innocent people. I don't believe for a moment that *you* call it love, either.'

'Thanks for the compliment,' she said with a laugh that held little humour. 'I didn't think you would believe me capable of love at all.'

He looked away from her.

'I haven't known what to believe. You've had me absolutely baffled. I did think you loved me at one time, but . . .'

'And I thought you loved me,' she broke in. 'But you didn't . . . At the first real test you walked out on me.'

He turned to her indignantly.

'Are you going to blame me for that? I loved you, believing you were somebody else, and . . .'

'Oh, yes, I know,' she interrupted. 'And I

know it was a dreadful thing I did, and I own up to all the lies I told; but I loathed them, and loathed the whole thing. Only once I started I couldn't stop. If you had any knowledge of human nature you would know how I suffered over it. But you're not human yourself. You're just too high-minded to live. Oh, I hate you!'

She broke off passionately and hid her face in her hands.

He came slowly towards her, his face puckered.

'I am sorry that you think me inhuman. Perhaps I *am* difficult and I don't forgive things very easily, but then I don't give my affections easily, and you smashed an ideal for me when you told that story last night. It wasn't easy for me . . . you don't know what it did to me . . .'

'And you don't know what you did to me,' she said in a muffled voice.

He felt his heart throb with the old wild surge of love and longing for her, but he suppressed it. He said:

'We seem to have hurt each other rather badly. The whole business is damnable.'

She looked up at him, her eyes suffused.

'Can't you see how awful it's been for me? When I fell in love with you I wanted to tell you the truth, but Fiona wouldn't let me. All those things you said that you wished I wasn't, an heiress and that sort of thing, I longed to tell you I was just nothing and nobody. An

301

orphan . . . a typist . . . earning my own living for a few pounds a week until Fiona dragged me into this wretched affair.'

Martin looked at her.

'My dear,' he said in a shaking voice, 'believe me, I would have been only too thankful to have known all along that you were an orphan and a typist. Thinking you William Challis's daughter was the one fly in the ointment as far as I was concerned, and last night I imagined you were just a society girl friend of Fiona's who had done this thing for a laugh.'

'You have never been more wrong.'

'No,' said Martin, 'I think perhaps I have been wrong about a good many things.'

She cast a glance at him. He looked worried and weary, and oh! so inexpressibly dear to her still. She turned from him and moved toward the door of the barn.

'I'd better go. There's no sense in us talking. You don't understand. You never will.'

He called her back.

'Christine,' he said, using her real name for the first time, 'don't go.'

She turned round.

'I like to hear you call me that. I wish it were the only name you had ever called me.'

'I wish it, too,' he said, and turned his gaze from her. He did not know why he had called her back. He could not recover from the blow she had dealt him, nor forgive her. He said:

302

'I don't want to go away feeling that we are enemies. Let's leave it like this . . . that we are friends.'

'Friends!' she echoed bitterly.

'Perhaps it isn't even possible for us to be that,' he said painfully, 'but I can't get over this business . . . I just can't.'

She felt that if she stayed here a moment longer her pride would desert her entirely and she would throw herself into his arms and beg him to forgive her—to try to understand the mad foolish thing that she had done for Fiona's sake. In a muffled voice she said:

'Oh, it's no good us talking any more. I don't want us to be enemies. By all means let's be friends, but I don't suppose we'll ever see each other again. But I wish you luck, Martin, I hope you'll like being a soldier, and that all through this war you'll have the very best of luck. Good-bye.'

He stood irresolute, wanting to say so much more to her, but unable to find the words. In a queer way, he felt that the torrent of his former passionate feeling for her had dried up. He felt sterile of all emotions. There was only one thing he wanted to do—get away from Stonehead and give himself up to fighting in this war.

He let Christine go. He saw her small familiar figure move out of the barn, letting in a shaft of sunlight in which the dust and chaff danced and glittered. The door swung behind

303

her, creaking on its rusty hinges. He covered his face with his hands and stood there. His dream of love was lying in wreckage around him.

Christine went back to the Manor. She was beyond weeping. Her eyes were dry, and her lips shut tightly together. She was suffering as she had never thought it possible to suffer. That short interview with Martin had done her no good . . . done neither of them any good. It had only served to show her how completely she had lost him. She might have known that Martin Farlong would be relentless—that he was not a man who could ever forgive a tissue of lies, no matter the reason for them. Against that granite wall of his ruthless honesty, his own unshakable integrity, she had hurt herself beyond healing. She was being punished for what had started as a crazy escapade to aid and abet Fiona's romance, and had ended in tragedy. Her only wish now was to leave this place which she had grown to love, and to start again. How that could be done she did not know. She had no real desire to go on living, since her life must be led without Martin. She would love him until she died. She only wished that she *had* died when she had been bombed down in Bremhaven. Anything was better than this pain . . . this complete despair.

She went straight into Fiona's room. Fiona was still writing a long letter to Peter and the moment Christine entered the room she looked up and started to enumerate the list of things which Christine must do. But Christine had hardened her heart against Fiona and the whole episode. She had done with sacrificing herself for her friend. She was not going to stay at Wyckam Manor one day longer. She told Fiona so, without mincing matters.

At once Fiona started to weep.

'You promised you'd see me through these next few days. You can't leave me alone.'

But something of Martin's ruthlessness seemed to have entered Christine. She was adamant.

'I'm sorry, Fiona, but I've come to the end of my tether. One can go on for a time and then one comes to an end. I can't bear this any more. I can't stand being here and having to go on seeing any of the people I've deceived, or go to any of the places I have been with Martin. I've got to go.'

Fiona sobbed into her handkerchief.

'Well, it's very hard lines on me. I think Martin Farlong is an absolute brute and if he really loved you he'd have been more understanding.'

Christine smiled grimly.

'Perhaps it's because he loved me so much that he can't forgive me,' she said. 'It isn't easy to forgive someone you care for very deeply when they've let you down.'

'Didn't you tell him it was all my fault?'

'My dear, I told him everything, but it's no

use our trying to whitewash what we have done between us. I'm just as much to blame as you. After all I was the one who carried out the impersonation. B.J. begged me not to. I ought to have listened to her.'

'Oh, dear,' moaned Fiona. 'Everything seems to have gone wrong. And poor darling Daddy is dead. If only I'd known that was going to happen, we need never have done this at all. And yet if we'd waited, Peter would have been gone and I wouldn't be his wife now.'

Christine gave a deep sigh and looked with her sore, tired eyes down at the frost-whitened garden. It was so typical of Fiona to be so self-centred. Still thinking only of her own misfortunes. She did not seem to understand what Martin had meant to her, Christine. And while Christine stood there arguing with the other girl, her mind was not really here at all. It was with Martin, following him in the train to Manchester, visualising what lay before him. Martin as a recruit, drilling and training. Martin qualifying to be a soldier. Martin, feeling perhaps as wretched as she did—the more wretched because he could not find it in him to forgive her for what she had done.

She had hurt him profoundly.

'Do stay with me a little longer, Christine darling,' begged Fiona.

But Christine, her whole heart one agony of pain with the thought of Martin and the futile remorse which she suffered now, not only because she had lost him but because she was the cause of his hurt, was not to be moved.

'No, Fiona,' she said quietly, 'I'm going. I'm going tomorrow. You aren't really ill, my dear. Agnes and Mr. Standing will look after you very nicely while you are here. I must go away.'

'Oh!' moaned Fiona, burying her face in her hands again. 'And I haven't got Daddy now or anybody and I mightn't see Peter again for years.'

Somehow, this morning, the sight of Fiona's wretchedness touched only the faintest chord of sympathy in Christine. She had never felt so dead, so emotionless. She looked at the fair curly head of her friend and said:

'All your life you've had your own way. And I know I was wrong to help you get it by taking your place up here. Now you've got to stand on your own feet, and at least you've got Peter. You've been his wife, you've lived with him— with any luck you'll get him back. I can't be sorry for you. I'd give my life to know that I could belong to Martin and feel that he loved and trusted me as Peter loves and trusts you— if only for a little while.'

Fiona sniffed and blew her nose.

'Oh dear! I never dreamed all this trouble would come of it. I know I was lucky to have had Peter for a bit, but he has gone now and I have been injured in an air-raid and . . . oh, dear, you don't seem to care for me any more.'

Christine melted a little. Fiona was such a

spoiled child and there was something pathetic about her sitting up there in bed making a list of her present misfortunes. Christine moved forward, sat on the edge of the bed, and put her arms around her friend.

'Poor little Fiona! It's a nice mess for both of us. But you will be happy again. Peter will come back to you and you'll get his letters, and you can tell the world now that you're his wife. But I've got nothing . . . nothing.'

Fiona hugged her.

'I'll always love you, Christine, because you helped me and I've got all this money now . . . I shan't know what to do with it. You can have as much as you like.'

Over Fiona's daffodil head Christine looked into the distance and smiled her grim, bitter little smile.

I don't want money, Fiona, thanks all the same. I want to work now. As soon as my eyes are quite healed I shall join one of the services. Now please let me go tomorrow . . . that's all I ask of you, let me get away from here. I just can't bear it!'

Her voice broke and she leaned her head against Fiona's shoulder and now it was the turn of the other girl to comfort her. And for a moment they clung together in tears and wretchedness.

Later that evening, Christine saw Robert Standing and told him that she would be leaving Wyckam Manor in the morning.

Mr. Standing was a little shocked at the sight of the girl whom he had known so long as Fiona Challis. She looked ill and pinched. She wore dark glasses, but behind them her eyes were red and strained.

He put out a hand and touched her shoulder.

'My dear, you've no need to rush away if you care to stay under my roof and help me take care of that bad girl upstairs.'

'Thank you, but I just couldn't stay. I must go. It's awfully good of you, but I must say "good-bye" to you and to everything up here at once.'

He raised his brows.

'Well—if you feel like that.'

'You understand, don't you?' she said painfully. 'And, in any case, surely you want to get rid of me. There is going to be such a scandal when people around here learn the truth, isn't there?'

Mr. Standing smiled a trifle wryly.

'The devil of a scandal. And it's all very disagreeable to me, but I've been thinking about you two girls all day and it seems to me that you are no more than a couple of foolish children who have carried out a crazy escapade. Fiona did it because she wasn't brave enough to defy her father, and you were misguided enough to believe that it was right to help her. Well, well, what a mistake you've both made!'

Christine turned from him.

'I know it only too well now.'

'Did you see Martin?'

She winced.

'Yes. Of course, he won't ever forgive me.'

Robert standing shook his head.

'Poor child—you're being punished and that girl upstairs has been punished. Well, you'll both have to make a fresh start and maybe one day you and Martin . . .'

'No,' Christine broke in. 'No, he'll never forgive me—never. And I shan't make any effort to see him. I shall join up . . . I shall try to get into the A.T.S. in the Motor-Transport Section because I can drive . . . as soon as possible.'

Mr. Standing made no protest against this. He thought it was probably the best thing the girl could do. And so that long dark day at Wyckam Manor, the darkest Christine had ever known, gradually came to an end, and in the morning she said 'good-bye' to a weeping Fiona and was driven into Grange to catch her train for the South.

She could hardly bear to look in the direction of Stonehead Farm. The frost-whitened beauty of Cartmel Fell cut into her heart like a knife. And she looked in the direction of Cartmel and the steeple of the Priory and felt that that heart would surely break in two. This was Martin's home—there were the fields and hills and fells that Martin loved and which he had taught her to love. She was going away, never to return.

Mr. Standing was kindness itself. When he said 'good-bye' at the station he begged her to keep in touch with him.

'I shall always be fond of you, my dear. Now, please do write to me and if you want somewhere to come on leave . . . Wyckam Manor will always be ready to receive you.'

Her eyes filled with tears as she clasped his hand.

'I don't know why you are so good to me after all the wrong I've done.'

'We'll wipe that out, my dear. Come back if you want to.'

She was too moved to answer, but when she was in the train moving slowly away from the familiar landscape, she felt, in an agony of regret and of self reproach, that what she had done could never be wiped out and that she would never see Martin or this wild and beautiful countryside again.

CHAPTER TWENTY-EIGHT

One day in April, about six months after Christine Shaw had left Wyckam Manor, two girls, one wearing a tweed suit and the other the khaki uniform of the A.T.S., sat together in the garden of a small house on the borders of

Dartmoor.

It was one of those warm spring days which, in Devonshire, can be so exquisitely soft and beautiful. It was the first real day of spring, for yesterday there had been a cool wind. Today was windless and the sun shone bravely from a clear blue sky. Christine had taken off her khaki tunic and rolled up the sleeves of her shirt, and sat back in a deck-chair with her arms laced behind her head, looking dreamily at the scene before her. An enchanting scene of which she felt she would never grow tired. The little old-world garden, gay with spring flowers . . . the trees in the orchard beyond, snowy and pink with fruit blossom . . . the rockery ablaze with purple aubretia. And away to the right the fringe of the moors, splendid and lonely, giving her a pang now and again because there was some similarity between this portion of the Devonshire moorland and Cartmel Fell. It seemed to her years rather than months since she had lived up in the North—lived that reckless life as 'Fiona Challis' which had brought the one great love into her life and at the same time precipitated her into such disaster.

During those months she had become a driver in the A.T.S. and had undergone a gruelling training which had done her good, mentally and physically. It seemed to have taken away some of her individuality and made her a mere cog in a machine; but since it was a machine directed against the Germans and designed for winning the war, that was quite satisfactory to her. Besides, she no longer wanted to be Christine Shaw. She still hated herself and the memory of what she had done. In order to blot out that memory she had been glad to become one of hundreds of women drilling and marching and learning and having recovered from the effects of that raid at Bremhaven, she soon grew fit and strong again. For five months she had been driving motor transport, in an anti-aircraft unit stationed somewhere on the East Coast. There had been raids there, and once or twice they had been bad ones, but nobody in the unit had cared less than Christine. She had won a name for herself for being the coolest among them— she seemed without fear and she had no home ties or connections to take her mind off her job. So she had done well and was expecting to go up next week before a Selection Board to be recommended for a commission.

This was the second leave that she had spent down in Devonshire with B.J. The first had been when Alan was at home and they were still at Plymouth. And although they had both been very kind to her and anxious to give her a good time, she had not enjoyed herself overmuch. Dear old B.J., trying to help, sorry for the disaster which had overtaken her friend, would keep introducing her to Naval officers, friends of Alan's, and so obviously hoped to take Christine's mind off the man she had loved and lost. But Christine had found no pleasure in the company of any of these men. She wanted no man in her life except Martin, and about Martin, all these months, she had received only the most indirect news. Once from Fiona, who was still up at Wyckam Manor and appeared to be making her home there with her father's friend. Fiona had heard in the district that Mr. Farlong was training 'somewhere in the North' but nobody seemed to have had a letter from him except his previous employer, who was inclined to be reticent on the subject of his factor.

And then Christine received a letter from Mr. Standing himself, in which he had said:

It may interest you to know that Martin had to come and see me on business when he was on leave last week and he stayed a couple of nights at the farm. He looks thin but very fit, is now a sergeant, and expects to be recommended for a commission shortly. His main object appears to be to get abroad as soon as possible.

That news had been of the most intense interest to Christine and for a long time she had brooded over the thought of Martin— Sergeant Farlong—like herself, shortly to become an officer. She wondered if he worked as hard as she did and with as little real inspiration . . . whether he was as miserable as she was . . . whether he ever thought of her in the way that she thought of him . . . with untold longing and regret.

But he was luckier than she. He was a man and he could get abroad and fight. That was what she would have liked to have done.

She sat here in B.J.'s little garden, her thoughts turning toward Martin even at this moment, wondering how and where he was.

B.J. sat opposite her, the inevitable piece of knitting in her hands. Dear B.J. So much to be envied, thought Christine. Alan had only just gone back to sea and she had reasonable expectations of seeing him back again before the end of the summer. He had found this adorable little cottage for her near Yelverton. She shared it with the wife of an N.O., who was a grass-widow like herself and who worked in the W.V.S. and was out most of the day. It was a good arrangement because B.J. particularly needed peace and the comfort of a small home just now. She expected a child in July. And that to her would be a crowning happiness. Lucky B.J., thought Christine. How wonderful to be married to the man one loved and to be bearing him a child.

B.J. glanced up from her knitting and regarded her friend. Christine looked absurdly young in the khaki shirt, collar and tie, and short skirt—young and sunbrowned . . . she was out driving all day in her job . . . but on the thin side. And those big eyes of hers were always too sad these days for B.J.'s liking. Poor little Christine! She had come through the mill all right, B.J. thought. Things had turned out badly just as B.J. had prophesied. She could not help resenting the fact that Martin Farlong preserved such an unbending and unforgiving attitude. It seemed such a waste of love . . . if they still loved each other . . . for them to be totally cut off like this.

This was the last day of Christine's leave. The two girls had had a delightful week together. Tomorrow B.J. would miss her friend, but Christine had to go back. She must travel all night, tonight, in order to present herself to her company tomorrow.

'I suppose,' said B.J., 'the next time you come down here you'll be wearing an officer's uniform and much too important to share my humble life.'

Christine smiled.

'Oh, much too important, idiot!'

'Well, you'll look nice as an officer. You've got the right figure; only don't get any thinner.'

'Oh, I'm fine!' Christine moved restlessly and taking a cigarette from a packet on her lap, lit one.

'Have you heard from Fiona lately?'

'Not for a week or two.'

'She seems to have settled down at Wyckam Manor.'

'Yes, it surprised me. I felt sure she would go back to London or thereabouts, but I suppose after that bombing and her father's death, she is content with the country, and Mr.

Standing is very good to her. They keep trying to get me up there but I shall never go.'

'I don't blame you,' said her friend.

Christine turned her gaze to a meadow beyond in which sheep were grazing. The sight of those sheep brought a vivid recollection of those other sheep which she had so often watched and helped to tend on the hills above Stonehead. The sight gave her a definite pang. She knew that more than anything in the world she would like to go back to Martin's country.

A bicycle bell broke the stillness of the golden afternoon.

'That's the post,' said B.J. 'Go and get my love-letter for me. I'm due one.'

Christine walked through the little whitewashed cottage and took the letters from the postman at the door. Two for B.J.—one with the censor's stamp and with Alan's handwriting; so dear B.J. would have her love-letter. And one for Christine. The sight of the postmark made her catch her breath just as the sight of those sheep in the meadow had done.

Grange-over-Sands! Fiona's big loopy handwriting, addressed to Driver C. Shaw, A.T.S., A.A., M.T. Unit, and forwarded from the East Coast. Funny that there should be a letter from Fiona when they had just been talking about her. The two girls settled down to their post, B.J. to luxuriate in the long letter from her husband, and Christine to read news far more exciting than she had ever expected.

317

For Fiona's letter was almost entirely about Martin. Fiona had *seen* Martin and spoken to him. He had spoken about *her*.

Christine grew hot and her heart raced as she read all that Fiona had to say, written with her usual extravagance and lack of restraint.

Darling—I've got the most thrilling news for you. First about myself . . . (it would be, Christine thought amusedly) *. . . I have heard from Peter and he is in Cairo. He got a flesh wound during one of the Libyan drives and is now at H. Q. and is a staff captain, so I shall hear often and I don't have to be so worried, which is marvellous.*

Now, about you—I actually met and spoke to your Martin on Saturday . . . (now the hot colour flamed into Christine's cheeks and she sat up and read the letter more intently—*her* Martin!) *. . . Whenever he has been in the district he has always avoided me, but I happened to be in Cartmel with Uncle Bob and I had just come out of the P.O. when I ran straight into his lordship. What do you think? He is a Commando . . . (he would be) all iron and steel, no nerves and ruthlessness, etc., etc. But joking apart, I admit he looks pretty good in the uniform and there are all sorts of rumours going about that the Commandos will soon be in action. At any rate he tried to avoid me as usual but I wasn't having any. I just stopped him and said: 'I know you hate me but you're going to speak to me, Mr. Commando.' He saluted, all* *stiff like, and didn't even smile and mumbled something about 'Good afternoon, Mrs. Hollis' and then I just let go. I don't suppose you'll ever forgive me but I told him what I thought of him since there was nothing to be lost by it except that you might be annoyed. I told him that he'd broken your heart and that he was a ruthless monster and that he didn't seem to understand that it was little me who was all to blame. I told him how frightfully hard you always worked in your life and how badly you needed that change in the country and how you hated the deception all along but that I made you stick to it.*

My dear, he listened and you would have thought the man was made of iron—not a muscle twitched—but he couldn't control his eyes. You know how blue they are and they seemed simply to blaze down. I think he would have liked to have levelled a Tommy-gun at me. And then I said: 'Oh, don't stand there like a graven image putting yourself up as a judge. Anybody would think you were a dictator. And you're not so perfect yourself. You're just an insufferable prig and I despise you. Christine is the sweetest thing that ever lived and you've made her absolutely wretched and she is lonely and, oh! anyhow you're the loser and she's well rid of you . . .' And then, do you know, darling, I daresay you'll be livid with me for all this but I am uncontrolled and know it: I just began to cry, standing there in the village like an idiot, sniffing into my handkerchief . . .

Christine looked up from the letter. Her hands were trembling so that she could hardly turn over the sheets. Pages and pages scrawled from top to bottom. Never had Fiona written such a diary, and the contents made Christine feel first of all hot and then cold; like one with an ague she sat there in the sunshine shivering, horrified that this should have happened and yet madly anxious to know the result.

'How could Fiona have done it?' she inwardly asked herself, and then, feeling as though she were choking, read on:

Something awfully odd happened then. I looked up expecting to find that the gallant Commando had marched off in a huff; instead he was looking down at me completely changed. His face was all broken up. His lips were twitching. He said: 'For the love of Mike, don't cry. You're embarrassing me beyond words, Mrs. Hollis. Look here . . . I'm sorry you feel like this about me. I didn't wish to hurt Christine. But you don't seem to see how I was hurt. I idealised her. Surely you must see that everything fell to pieces around me when I heard the truth. It isn't that I minded her being just a girl who worked for her living instead of the rich Miss Challis—I prefer it that way—but I had grown to love someone named "Fiona Challis," and suddenly I found she didn't exist. The whole thing was a fabrication and a long deception. It seemed just unforgivable, that's all.'

Well, I said: 'Nothing is unforgivable. How

320

would you like to make a mistake and feel that she would never forgive you? But she would have forgiven you anything. She is much more generous. And you've no sense of humour. That's your trouble. Why couldn't you have laughed a bit when you got over the first shock? Thank goodness I don't love you. You're too hatefully pompous for words.'

I honestly thought he'd run away then, but to my amazement he smiled. And I must admit when Martin smiles he is full of S.A. I like those crinkles on either side of his mouth and how it narrows up his eyes. He said: 'You're an amazing person, Mrs. Hollis. And it's colossally impertinent of you to talk to me like this; but I think I admire your spirit. As for being pompous and a prig, I've no wish to be either. You make me feel insufferable.'

Then I said: 'Oh, why can't you forget yourself and your side and think of Christine, working away driving an ambulance, eating her heart out for you.' Then his face went all queer again, and he said: 'Is that strictly true?' And . . . I don't know whether you'll ever forgive me, Christine, darling, but I said: 'It's the absolute truth and I think it's time you wrote to her and said you were sorry for being so hard on her. You do still love her, don't you?' And now, brace yourself up, darling . . . his answer was: 'Yes, I do. I've never stopped loving her. You needn't think she's the only one who has suffered. I've been through hell, only I've tried to concentrate on my work

321

and cut it out.'

Then I said: 'Why try to cut it out? It's such a waste for both of you when you're still in love with one another.' And then, darling, he took out a little notebook and asked for your address and he thanked me. He was rather sweet. He said: 'I'm sorry you have such a poor opinion of me. You're probably quite right, but I'll see what can be done about it.' And that was how it ended. And oh, Christine, darling, you were always so good to me, I do hope now your happiness will come. I feel sure you will hear from Martin quite soon . . .

The letter dropped on to Christine's lap. Her fingers seemed to have become nerveless so that she could no longer hold the thin pages. Her eyes were blinded by tears. So many and varied were her emotions in that moment that her thoughts were neither consecutive or clear, but one salient fact stood out amongst the rest; Martin had told Fiona that he still loved her. *Still loved her.* And that he had suffered these last six months. He had not forgotten, nor had the wrong she committed destroyed the foundations of his initial feelings toward her.

She heard B.J.'s soft voice:

'Darling—is anything wrong? Have you had bad news?'

Christine shook her head. She covered her flaming cheeks with both hands and strove to master her surging emotions. This letter from

Fiona seemed to have turned her world upside down again . . . caused a complete upheaval of body and mind. She said:

'Oh, B.J., B.J., it's wonderful news, really! I can't begin to tell you all about it so you had better read this epistle from Fiona. It's come as such a surprise, I can hardly believe it.'

The other girl took the letter and scanned through it quickly. When she had finished she raised shining eyes to her friend.

'But, Christine, this is wonderful, my dear. I *am* so happy for you. You really do deserve a break and it's the only decent thing Fiona has ever done. I take off my hat to her.'

Christine stood up and threw her arms above her head with an ecstatic gesture.

'B.J., he's told Fiona that he still loves me. And he's got my address. Oh! Do you think he'll get in touch with me? Do you think he really wants to see me again, or did he just say those things to pacify Fiona?'

B.J. shook her head.

'Most unlikely. Your Martin doesn't seem to be the kind of man who does or says anything unless he means it. I expect when you get back to your billet tomorrow you'll find a letter waiting for you or a message of some kind.'

Once again Christine stretched her arms above her head.

'Oh! I could *die*—I feel a changed being. There is something to live and hope for now. I've been dead all these months, absolutely *dead*, without him.'

B.J. looked almost with awe at the young tense figure in khaki . , . at the tilted head, the shut eyes, the whole attitude that suggested suppressed rapture . . . supplication to the very gods themselves. It was not in Barbara's own quiet nature to love a man quite like this. She could not have cared more for Alan than she did, but it was an emotion of a quieter, more humdrum variety—and she knew it. She had always said that one day Christine would love very deeply and passionately, and from what she had heard of Martin Farlong, she was glad, now, that it was he who had touched the mainspring of that passion. Hard he might be, but obviously he was every inch a man. Someone whose feelings ran as strongly and as deeply as Christine's. It would be a wonderful day, B.J. thought, when those two were reunited.

Christine dropped back into her chair.

'I'm making an ass of myself. I really must try and keep sane, but I don't know how to wait until I get back to my billet and see if he *has* written.'

'Don't you dare exhibit such anxiety to leave me.'

Christine laughed and reaching forward took her friend's hand and pressed it.

'Darling, you've given me a heavenly week and I owe you so much. You must try to understand what this news means to me.'

'I do, my dear, bless you. And you know my one wish is to see you happy again.'

'He's a Commando, B.J. Isn't that exciting? It's the sort of thing he would do, as Fiona says. Martin wouldn't know any fear.'

And she fell to thinking what he must look like in his uniform. He would have just recently got a commission. He would be in hard training. And soon he might be in action if the British started to invade the enemy coast.

She felt her heart knock at the thought. Martin as a Commando would have to risk his life in the most hazardous and daring adventures. *(Oh, dear, dear Martin, let me see you . . . let me hear your voice . . . let me feel your touch just once more if never again, was her wild inner prayer.)*

Never had the long night journey from Yelverton back to the little coastal town where she was billeted seemed so tedious and unending. She felt half-crazy with irritation every time the train slowed down or there was a hold-up at a station. She *must* get home and see if Martin had carried out the promise that he had made to Fiona to get in touch with her.

She was tired and heavy-eyed after a sleepless night when at length she reached her billet and deposited Army greatcoat, steel helmet, gas mask and suitcase on the floor. She had walked from the station carrying the heavy load and she was hot and weary, for it was one of those close April mornings on which the sun was hidden by a faint haze and made one feel damp and sticky, especially in a thick uniform.

The girls in Christine's company were comfortably quartered in a big empty country-house on the outskirts of the town. In the entrance hall was a table on which lay letters and parcels. Christine was about to make a dash for that table when her company commander appeared, so she had to hold back and stand to attention (this was the value of discipline and training, but, oh, how she longed to disregard the commander's presence and look for a letter from Martin).

A Junior Commander, a pleasant-faced woman, wearing a smart uniform with three 'pips' on her shoulder, looked in a kindly fashion at the pretty driver.

'Well, Shaw, did you have a good leave?'

'Very, thank you, Ma'am.'

'I want to see you as soon as you can come over to the office. You are being transferred at once.'

Christine's eyes widened.

'Transferred, Ma'am? But I thought I was going up before the Selection Board next week, Ma'am?'

'That is so, Shaw, but Command asked me to let them have an extra driver in S— . . .' she mentioned the name of a town on the outskirts of London, '. . . I said you were one of my best drivers so I am sending you down there this afternoon.'

Christine blinked and drew breath. Everything seemed to be happening to her at once, but one had to grow used to sudden transfers and changes in the Army. The company commander passed on, Christine saluted, then rushed to the table, her heart on fire.

There were two letters for her. She picked them up with trembling fingers and then that flaming heart seemed to sink into a cold abyss. Neither of the letters was from Martin. One was a bill and the other from Kenneth Howell . . . faithful admirer, who, since she had joined the A.T.S., had kept in touch with her and taken her out in London once or twice.

Never before had Christine felt such a crushing disappointment.

'Oh, damn, damn!' she said to herself miserably.

The next moment she was chiding herself for a fool. Possibly it was just as she had told B.J . . . Martin had asked for her address to pacify Fiona, but he hadn't meant to write. He didn't want to get in touch with her and reopen their association. The disappointment was cruel. She wished that Fiona had never told her about that meeting with Martin. She wished she had never allowed herself to hope so intensely all last night as she journeyed up from Devon.

There was a mist of bitter tears in her eyes as she turned away from the correspondence table and, picking up her kit, began to trudge wearily up the stairs to the room which she shared with three other girls.

One of the drivers, an attractive-looking girl, who was a special friend of Christine's met her coming down the stairs.

'Oh, hello, Christine. So you're back.'

'Hello, Ann,' said Christine briefly.

'Had a good leave?'

'Lovely. How are you?'

'Oki-doke. Got a beast of a car to drive at the moment, and I've been under it all the week-end messing about in the garage, but I've been promised one of the new Merks next week. By the way, I hear you're being transferred?'

'Yes. To S——. I shall be sorry to leave here and say "good-bye" to you.'

'I shall miss you too, my dear,' said Ann Wilson. 'But S—— is beautifully handy for the gay lights of London.'

Christine took off her peaked cap and passed a hand over her chestnut waves of hair. Her head had begun to ache and she felt utterly miserable. Martin hadn't written. Martin would never write. Life would be just as it had been before . . . without real meaning. She would go on as a cog in the war machinery, stripped of personal happiness. And she didn't care whether she stayed here or

328

went to S—. The 'gay lights of London' meant nothing to her anyway.

Then she heard Ann's voice:

'Oh, I say, Christine, so sorry . . . there was a telegram for you this morning and I've got it here in my tunic pocket. I've been waiting to see you. Here it is.'

Christine almost snatched at the orange envelope, a dozen crazy hopes surging within her again. It might be from Martin. *It might be.*

Then, as she read the printed words, hope soared into blissful certainty. It *was* from Martin. It was all and more than she had hoped for.

'*Must see you very urgently will be London April 21st can you meet me Berkeley 1 o'clock.*'

The telegram was reply-paid and Martin gave an address near Aldershot.

Once or twice Christine read this invitation, her eyes very bright. Martin wanted to see her 'very urgently'. Could anything be more wonderful? And now she could not grumble that she was being transferred to S—. The 'gay lights of London' as Ann called them were going to be of vital importance to her. In fact, everything was working out wonderfully. Once she got to S— she could ask for special leave to meet Martin.

All her feelings of fatigue and depression left her. She ran upstairs to her room, her heavy kit no longer a weight. Her heart was singing. At lunch-time she would nip down to

329

the post office and get off her answer to Martin.

She would meet him at the Berkeley on April 21st . . . that was the day after tomorrow . . . even if she had to desert, she laughingly told herself, she would keep that date.

CHAPTER TWENTY-NINE

At a quarter to one on April 21st, Second Lieutenant Martin Farlong sat in the lounge of the Berkeley smoking a cigarette and keeping an anxious eye on the stream of people who came in and out of the hotel.

He had asked Christine to meet him at one o'clock, and he knew he was fifteen minutes too early. So anxious had he been for this meeting that he had hardly known how to fill in time this morning until the hour came. He knew now that Christine Shaw mattered to him more than anyone or anything on this earth. To get into contact with her again was of vital importance. He had been conscious of that fact ever since his meeting in Cartmel with Fiona.

Of course, Christine had always been of vital importance to him since the days when she had worked on his farm as a land-girl, in the guise of Fiona Challis. He had thought, after the débâcle that had ensued, that he could put her out of his life and out of his heart. But he had been able to do neither. All through the months spent in the Army he had known two desperate desires . . . one for her and one for his farm, for the wild lovely countryside of his boyhood. The first had seemed to him lost beyond recall and the second to be gained only after peace was declared. But now it seemed that the first and foremost . . . Christine herself . . . was to be given back to him.

Fiona had opened the door. He had never liked Fiona. He had despised her conduct just as he blamed her for being the real cause of all the trouble. But at least now he was grateful to her for having shown him what a fool he was. She had pulled him up with a jolt. She had made him realise that he was all that she had called him. A pompous prig . . . a man who dared set himself up as a judge . . . a fool who had cast love out and tortured himself, as well as the woman he loved.

When he had wired to Christine, he had felt that he was taking a risk, the risk of being turned down; in fact paid back in his own coin, since she might, out of sheer pride, refuse to meet him. But when her answer to his telegram had come, saying she would meet him, he had felt a new man. For surely she would not meet him unless she was prepared to forgive. And there were things that must be forgiven . . his stubborn pride and lack of generosity. He had failed her because she had seemed to fail him, but that had been a poor thing to do and he knew it now.

He tried to picture in his mind what she would look like in her uniform, and how she would be after the long months of their separation and the complete alteration in both their ways of living. His restless blue eyes kept watching the women who passed by. One or two in uniform, which made his heart jolt, but so far not Christine. One or two beautiful glamorous-looking creatures but none of them Christine.

Most of the women took a second look at the tall handsome young officer with the letters 'COMMANDOS' on his shoulder. His good looks coupled with that name, which in itself spelled all that was most thrilling in this war, were enough to excite the interest and imagination of the average woman. But the young Commando had no eyes for anybody. There was only one woman in the world in whom he had any interest. Only one in whom he had ever been interested.

Then he saw her. He rose, stubbing his cigarette end on an ashtray. His heart thudded as Christine came towards him and he took in the first glimpse of her . . . the slim neat figure full of grace despite the roughness of the private's uniform. The peaked cap, hiding most of the lovely chestnut hair. The respirator hanging over her shoulder. Brown leather gloves. Long slim legs in khaki stockings, small feet in brown flat-heeled shoes. Christine of the A.T.S . . . a stranger whom he did not know. Yet when she reached him, it was a Christine whom he knew intimately . . . for the beautiful sun-browned face was the face of the girl whom he had known and loved as 'Fiona' up in the North. The same, except that it was thinner. Eyes and lips were a trifle more grave. He could see that she had suffered.

All his heart went out to her as he held out a hand.

'My dear,' he said. 'It's good to see you.'

She placed a hand in his and her body trembled a little.

'Martin,' she said.

For a moment they stood there gazing rather foolishly at each other, unable to speak. His gaze swept her again from head to foot and he shook his head, smiling a little.

'You in the Army . . . it doesn't seem possible.'

She looked at him, at the brand new leather belt and the 'pip' on his shoulder.

'You, too.'

'A bit different from the old days.'

'Quite different.'

'I rather like you in this,' he indicated her uniform.

'I like you in yours, Martin, but mine is rather awful. It fits where it touches, but if I get my commission I'll be able to have a beautiful tailored one.'

'You look all right to me as you are.'

She gave an excited little laugh.

'Thank you.'

'Thank you for coming,' he said.

'It was good of you to ask me.'

'I wanted to see you. I may be in some other part of the country soon, and unable to see you. I had to get in touch with you at once.'

'Do you mean you are going into action?'

He smiled.

'I can't answer any questions. But I just wanted to see you now when I *knew* I would be in town.'

Her eyes drank in the sight of him. She thought how lean and brown and marvellous in every way he looked and she knew that she loved him almost unbearably. And she thought:

'He is going into action and he knows it. He might never come back. Oh, Martin, *Martin*!'

He said:

'Do sit down and have a drink.'

She let her gasmask drop to the ground, took off her hat and shook back her curls. He looked with tenderness at those curls.

'Now you are still more like the girl I used o know.'

'Oh, I'm still the same really,' she laughed a ittle nervously. 'Inside I haven't changed. Iave you?'

334

'No. I'm still the dumb, difficult fellow who used to annoy you and I still hate this sort of place, really, and want to get back to my farm and watch the wheat coming up and the sheep grazing on the hills.'

She drew a deep sigh.

'Don't. It makes me heart-sick for Stonehead and Burnt Hollow and dear little Cartmel.'

'Have you missed it all then?'

'You've no idea how much.'

'I like to hear you say that.'

'You know how much I had grown to love it, Martin.'

'Yes, I believe you.'

There was a moment's awkward silence, then he added:

'I don't know how to begin to talk to you, Christine, but I do want to say this straight away and get it over. I had no right to walk out, or to be so infernally critical and ready to condemn. I behaved very badly and I want you to forgive me if you can. I have one excuse, and one only. It was all a shock. I took rather a long time to recover from it.'

Her cheeks coloured hotly.

'I understand. Please don't think I blame you. You had every right to condemn me and I've no excuse to offer.'

'Except that you did it all for someone else's sake. Fiona made me see that.'

'Oh, don't let's talk of it, please.'

335

'No. I don't want to talk of it. I want to forget it ever happened. I just want to think of you as you are . . . Christine.'

Nervously she took a cigarette case out of her tunic pocket. Martin hailed a passing waiter and ordered drinks.

'Tell me all that you've been doing . . . that is without giving away any secrets,' she said. 'It's such a long time since we met.'

'Much too long.'

'How have you been liking the Army, Martin?' she asked softly, her pulses thrilling at his last words.

'Oh, quite well, especially since I joined this lot. They're grand fellows and I get out more in the open air.'

'You look well.'

'I'm fit as a fiddle. And you? You look well except that you're too thin.'

'I've been all right,' she said laughing.

But he knew that she hadn't and he could see the marks that unhappiness had carved faintly about her lips and her big luminous eyes. He was filled with remorse because it was his own ungenerous conduct that had helped to etch those lines. He wished intensely that they were not in this crowded hotel lounge, but alone in the old familiar countryside where he could see the wind stir her hair as it blew across the fells, and where they could hear the birds singing in the trees above them. His blood was racing at the sight and sound of her.

336

He wanted to snatch her into his arms and hold her close and tell her how inexpressibly dear she was and always would be.

And instead he had to take her into the restaurant and order a meal and they had to sit there talking . . . just talking aimlessly with the eyes of the crowd upon them.

He was touched when she remembered to ask after Jess, his spaniel.

'She's still at the farm with Emmy. I'm afraid she fretted for the fist week or two after I left and sat on an old coat of mine and wouldn't eat. But Emmy coaxed her and she is all right now. When I go back to the farm I get a tremendous welcome.'

'I'm sure you do. And Emmy?'

'Just the same. A bit more rheumaticky, poor old soul.'

'And the granddaughter, Susan?'

'Oh, Susan is in a munitions factory near Manchester.'

'I was always jealous of her,' smiled Christine, and looked a trifle mischievously at Martin, but he gave her a long serious look in return and shook his head.

'You had no need to be. Why, my dear, you've no need to be jealous of any woman in the world. You must know you are the only one who interests me.'

She looked at him over the rim of the coffee cup which she had just lifted to her lips and was enraptured by the meaning in his glance and his words. She had come to this meeting with many heartburnings and misgivings but now, after being an hour with him, she knew that she had no cause for either. He was the same Martin who had loved her up in the North. Nothing really had changed.

When the meal was over and Martin had settled the bill, he asked her what she would like to do.

'My whole afternoon and evening are at your disposal,' he said. 'Probably you'd like to do a show, and then we'll have dinner.'

'It sounds perfect. I've got the day off, too, but I've got to be back in S— by midnight. As a matter of fact I wangled this day by saying I had to meet a relative who was on special leave and wanted urgently to see me,' she smiled.

'I don't know about the relative but the last part is quite true.'

They stood outside the Berkeley together. The man and the girl in their respective uniforms, strong and brown and ready for any emergency, thrilled with each other and with their reunion.

Then Martin said:

'I'm going to get a taxi and we'll drive through the park. It's a lovely day. Let's see some trees and some grass and pretend that we are in the country.'

She nodded. And the next moment they were in a taxi driving into Piccadilly and down toward Hyde Park.

No April day that Christine could remember had ever seemed more lovely. The Park was exquisitely green, the sky a translucent blue, the sun glittered on the water in the fountain opposite the gates of Buckingham Palace. Outside the sentries in their steel helmets and khaki uniforms were about to change guard. It was a London stripped and ready for war, thought Christine, and she and Martin, too, were ready for war. But war seemed a long way from her just at the moment. She was trying to capture Martin's spirit, his flight of fancy, and move with him across the fields of the farm whereon they had both worked and loved.

'What orders for today, Mr. Factor?' she asked demurely.

His fingers reached for hers and held them fast.

'I think I'll let you off work today and we'll drive into Cartmel and interview the Vicar at the Priory.'

'What will we do that for?'

'To see about putting up our banns . . . that is, if you are willing.'

She turned to him quickly, her heart racing, her face on fire.

'Martin!'

'Oh, my dear,' he said huskily. 'My darling, darling Christine. Once before, I asked you to marry me and you couldn't give me an answer but this time I am asking you and I want you to say "yes" straight away. I don't suppose we can be married at Cartmel Priory as we would like to do because there is no time, but please let me get a special licence and you get special leave and let's be married in London before I go . . . to wherever I'm going.'

She sat still, no longer seeing the brave young green of the Park . . . but only Martin's strong, tender face . . . yes, it was unutterably tender now; all ruthlessness wiped from it. And she answered without hesitation:

'I'll marry you whenever and wherever you wish. I love you, Martin. You know what held me back before, but if you want me now, nothing will hold me back . . . nothing, ever again.'

'Darling,' he said. 'Darling . . .'

And his long hard kiss against her mouth assuaged the pain and the bitterness of those last difficult months and told her that all was well with her love again.

Again and again they exchanged long breathless kisses, each with so much to give, each realising what a lot of time had been wasted and must be made up. At last Martin let her go and said, laughing:

'This won't do. I'm supposed to be a fellow who's trained to keep his head in any emergency, and you are making me lose it.'

'Darling, I'm trained to keep mine, too; but it is so lovely for us both to lose our heads together,' she laughed back, and put on her cap again and searched for powder puff and comb.

He said:

'I'm going to tell the taxi-man to drive straight down to Bond Street. I must buy you a ring—two rings—engagement and wedding!'

She gave a great sigh.

'Sounds too marvellous to be true. Are we really going to get married, Martin?'

'If you don't mind tying yourself up to a dull fellow like myself. You know, after the war, darling, if I survive, I shall want to get out of the Army and get back to farming.'

'So shall I, Martin. We'll have a farm of our own together somewhere.'

'Up North?'

'Yes, near Cartmel,' she said softly.

'We'll both get a week's marriage leave. Shall we spend our honeymoon somewhere there, on the Lakes?'

'I'd adore that, Martin.'

'My darling,' he said, and raised her hand to his lips. 'You are going to be the ideal wife, who likes just the same things as her husband.'

'It's going to be an ideal marriage,' said Christine.

Still holding on to her hand, Martin knocked on the glass partition separating them from the driver. The driver pulled up and put his head round for orders.

'Bond Street,' said Martin.

The driver touched his cap.

'Right you are, Captain.'

Martin's blue eyes laughed at the girl.

'I've been promoted. That's because I'm with you. I shall obviously be promoted for having the sense to choose such a beautiful, adorable girl for a future wife.'

'And what about me? I'm supposed to be an officer next week, but it's all going to be a mix up if I'm getting married. I'll have to go back to my job afterwards. We won't be together very much.'

'No, that's a snag,' he agreed. 'But we'll have lovely leaves, darling, and the day will come . . . perhaps not too far ahead, when we can both lay aside our uniforms and get back to the land.'

Christine sighed.

'What a wonderful day that will be.'

A moment's pause, during which Martin lifted the girl's left hand and brushed it with his lips. Then he said, almost shyly:

'There is rather a wonderful poem about Cartmel which a poet named Gordon Bottomley wrote one New Year's Eve way back in 1913—before the last war. I've known it by heart ever since I was a boy. Would you like to hear it?'

She looked up at him gravely.

'I learn something new and wonderful about you every time we meet, Martin. Not very many men these days seem to like poetry.'

He gave a little laugh.

'Well, a Commando can be a tough guy outside and keep the essence of poetry in his soul.'

'Say it to me, Martin.'

Still holding her hand he quoted:

'Oh, Cartmel bells ring soft tonight
  And Cartmel bells ring clear,
But I lie far away tonight,
  Listening with my dear.

'Listening in a frosty land
  Where all the bells are still
And the small-windowed bell-towers
      stand
  Dark under heath and hill.

'I thought that with each dying year,
  As long as life should last,
The bells of Cartmel I should hear
  Ring out an aged past.

'The plunging, mingling sounds increase
  Darkness's depth and height,
The hollow valley gains more peace
  And ancientness tonight.

'The loveliness, the fruitfulness,
  The power of life lived there,
Return, revive, more closely press
  Upon that midnight air.'

He paused. Christine drew a deep breath, and said:

'Those are wonderful words. That's how I should feel if I were you. *'As long as life should last'* you would hear those Cartmel bells. They haven't rang since the war, have they? But when the war is over I shall hear them with you.'

' *"The power of life lived there,"* ' repeated Martin. 'And the power of love, too, learned there with you, Christine.'

We hope you have enjoyed this Large Print book. Other Chivers Press or Thorndike Press Large Print books are available at your library or directly from the publishers.

For more information about current and forthcoming titles, please call or write, without obligation, to:

Chivers Press Limited
Windsor Bridge Road
Bath BA2 3AX
England
Tel. (01225) 335336

OR

Thorndike Press
295 Kennedy Memorial Drive
Waterville
Maine 04901
USA

All our Large Print titles are designed for easy reading, and all our books are made to last.